YIELDING

LIFE UNRAVELED

BY

S. SIMONE KAMASSAH

Yielding: Life Unraveled

Kamassah, S. Simone
ISBN 978-1-7779352-2-1 (Paperback)
ISBN 978-1-7779352-1-4 (eBook)

Edited by Christine Bode.
Book production and cover design by Publish and Promote.
Interior layout and design by Davor Nikolic.
Printed and bound in Canada.

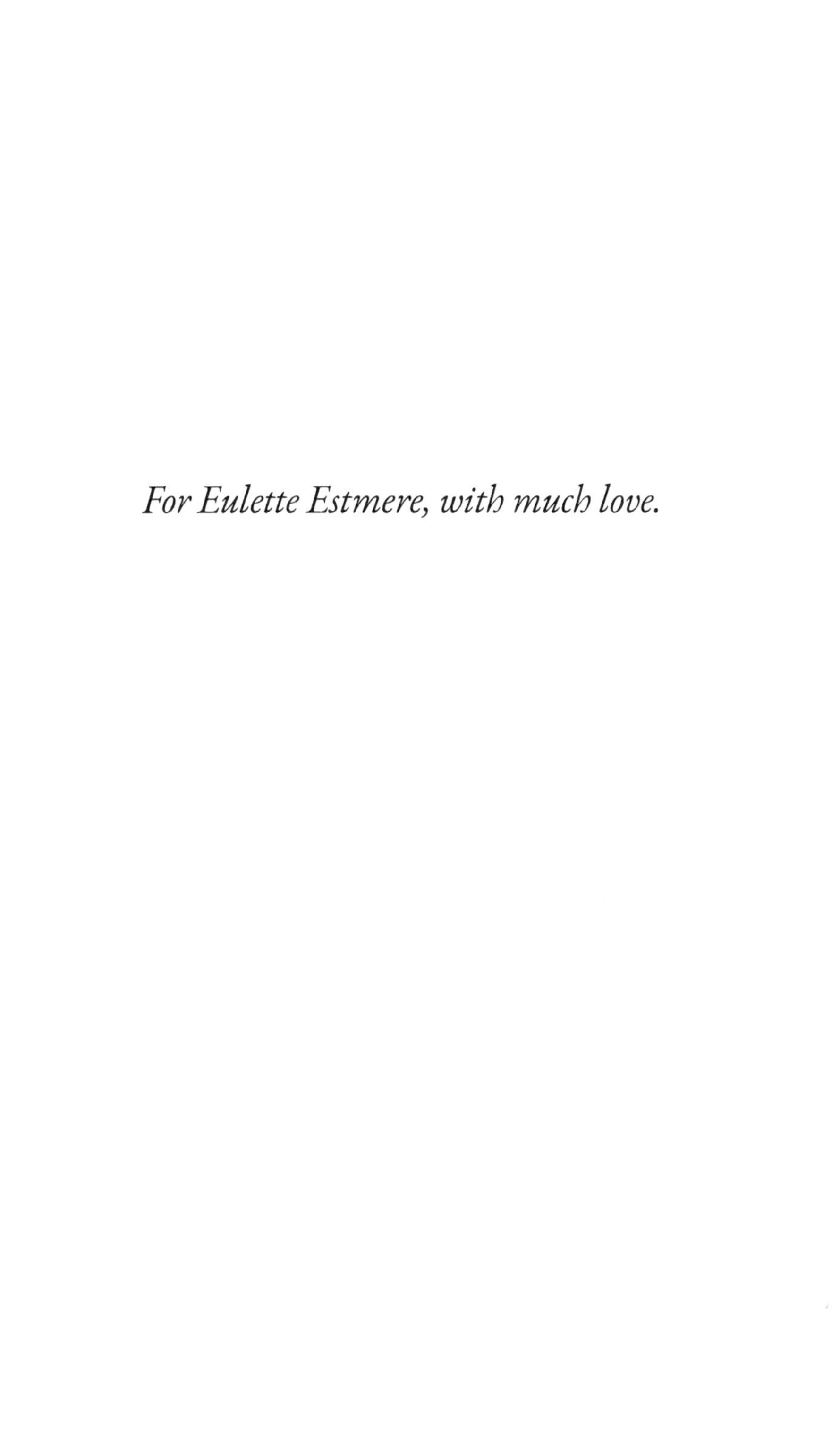

For Eulette Estmere, with much love.

TABLE OF CONTENTS

ONE

Four fifty-eight a.m. is burning hot.

The alarm will soon sound.

I rub my eyes to force the fog away, before gently nudging the snore. "Qu," I whisper. The snore continues without missing a rise and fall. "Qu!" I say a little louder.

"Five more minutes," Qu pleads groggily, roughly dragging the covers over his head.

"You know what? Fine!"

I'm tired too, but you know the drill!

Gritting my teeth, I throw off the covers, allowing the frigid air to attack. My legs refuse to move despite the goosebumps raiding my body. *How did I get here?*

"Mom, you up?" A soft voice pierces my thoughts, drawing my attention.

"Yes, Faith. I'm up."

"Mom, you remember you said you'd proofread my essay before work?"

The alarm's scream jolts me to my feet. I slap it off and spin around to face my daughter. "Faith, it's barely five o'clock," I plead. "I barely remember my name let alone what I promised you yesterday."

With a grin, she snaps on the light and roughly shakes my arm. "I know! That's why I got up now so you wouldn't forget. Here it is."

"Five more minutes," comes a muffled voice from deep under the quilt.

"Whatever," I sigh to no one in particular. Yawning, I stretch my arms skyward allowing my head to fall back.

"Mom!"

"Faith."

"Did you hear me?"

"Am I deaf?"

"Good. Gotta go bat'room," and with a shove of the binder and flash of her robe, Faith vanishes.

I stare blankly at the door for a few moments. A slight movement draws my eyes back to the bed. Kissing my teeth, I flick off the lights and shuffle to the kitchen.

Falling into a wooden chair I crack open to the cover page. *The Great Depression* in bold red letters stares back at me.

"Great," I grimace as I try to get my mind to understand what my eyes are reading.

Yadda, yadda, yadda...

"So, what you think?" Faith asks excitedly.

"What?"

"So, what do you think, Mom?" she draws out slowly.

"Please, give me a brea..."

"Wha' you mean?!"

"Faith. It's been five minutes!" My frustration boils under the surface.

"Mom, it's been longer than that."

Lord, this girl is testing me! I point at the wall clock. "No..." I glance up stunned to realize an hour and a half has already passed. "Forget it," I murmur, annoyed with myself. "I need a shower."

"Mom, this thing is due..."

I spin around, index finger loaded. "Faith, back off! I'll figure it out after I shower."

"Hey, Viv! Why didn't you wake me?" accuses Qu, sprinting across the upstairs hallway to the bathroom.

My head is pounding. I rest my face in my hands, leaning my elbows against the table.

"Mom!"

"Faith."

"I need—"

"Faith now's not the time."

"Fine," she shoots back at me. Yanking her binder, Faith huffs towards her room. She thinks twice before firmly closing her door.

Good... Anyhow she slam that door it would have been me and she!

I knead my temples. *I ain't able with drama this morning. My head... I wonder if we got any aspirin. Times tickin.' I got to get moving.* The room swims around me as I lift my head. *Not this morning. I don't have time for this this morning!* Rising, I jerk open drawer after drawer. *This aspirin is hiding from me. When I gonna clean out this junk? I can't find anything in here!*

Slamming the last drawer, I turn around and lean against the counter. I quickly rub my hands together in circles. Once fired up, I place them on my cold cheeks. I then take my newly warmed fingers and massage life back into my lids. Opening my eyes, they rest on the wooden cross. Qu hung it above our doorway years ago when we just bought, or should I say mortgaged this place.

I forgot we even had it. How many times have I walked into the kitchen, right underneath the two wooden sticks, oblivious it was even there?

How did I get here?

"' Kay Viv, I'm gone!" Qu says racing to the door.

"Hmm...?"

"I'm gone. Later!"

"Right."

The front latch clicks before I realize I didn't get a chance to peck Qu on the cheek. He didn't seem to mind.

I have to get moving.

I pour the bitter liquid into my steel travel mug, smoothing the strands off my forehead with my other hand. *I remember a time I wouldn't touch coffee. Too strong, too foul, too bitter. Amazing, now I can't seem to do without it. Do I have everything?*

"Faith! Justin! Get a move on!" I scream over my shoulder.

Stone-faced, Faith drops her knapsack near my feet and tugs at her kilt.

"How'd your kilt shrink? Didn't we just buy that the other day?"

Faith rolls her eyes, "It wasn't the other day, and it didn't shrink."

"It's barely covering your butt."

"My butt's covered fine, Mother."

She is playing piano on my last nerve. "Faith, go put on some pants."

"But..."

"Faith, just do it."

"There's nothing wrong with this skirt!" she defies.

"Watch. Your. Tone." I seethe.

Breathe girl, breathe. One. Inhale. Two. Exhale. Three. Inhale.

Flames still blaze from my eyes as I try to remember what comes after three. Feeling the heat, Faith makes a beeline out the room. *Close call.*

Startled, I realize Justin is sitting at the table reading a paperback.

"Justin?"

Without raising his eyes, he drawls, "Why do you two have to go at it every morning?

Doesn't it ever get old?"

"How long you've been sitting there?" I deflect.

"Couple minutes," Justin replies nonchalantly. He licks his finger and turns the page.

My eyes cool on his face. *My children are like night and day. One I have to beg to stop talking and the other I have to bribe. So handsome. As a toddler, all I wanted to do was squeeze Justin as I held him on my lap. That was my joy. Just to hold him, rubbing his cheek against mine. Given the chance, I would be like that for hours. When was the last time I gave Justin a hug?*

My fingers brush his sleeve. He recoils as he grabs his bag.

"You ready?" Justin asks in the same monotone voice.

"Yeah, yeah, I'll meet you in the car."

Giving a sharp nod, he tosses the bag over his shoulder and is gone.

Right. He's not little anymore. I feel cold again. Silence hangs in the air for two beats before I realize... I'm forgetting something.

"Happy now?" Miss Sarcastic curtseys in the doorway.

"Hmm?"

"My pants!"

"Why is it hanging below your belly button?! Pull it up!"

"Pull it up, pull it down. There is no pleasing you!" Faith retorts between clenched teeth.

"Just get in the car! Oh," I tap my head, "you got your paper?"

"I took it from you earlier, remember?"

"Right, right. My head is just killing—"

"Then take an aspirin. Can I drive?"

"No. I value my life."

"Very funny. Come on, Mom. Ticktock."

"Ka boom," I sigh, grasping my coffee in one hand, book bag in the other, and keys jangling off my pinky as I race out behind her.

Wait...

I look down and see oversized, fuzzy slippers peering back at me. I tear back into the house.

Traffic is so slow today. *I have to remember to pick up some aspirin.*

"Mom!"

"Sorry?"

Faith rests her hand on my shoulder. "Remember, I have swim practice tonight, so I'll need a ride."

"OK. Justin, on the way home can you pick up Dad's dry cleaning?" I shove my hand in my purse, fishing for my wallet while keeping my eyes on the road.

"OK. Wait, I'll get it. How much should I take?" Justin gently places my hand back on the steering wheel, lifting my purse onto his lap.

"Twenty dollars should do. Thanks," I respond.

He riffles through the bills, rezips the wallet and drops it back into my bag.

I turn into the Kiss and Ride. *They should change the name. What self-respecting teenager is going to allow their parent to kiss them in front of their crew? Do they still say, crew?*

"Alright guys, see you later! Have a good day!"

"Alright Mom, later," they say almost in unison, slamming the doors behind them. They walk off in separate directions. Hesitating, I grip my steering wheel, watching their backs walk away. My temples throb. I reach down and thrust myself into drive.

Ticktock... Why does everyone slow down when I'm moments away from missing my train?

"Hello people! Lady here needs to merge! Ahh! Thank you, kind sir," I sigh to myself as if my fellow drivers can hear me.

Beads of sweat drip into my eyes as I dance from one lane to the next.

OK, five miles over the speed limit. I'm still in control. My calves tense. *OK, ten miles... fifteen... is it me or is nobody moving?*

"Come on, come on, hold on yellow... Damn! I was that close!" I slap the steering wheel as if it failed me. *I got five minutes. I can do this. OK, green.* I race down the street like it's life or death.

Come on, come on parking. Is everyone a moron? Lines people! Park between the lines! Aah, a spot. Looking good. Seasoned stunt driver style, I jerk backwards into the space, slap everything off, and dart from the car in one fluid motion. Head and feet pounding, I flash my card and dive for the doors as the conductor rattles off the 'stand clear' warning.

"Speaking of moron," I moan as I catch a glimpse of myself in the window. The platform whizzes by me as I frantically attempt to paste my hair in place with my fingers. *Forget it. I'll redeem myself at work.*

"Excuse me," I murmur as I brush past fellow commuters to the upper deck of the coach. I target a prime seat. Against my will, I'm racing again. *A window seat is gold on a grey rush hour morning. A window to rest my head. Passing scenery to dream by without the obstruction of people blocking my view. Absolute gold.* Flopping in the seat, I let my bag fall on my feet. Resting my head against the pane, I immediately close my heavy eyes. *Until the next round,* I muse.

Aspirin...swimming lesson...change for coffee...forgot mug in car... Do I have everything? Qu, you awake? Dry cleaning... The Great Depression... forgot to sort laundry. When were parent-teacher meetings again? Test in email, got to print it out. Two wooden sticks... How did I get here?

"We are arriving at Lewis. Lewis Station," the conductor scratchily announces through the intercom.

That was fast!

Flurry. People racing in every direction, pour onto the street. Crisp suits, colourful dresses, contrasting masks, backward baseball caps, heels clicking, basketball shoes pumping, and pieces of conversation wrapping around one another in a general din. Cell phones sounding, bags being hoisted, tossed, and swung, just missing contact with the masses. White lines drawn from ears to tunes, teardrop plugs glowing in ears answering to head nods, and kids keeping pace with their parents tightly squeezing their hands. Concrete buildings hover overhead. Heat and odour rise from the holes in the pavement. Storefronts with closed, darkened eyes. Homeless hands thrust forward as people dodge in response. I turn on the side street, relieved to see the paved yard leading to my school.

I'm almost there.

"Are you alright?"

Her words roll around my head and for a minute I don't understand her question. I glance up and we lock eyes. Her intensity startles me. I look away, ashamed.

"No, of course, yes, yes, I'm alright. Just need to get my stuff. You know how it is."

"Aha. Too well," Sarah pauses. The seconds of silence seem deafeningly loud to me.

"Listen, you are the teacher. You need a few minutes to get it together, splash water on your face, take it! Shoot. They just have to wait, right?" she bubbles with a strained laugh, squeezing my arm before heading for the door.

Conflicted, I stand there watching her back. *Splash water on my face? How bad do I look? What is happening...? Stop it! Just stop it. If you hurry, you can get coffee and the photocopying done with a minute to spare.*

I slam the locker shut, trip across the staff room and head straight for the half-done coffee pot. "Come on, come on..." I coax the brew as it splashes outside the mug, burning my hand. *No time.* I shoot the bitter down my throat as I fly into the copy room.

The bell sounds as I drop my load on the desk. *Lord, I made it! Ha!*

"Morning everyone," I greet the class. "It's Test Monday. Take a seat. Take a seat. Here Afi. Please take one and pass it along. Don't turn them over until everyone has received one." Afi slides sideways out of her seat, outstretches a reluctant hand, and grabs the pile from my grasp. She drags the top sheet off, before lifting the rest over her shoulder expectantly. I lean back against the desk and cross my arms. Watching the papers go from person to person, I look at the faces of my children.

You couldn't pay me to be thirteen years old again. Half of them look like they literally woke up five minutes ago. Trish at the back always seems to be pulled together though. Nothing particularly rattles her. Prepared for whatever's tossed her way. May she never change. What has Wayne done now? How many piercings can a body sustain before revolting?

"Ms. Moji?"

"Hmm, yes?"

"I asked if we could begin now?"

"Right. Does everyone have a paper?" I take their grumblings as affirmations. "Good. You can turn them over. You have an hour to complete the test starting now."

After a brief hush, pages start rustling and the pencil scratching begins. I yawn and circle the desk. *Let me take some time and iron out the next lesson plan.* Another yawn escapes me, only this time it is drawn out and sends a shiver through my body. *Hmph. I need this coffee more than I thought.* Taking another bitter draw from my cup, I glance at the door. Framed in the window is Principal Dour. The fluorescents reflecting off his smooth head give him a strange glow. I shoot him a quick smile before returning to the cup in my hand.

He returns the false grin as he knocks lightly. He pushes the door slightly ajar.

"Morning, Madame Moohee," Dour loudly whispers.

He will never get my name right.

"Good morning," I answer.

"After your class, could you please stop by my office?"

"Alright," I say slowly. "Anything I should be concerned about?"

"No. Just need to go over a few things with you. I'll see you at 10:30."

"Yes, 10:30."

"Bye," he replies, stepping back into the hallway.

Ten-thirty. I wonder what's on his mind. A low rumbling rises from my core. *Great!*

First my head, now my stomach. I pat my lap lightly, hoping it will subside. I shuffle my papers and poise my pen, preparing to review my lesson plan. My eyes blur. The words wash away. Time slugs on.

"This is bull," Todd mumbles.

I look up quickly, wiping my eyes. *Maybe I heard wrong.*

"Excuse me?"

"Nothing."

"Didn't sound like nothing. Swearing isn't permitted in this class. Hand in your paper."

Todd defiantly sits stock-still. He continues to stare me down. My eyes start to haze again. The roar inside me steadily rises. "Bull isn't swearing. Besides, why the hell should I care about a bunch of dead White people and their battles? I got my own!"

My ears grow hotter, and my mouth dries shut. I swallow. "Well, maybe if you studied—"

"What's the point?" he throws back.

I stumble on. "We learn history, so we have a better sense of—"

"What we? We are just a freakin' paragraph in this book!"

Half the class starts to fidget nervously. The other half keep their heads down pretending to be engrossed in their writing.

"We are more than a paragraph! History is packed with lessons for us to know."

"What the hell do you know?" he snaps.

My mouth hangs slightly open. *How did I get here?*

"This is *bullshit*!" he punctuates as he shoves his stuff into his knapsack. "I need to learn how to make money, not this shit," he snatches the door open.

"Make, make, make sure you go *straight* to the Principal's office!" I fail at trying to steady my voice.

Todd doesn't answer. The door hits the frame and vibrates. The roar in the pit of me is growing louder. I take a gulp of coffee before unsteadily crossing the front of the room. I gently close the door. Leaning there a moment, hands pressed against the gap, I try to digest what just happened.

I should call down to the office and tell them Todd is out there wandering. I should call...I should call...

I turn around to return to my desk, only to find twenty-four pairs of eyes staring at me keenly. "Please, you have fifteen minutes left. Begin to wrap up."

Heads self-consciously drop back down. Pencils scribble frantically. I pass my desk and walk along the row to Todd's empty chair. I finger his blank answer booklet. Turning it over, and over again, I hope to see any sign of effort. Looking up, I catch multiple eyes dart back to their papers. *The roar is deafening.* Mercifully, the bell rings. The students hastily hand in their papers and scurry for the exit. I thank them one by one as I watch them go.

Ten-thirty. I'll tell the Principal about Todd when I see him.

"Hi Dour, I mean Etienne. You wanted to see me?"

"Yes, please come in and close the door."

I step inside, talking all the while to drown out my rumbling stomach. "Thanks. Before I forget, I had an inci...dent...Sarah?"

"Hi, Viv."

Dour nods in Sarah's direction. "Yes, I asked Sarah to join us."

"Alright," I say hesitantly. My blood flows cold. I reach for the nearest armrest and lower myself.

"You were saying something about an incident,"

"It's nothing."

"Sure?"

"Very."

The office hangs in suspended silence. Sarah twitches in her seat, eying Dour intensely.

"Well, Viv, before I begin, I just want to say, you've been working at St. Mike's for over ten years now and I've always found you to be a woman of integrity,"

"Yes," I reply. *Just spit it out!*

"However, I've noticed, as has Sarah, that these past few months you seem to be... well... struggling."

"Struggling," I repeat.

Sarah briskly turns to face me. "You are often late for work and forgetful. Sometimes, I or another teacher may be talking to you, and you seem... preoccupied."

I stare at her mouth flapping all my transgressions at me, fanning the flame hotter and hotter. *How dare she?* I'm perspiring. *How do I defend myself without losing it?* The fierce rumble keeps rocking me back and forth. *I can't stop rocking.*

"Viv?"

"Yes, sorry?"

"I asked if there was anything wrong that you would like to talk about."

I turn to Dour and swallow. "As a matter of fact, everything is wrong. I give 100% every day. Every year my class responsibilities grow. More students, more subjects, more homeroom duty, sometimes supply, extracurricular, Black Heritage Month preparation because God forbid any of the other teachers take the initiative—"

"That's enough!" Dour bellows.

Say what?!

"We are not having this meeting to point fingers at you. No one is saying you don't do good work..."

"Well, that's funny because that's exactly what I heard Sarah—"

"Then you heard wrong!"

I fall into a shocked stupor. I'm completely confused. *One inhale... one inhale... one inhale.... Why can't I breathe?*

Dour clears his throat. "We are here because it seems like you are struggling."

"I'm not struggling. I'm fine."

"It seems like you may need some time."

"Don't need time. I'm fine."

"Viv," Dour's voice evens. He addresses Sarah. "Sarah, can you please give us a moment?"

"Sure," Sarah hastens. The door closes gently behind her.

Dour comes around the desk and sits in the now empty seat beside me. *I can't bring myself to look at him.* "Viv, can you honestly say nothing we've said here holds any truth?"

My head hurts. *What does he want? Blood? I don't give blood.* I shake my head, lying to myself. "Etienne, everything is under control."

I wait. Dour eventually returns to his chair, obviously exasperated. The uncomfortable silence returns.

"Can I go now?" I say meekly.

"No," he says leaning forward abruptly.

"I can't leave, Etienne! I've got tests to grade, lesson plans to finalize, I'm working on that research project we discussed last month, it's too close to—"

"Viv, I don't care what your excuses are, you are on leave, effective immediately!"

He can't just fire me like this! I'm fine!

"I have responsibilities, Dour. Bills." *If only he knew how much.* He reaches for my hand. I dodge just in time.

"Etienne, not Dour," he gently corrects. "And of course, you'll still be on payroll."

"I was saving my vacation time for—"

"Consider it a paid leave."

"Dour, sorry, Etienne. I'm fine!"

"Viv, you're not! Now I can't make you tell me what's going on with you, but I can, as your supervisor, give you some time to sort it out before..." he trails off.

Before what? How do I defend myself? I don't know what to say that will make him hear me.

Agitated, Dour starts fidgeting with the papers on his desk. "Believe it or not, I'm on your side. Just leave me your notes and I'll deal with your tasks. That's what supply teachers are for," he jokes.

I'm replaceable. "How can I leave my kids?" *I've failed.*

Dour stops and folds his hands. He looks at me like he can read my mind. "This isn't punishment. You are not on suspension. I'm actually trying to support you."

I can't let him see me cry. "Dour, can I leave now?" I plead.

He grimaces but decides not to correct me again, "Fine."

I spring up and charge the door.

"Don't forget to leave me your notes," he yells.

I'm too busy finding cover to answer him.

TWO

How could Sarah do this to me? I could just...

The tears are running into my mouth. I try to wipe them as quickly as they fall but I'm losing the battle. *Keep it together girl. Don't let anyone see you like this!* The rumbling quickens with every tear. *Keep it together. Keep it together.*

I clear my desk, dropping notes haphazardly into an interoffice envelope before venomously twisting the string shut.

"He wants me to go? Fine! I'll go! Support what? Do I look like a charity case? Did I ask for his support? Since when is he, Mother Teresa?" I huff to the teachers' lounge thankful none of my gossipy colleagues are around to hear my muttering. I jam the envelope into Dour's slot.

Fine, I'm going. I'm going!

I empty my locker into my knapsack unseeingly.

Twenty years and he figures NOW I need support, I think, sardonically. *I'm gone alright.* With that, I slam the locker shut.

I can barely see. I push through door after double door, cocking my head low to avoid any potential eye contact. I notice blonde Mary walking towards me. She smugly rolls her eyes as she edges away from me. *I must look a mess. If I had gotten here earlier, I wouldn't have to hike it to Siberia.*

I pass car after endless car in the staff parking lot. The heat off the line of metal burns me. *Where are my keys?!* Shoving my hand deeper into my sack, I pull out a handful of stuff, look, drop, and start rummaging again, hoping my hand will discover the prize. Ah! I snatch the keys flipping through until the car key hits my index finger.

Wait... I stop mid-stride. I hit the keys *against my forehead. I took the train!*

Frustrated, I turn back towards the street, dabbing at my face from time to time with what's left of the tissue I swiped from the lounge. *I'll soon be at the station. I'll be home soon,* I comfort myself.

Feeling like a pariah, I swerve around people and brush past storefronts. The heat is beating down on me. My pulse quickens. A deep moan escapes me. The *I'll soon be home; I'll soon be home* mantra continues to propel me.

Flurry. People racing in every direction. Worn jeans, colourful dresses, backward baseball caps, heels clicking, exposed jewelled belly buttons, and pieces of conversation wrapping around one another in a general din. Eyes cocked downward, cell phones sounding, and bags being hoisted, tossed, swung, just missing contact with the masses. White lines drawn from ears to tunes, teardrop plugs glowing in ears answering to head nods, women staring into windows with cupped hands. Concrete buildings hover overhead. Heat and odour rise from holes in the pavement. Storefronts with bright neon signs entice. Homeless hands thrust forward as people hold their breath and sidestep in response.

I'll soon be home; I'll soon be home...

Thank God for air conditioning!

Fumbling, I find my ticket. Glancing up, I check the prompter. *Good, it leaves in ten minutes.* I start to pick off the pieces of damp tissue from my cheek as I walk towards the platform. *It's not here yet!*

"Attention, train passengers. Those on Platform B Northbound, please note the train will be delayed by approximately fifteen minutes. I repeat..." the announcement rattles on overhead.

"Delayed," I sigh. Looking around, I spot a bench and shuffle towards it. A sharp pain pierces my temples again. Dropping down, I rest my face in my hands.

How did I get here? I'm going nowhere fast.

What am I going to tell Qu? Oh, by the way, my boss thinks I'm incompetent, no, maybe cracked is a better word, and he relieved me of my duties temporarily instead of firing my ass. Or how about, it's come to my attention that I'm "struggling" so like the mess that I am, I've been sent home for my own good. This whole thing is ridiculous! I had everything under control.

The horn sounds. I stand and wait for the door to roll to me. Off by a few steps, I reposition myself, clutching the railing, and pull myself up and into the coach. After showing my ticket, I trudge up the stairs. It's emptier than at rush hour. What a relief. Less people to see me crying like a baby. Dropping into a two-seater, I begin searching my bag for another tissue.

What am I going to tell them? I don't want to tell them anything! Be great if I could start this day over. If I hadn't been late and let that Judas, Sarah, catch me... Shoot! I should have told Dour about Todd walking out. I won't be able to follow up. I handled that badly. What was I thinking? Todd had a real complaint and all I could think to give him was some trite answer. If I were him, I'd walk out too! Seriously, what the shit do I know?!

How did I end up here?

I watch as grey buildings meld into lush trees as they rush past my window. For a moment, I forget myself and relax in the stillness of the coach. I look around, and there isn't anyone else in the upper deck. I exhale and relax a little more. I pat my stomach, attempting to calm it. My eyes return to the window. I've run out of tears.

I need to put this in perspective.

I can always call Dour and tell him about Todd. But I can't hide this 'leave' from Qu or the kids, can I? I feel so ashamed. This is not me. I'm the one people rely on. I'm the person that will stay late to get the job done; NOT be sent home for 'struggling.'

"Breathe, Viv," I remind myself.

What do they see? What do they define as struggling? Because I was late a couple of times? Because I didn't hear them when they may have been talking to me? What else did Sarah accuse me of again? I laugh at the irony. Right, I didn't hear anything else. I was too busy trying to defend myself. Fabulous. In this instance, I prove her right.

I shake my head and return my gaze to the window. *What a mess.* Looking out distracts me. I knead my right shoulder. My neck, shoulders and back are in a vice. The sun is trying to peak through the clouds. *It may not rain after all. This morning was so grey, I assumed a thunderstorm was coming. I was wrong.*

Older houses and low apartments whiz past, merging into an elongated brown-beige palate. I continue to stare, hoping to keep my thoughts at bay.

My stop is coming up. I still don't know what to do. Of course, I'll tell them, but how?

Besides that, what am I going to do with myself for a whole week? Clean my house? Who wants to do that? Not even I want to face my dust bunnies. I laugh at my joke. Seriously, a week to do what? Dour and his sort out stuff—struggling talk. What am I going to do? How did I get here? That question has been constantly nagging me...for a long time now...creeps in when I'm not even facing... that...not even facing that question.

"Next stop is Main, Main Station," the automated voice broadcasts.

I look at my bag lying beside me, not sure if I should pick it up. The train screeches to an eventual stop. Not knowing what else to do, I make my descent to the sliding doors and step onto the pavement. I stand there a while. The train speeds past my back, blowing dust up into my hair. I feel the salt sheen crusting my face. I look left and right. *Where did I park?* I am oblivious to the few other passengers who walk a safe distance around me. I choose a direction, not knowing if I've made the right move.

It has to be here somewhere. I make my way down yet another aisle. *In my mood, I might as well hop a bus. Oh, there it is.* I open the door and a wave of fire hits me. I crawl in and repeatedly press all the window buttons frantically. Drained, I stop.

"Right. If the car is not on, the buttons are useless," I scold myself. Sitting back in the driver's seat, I close the door and lay back on the headrest, letting the fire engulf me.

Alright, I'm in the car. I'm in and don't want to go home. I don't want to face anybody.

Then, where?

I've got… I take out my wallet and count my few bills. *Fourteen bucks, not a bad day! Wait! I also have a credit card, a debit card, and I get paid in a few days. Maybe I don't have to go home.* A slow thrill runs through me. I slowly twirl the idea around my head for a while. *What if I didn't go home? Where can I go?* The rumble gains intensity.

I've been so wrapped up in my thoughts, my body's a twisted vice, I'm dejected… Maybe Dour's right! Maybe I am screwed and need to take care of my business. I grip the steering wheel. "I'm going to start with food," I decide as I spark the car. *Big, rich, melt in your mouth, laden with fat, completely indulgent…something. I'm on a mission!*

I press the window buttons down and a cool breeze fills the vehicle. I turn onto the road feeling purposeful again.

What do I want to eat? Burgers? Pasta? West Indian? Thai? I slow to a halt at the light. I briefly catch a glimpse of myself in the rearview mirror. I look wretched. *Maybe I should eat in the car. Drive-through. Definitely drive-through.* I follow the road southbound. The traffic isn't too heavy, but I decide to stay in the right lane and take my time.

Driving further and further from my house, the tension slowly loosens its grip on my neck. I wipe my fingers under my eyes and blink. *I'm in a rush to go nowhere in particular, and it feels oddly comforting. This is my time. Mine. I'm going to find something to eat and enjoy it,* I try to convince myself. *I am going to be alright. I'll find a place to eat and feel better.*

I fix my gaze far down the road. It's been a long time since I went down this street. *It's changed a lot! I don't recognize most of these buildings. It's become trendy! It's been barely half an hour and I've passed at least five coffee shops!* "You know it's a trendy area when the coffee culture is blatant," I laugh lightly to myself. *A whole lot of caffeine.*

I drive aimlessly. I pass burger joints, Italian restaurants, and Indian cuisine. Nothing entices me to stop. Despite the constant rumbling, I can't make up my mind. Nothing seems good enough for me to stop. Nothing seems good. The pain in my head is now a grey drone I've grown used to. Being in control of the wheel is soothing. I'm not ready to give up the drive. One community blends into another. The sounds float past me in droves. Car radio buzz, storefront Latin beats, fragments of conversation, cell ringtones, dogs barking, and laughter float in and out my car windows with every passing block. Houses, to lofts, to malls, to high-rises, I pass them all on my journey. Time slips by.

I follow the road as it curves along the lakefront. I find myself pulling up into a parking lot of a low-rise white hotel. I turn off the ignition and wait. I glance at my watch. It's 4:07 p.m. I look up and stare at the hotel. Lethargically, I lift the passenger window buttons first and then close the driver's side window. I sit. Waiting. Lifting my bag, I slowly open the car door and step out.

"Hello Ma'am," greets the perky teenager behind the reception desk.

"Hello," I reply, haltingly.

"May I help you?"

I find myself saying, "Yes, I would like to book a room for a few nights."

I am totally bewildered. *I would?*

"How many? We just need to book the number of nights in the system."

"Alright, two, for now," I decide quickly.

"Okay, two nights. Just know that it's low season so if you need to stay longer, that's no problem," she assures. "Queen or king-size bed?"

"Queen."

"Smoking or non-smoking?"

"Non-smoking, please." I hand her my credit card and identification before nervously looking around the lobby. My eyes return to the girl's face, searching for clues. *What must she think? I arrive at a hotel for the night looking like Don King, with no luggage on a weekday. Ain't that a tiny bit suspicious?* The girl is absorbed in her typing.

"All set. Here are your cards back and the key card to your room. Do you know how to use it?"

"Yes," I lie. *I should be able to figure it out. It looks like a debit card and Lord knows I've mastered that.*

"The stairs and elevator are to your right. If you are interested in using the pool or weight room, it is just left of reception," she motions. "You're in room 212. If you need any assistance, please dial 0 and I'll be happy to help you."

"Thank you," I nod, hoping I remember everything.

"No problem. Enjoy your stay," and with an abrupt smile, she starts gathering the printouts.

How easy was that! I walk to the stairs with a new sense of freedom.

I tap the key around the door handle several times. On the ninth time, a flash of green releases the latch. Relieved, I flick the switch and this beautiful room illuminates. *It's so clean!* I think joyfully. I close the door and stand a while, taking it all in.

Small kitchenette on my left. *Look at that wood!* I run my fingers over the surfaces. *Coffee pot, drawers... I thought I asked for a queen bed. That looks like a king! Who cares? I am not giving this up now!* I roll over the covers in glee. *So silky, and the pillows!* I sit up and soak in the rest of the room. *Teal-coloured chaise lounge, side table, desk and armchair, TV—I may never leave!* I dash to the bathroom. *There are lights over the bathtub! Look at the marble sink bowl. And the towels! So luxurious!* I delicately replace the towel on the shelf and return to the bedroom. I exhale. "Thank you, God," I whisper, "this is an oasis."

Walking onto the balcony, I sit a moment and take in the lake's expanse.

Flopping on the bed, I empty my knapsack. I finger the contents: crumpled tissue, empty notebook, pens, pens, and more pens, funky cat-eye reading glasses, wallet, mints, sunglasses, lotion, hand sanitizer, dictionary (*dictionary?*), half-finished motivational book, pictures of the kids, half-falling apart address book, pay stubs, keys, expired train tickets, an old beauty magazine, miscellaneous receipts (*I may as well throw those out*), cell phone and a few forgotten tarnished pennies (*who carries a dictionary, address book or pennies anymore?*). *Okay, it's a start. I'll go get something to eat and pick up a few things to get by.* I open the side drawer and notice a Bible. I shove it aside and lay my belongings neatly beside it. After washing my face and rinsing my mouth with warm water, I place my hotel key in my wallet and step lightly into the hallway.

THREE

"Are you sure you didn't hear from Mom?" Faith whines as she throws Qu a look of disbelief.

"How could she just forget about me? It's nine o'clock for shit's sake!"

Qu keeps his eyes on the road and sighs. "Watch your mouth. I know you are upset, but Faith, why would I lie? I don't know where your mother is." He slows to turn the corner.

"And?" she pouts.

"And she's not at the school and there are no messages from her," he speeds up. "I'm sure she's fine. She probably went out with some other teachers and lost track of time. I wouldn't worry about it," he lies to keep the peace.

"Oh! I'm not worried! I'm pi—!" Faith spits back, glaring out her window.

Qu stops in the driveway and cuts her off. "Listen, go inside and see if Mom called. I have to pick up a few things at the store."

"OK."

Qu watches her back as she fiddles her key in the lock. Once inside, he gives her a quick wave before turning his head to back out of the driveway.

I called everyone I could think of and nothing! No one has heard from her all day. I called Memorial, Pacific General, and no Vivian Moji was admitted. What the hell is going on? Where the hell is she?

Qu's temple bulges as his jaw becomes more and more rigid. His grip on the steering wheel tightens as he weaves his way to 57 Division. Drawing closer to the building, he becomes aware of himself. *I can't roll up, all angry Black man. Keep it together. I can't believe I'm even here.* Eying a space close to the entrance, he swings the car between the lines and pushes the door open.

"Hi, can I help you?" The officer continues to stare into his screen.

I don't know, can you? Qu carefully chooses his words as he notes the number 3050 stitched on the officer's shoulder. "I'm not sure if this is where I should be, but I ran out of ideas," Qu leans his elbow on the counter.

The officer instinctively leans back in his chair behind the desk. Officer 3050's jaw visibly twitches.

"It's my wife. I saw her this morning, she went to work and then disappeared. I've checked the school where she works. I called all her friends, family. I've tried her on her cell. Nothing. I was thinking there may have been an accident in the city or something. If you could give me some advice on how to find her, I'd appreciate it. Her name is Vivian Moji."

The officer nods sharply and starts clicking on the computer. "You said that the last time you saw her was this morning?"

"That's right."

"V-I-V-I-A-N and how is her last name spelt?" he asks flatly.

"M-O-J-I."

"Date of birth?"

Qu rhymes it off.

"Your name, date of birth and address?"

Feeling interrogated, Qu reaches into his wallet and hands 3050 his driver's license to clear himself. The officer leans the card against the screen as he continues to type. With a final tap on the return key, the officer leans back slightly as his eyes dart back and forth across the screen.

"Do you see anything about my wife?" Qu finally asks after a prolonged silence.

"I'm sorry sir, but due to privacy legislation, I am not at liberty to tell you what we may or may not have in our records related to your wife," the officer answers mechanically.

"But she's my wife."

Officer 3050 stands and crosses his arms. Qu places his hands on the counter.

"She is an adult sir. I can't tell you if there are any prior records concerning your wife."

Qu takes a deep inhale. *Let's try this again.* "What can you tell me?"

"When was the last time you saw her again?"

"This morning around 6:30 a.m. She was getting ready for work."

"How was her mood this morning? How was her state of mind this week?"

How do I answer that? If I say she was overworked, forgetful and tired, how would that be interpreted? Depressed? Suicidal? I don't know. "Normal. Nothing out of the ordinary."

"Did she leave any notes?"

Now you're just pissing me off. "No notes."

"You mentioned you tried contacting her on her phone."

"Yes, but she wasn't answering so..."

"So, her phone was not left in the house?"

"Yes, the phone was not left in the house."

The officer continues to nod as if mulling over what Qu just said.

Why is he asking me all these questions and not writing anything down? What's that nod mean?

"Alright, I think I have enough information to relay to dispatch. Please go home and an officer will meet you there." Officer 3050 slaps Qu's driver's license on the counter, signalling his dismissal.

Qu stares at 3050 incredulously. *I don't want the cops near my house!* "I have kids and don't want them to worry. I'd rather stay and wait."

Irritated, 3050 sits. "Fine, once I give them the information for the missing person report, I'll ask an officer to come to the station and talk to you instead. Please take a seat to the left." The officer resumes typing and staring expressionlessly at the screen.

Qu's mind shuts down as he looks around the barren reception area. Shaking his head, he turns and walks away.

FOUR

I am totally reborn sitting in my fluffy terry robe, stretched out on my lounge chair, all scented and warm. The TV is tuned to an awards show as I savour every grain of my Chinese rice. The rumbling is a distant memory. Setting down the Styrofoam container, I wipe my lips on a napkin, rise, and retrieve my cell phone.

Five per cent. I stare at it a moment before plugging it in. 'You have 11 messages,' flashes on the screen. *I bet I do. Not listening.*

I lift the hotel phone receiver. Clearing my throat, I speak after the beep. "Ha-Hi! Qu, Faith, Justin. It's me, Mom. I'm alright. Ahh, umm...I had a rough day at work and was asked to take a few days' leave. But I'm alright! It's not a big deal, trust me (I give a stiff laugh). I just decided to take some time and sort out a few things (*there are those words again*) but I will call again and be home in a day or two (*a day or two?*). I don't want you to worry about me or feel you have to come looking for me. I'm fine. Be good to one another. Love you."

Did it sound breezy enough? Should I have told them where I was? Wait. I'm not breaking any law. Actually, that was terrible, I should re-record. Should I re-record?

I squeeze my eyes shut, holding tightly to the phone. Relaxing my grip, I hastily click the hashtag twice to send.

It's done. It will be fine. As it's on my mind, I also need to brief Dour about following up with Todd. Later.

I carefully return the receiver to the cradle and exhale. I curl up in my chaise and engross myself in the glitz of Hollywood. I glow as one of my favourite soul divas raises her statuette skyward, thanking the nation.

I don't know when I fell asleep. I wake up in pitch black, spare the brightness of the rectangular screen watching me. Stretching myself, I stand and power off the TV. The room glows in the moonlight. For a moment I'm motionless, lest I dispel the beauty of the room. I finally move towards the bed and burrow under the covers. *I feel almost guilty enjoying this luxury and not telling Qu where I am. The house is such a mess and here I am in this peaceful wonderland. This is not real. This is temporary, I can't stay here forever.*

Stop it! Just stop it!

Why did I have to go there? I'm here for a short time, why can't I just allow myself to enjoy this? In fact, this is the first time I've allowed myself any indulgence since I've been married. And why? Don't I deserve this? Why can't I just turn off my mind and enjoy this? I'm annoying myself.

I grimace, punch the pillow, and slam my head back down, angrily. *This is my time. I have a week to 'sort things out,' whatever that means.*

I yawn and feel my body relax again.

Sort things out...

My mind begins to float. I dream.

How did I get here?

Where is she?

Worried, Qu scratches his chest and glances at his wife's empty pillow beside him.

What kind of cryptic message was that anyway? Don't look for me. Has she left me? What if she didn't leave me and was taken? When was the last time I heard of a missing Black woman being found alive? What am I going to tell Justin and Faith? Should, should I contact the police again? That was a waste of time. I don't want the kids to worry, but I don't have any answers. Maybe I'll just lie and tell them she's visiting her cousin. I don't know.

Qu sighs heavily, now staring at the ceiling.

Lord, I know we haven't been on speaking terms lately, but I need you now. Please look after Viv and bring her home safely. I love her. Maybe I should have told her that, but you know I love her! Whatever she is going through, Lord, make her come back to me and we'll work it out. Promise!

Agitated, he turns over and focuses on the window. *Lord, bring her back to me.* The plea circles over and over. The moon's rays bring him little comfort as he continues to wrestle.

FIVE

How did I get here?

These words whisper me conscious. I listen to the morning waves outside my window. I'm so glad I left my balcony screen slightly ajar for the fresh air to flow throughout the suite last night. The cool air brushes my cheek, but I don't stir. I purposely keep my eyes shut. Cocooned in the duvet, my mind fixates on the question.

How did I get here? This question keeps haunting me. I'm forever moving in a frenzy of busyness. I never stop to think of why. Do I even have goals? I work because I have to. I have bills. A lot of bills. I have a family. I have responsibilities. The house, the car, my parents, my students, the women's haven. I need to be responsible. I am my mother's child, after all. Always doing what I have to do.

What do I do now?

Freaking out and driving for hours and miles on end without a destination, is, definitely not me! Spending a spontaneous night in a hotel by myself, without my family knowing where I am—what? Yet here I am. Sleeping in on a weekday in this gorgeous bed!

I rest my arm on my forehead and sigh.

If I look in the mirror right now, will I recognize myself? Did I ever know who I was?

I'm sober now. Eyes wide open. The sheets are still cosily wrapped around me. I sit up in bed and hug my knees close. I let my mind wander.

Did I ever know what I was capable of? I've always done what's expected. I went to school and was top of my class. There was no other choice. Good grades would win out over beatings every time.

University was a blink. I was good at writing papers and studying. Thank God, I love to read. I think that's what got me through. Even if I didn't particularly like the subject, I could read the required text without gagging. I enjoyed it.

Reading or listening to the content, then interpreting the words in my writing helped me better remember the lessons. But sometimes, just sitting there listening to professors drone on and on, I'd begin to daydream as I wrote. The lecture became alive for me. I'd be in Ghana, watching Nkrumah change a nation. I'd be floating amongst the stars, touching Venus. I'd play with fanciful chemical equations that professors tossed my way.

Hmm... Maybe not knowing what I wanted then was a good thing. It afforded me more... perspective. Being a generalist, I'd bounce from geography to science, to literature to charcoal drawing, drama, political science, whatever! Just out of curiosity. It didn't matter what direction I took, as long as I was in school and far away from my mother's belt.

I rock myself gently.

My parents tried so hard with me. They always wanted me to exceed. In their eyes, I wasn't meant to just survive.

I inhale deeply.

For them, coming here was about survival. Their survival together. Now that I think about it, I don't think they knew how rich they were back home! I don't think they knew any better. From the way they reminisce, their time there was richer than over here with all its currency. I remember my mom, Althea, telling me how she and her older twelve brothers and sisters lived on acres and acres of farmland. How they all had a role. Anyhow one member didn't comply, the whole family felt it. There was an unspoken understanding that every child and adult was important for the family to do well. Everyone was important. No one would question the equality of the work. Seeding, changing diapers, ploughing, washing floors, weeding, dusting, harvesting, making beds, boxing produce, washing siblings, selling in the market, hand-washing clothes—every task was weighed the same. This ensured the home ran smoothly.

On Sundays, no one worked. It was Sunday morning big breakfast with provisions and callaloo, Church, socializing, and soup for dinner. My mom would tell me how they all lived in a modest four-bedroom home with a dank outhouse, where not only did they manage, they also loved. Well, maybe not the outhouse so much, but the house itself.

I smile to myself.

Being close like that meant she was never alone. Infrequently in her youth, she would crave being alone, so she'd sneak into the fields, lie amongst the roots, and count the clouds. Her sisters and brothers were her best friends and still are. They would defend each other at a drop of a pin. Being one of the youngest also had its rewards. Wherever her older sisters would go, she'd be swung on a back, and off on the journey too. The exposure brought her early maturity. She has always been an old soul.

When Ma's father died, her siblings were already adults, looking after their own families. A few had moved into town away from the family land. Sister would raise niece. Brother would work alongside brother-in-law. They always looked after one another and were always up and in each other's business too! I could never tell which cousin was for which aunt or uncle because their lives were all so intertangled. They did what they could for Mooma, as they affectionately called Grandma Rose, but she still had to hire some neighbourhood youth to help her with the heavier farm chores. There was a steady stream. Unfortunately, what she could pay them was a "pittance," as Ma would say, so the quality of the work matched. My mother had to take on more tasks including managing the money. The way my mom describes it, Daddy's (as she called Grandpa) passing took a huge toll on Mooma. They were soul mates. They were deeply in love. Apparently, they made every decision together, every move together, and never had a harsh word to say to one another. They held hands till the day he died. After his passing, Mooma grew listless.

My father, Josiah's, family was not quite so big or so close. He had two sisters and a brother and lived off and on a few homes down from Ma. My father was raised by his Aunt Carol, in town, and would visit his mother, stepfather, and sisters, from time to time. He has been an earnest person for as long as I've known him. While Ma would tell me her whole life story and throw in tidbits of juicy gossip, usually exaggerated, my father was more reserved. I know very little about the way he grew up. I don't know why his mother didn't raise him. I don't know what happened to his father or even if he knew his father. I'm not sure if his sisters were full or half-sisters since back home, if you had a drop of the same blood, you were considered family no matter what. For all I know, his so-called sisters may be cousins or neighbourhood kids and not actual siblings. I like that though. Sisters and brothers, aunts and uncles, whether blood-related or not. We can always use more family. More people in our corner who accept us unconditionally. Love us unconditionally. Anyway, I suspect there was something wrong with his younger brother. I imagine he was possibly disabled or committed some crime, something serious like that. But again, the family rarely mentions him, so he's a complete mystery. I only heard about him by accident as a child eavesdropping on my parents' conversation one night.

When Mooma fell on hard times, Dad offered to work part-time on the farm. He already had a job in a tailor's shop, so he'd work there four days a week and the remaining days worked on the farm for room and board. The way my mom tells it, Dad just wanted to be close to her. The glint in her eyes also told me she wanted to be close to him as well. Of course, Mooma knew none of this.

They didn't actually date. They worked on the farm together and would have lunch in the field together and talk for hours at a time. Not that I would ever call my mom a liar, but it's still difficult for me to believe their relationship was all toil and talk. Part of me chooses to fantasize about this grand, passionate love affair between them. Her telling was way too mundane and chaste. I guess that's my twenty-first-century mind.

Somehow, my father got the opportunity to move abroad. He didn't want to go alone but didn't know how to ask Mooma for Ma's hand in marriage. Mooma depended on her. By that time, Ma was the only one left in the house and was managing the finances. Though he told Ma about his intention to leave, he kept his intentions concerning her to himself. Dad needed to stir up the courage to speak to Grandma. My father was—is—a gentle soul. Dad requested a meeting with Grandma one day and they sat on the porch, not knowing Ma, in her nosiness, had her ear pressed against the inside doorjamb. He asked for Ma's hand, assuring Mooma he would send her money every month and they would visit every year.

Hmm... I scratch my cheek. *The money promise was held, but the yearly visit promise was broken.*

The story goes, after he told her his intentions, Mooma cried "a river of mourning" (I love my mom and her dramatics). Days passed. Grandma never gave him an answer. I believe Mooma knew it was only right for Ma to live her life. I also believe that she was probably afraid to let her last child go, especially to some unknown country.

Dad waited. He continued to work, continued to lunch with Ma, but never spoke of the conversation he had with Grandma Rose. Now, if you know my mother, you know the whole situation drove her right around the bend! I laugh out loud.

Without any of them knowing, she had already packed her one meagre bag and was ready to elope at a moment's notice. But my dad may be a lot of things. Sometimes he could appear indifferent. Other times, thoughtful. These days, even outrageous! But no one could ever accuse Dad of being rash. In his heart, he was not a thief and to take Althea away without Mooma's permission would be equivalent to treason. So, he waited. And waited.

Three days before he was set to leave, Grandma still hadn't given Dad an answer, and Ma was itching. He stood firm. Still working the farm. Still saying nothing. Ma, however, was going crazy! She went to Grandma Rose and begged. I think this shamed Grandma. She had watched Dad grow up. She had him in her home when her husband was alive and observed his ways with her sons. In her heart of hearts, he <u>was</u> her son. She knew his character and loved him.

Tear-stained, the two women walked out into the field and approached Dad. Mooma, with a little tremble, looked Dad in his brimming eyes as she placed Ma's small hand in his. Overwhelmed, Dad reached into his satchel and took out an envelope and paper. Both were a bit crumpled. He must have had it on him since the talk. On the paper, he had written and signed the promises he made to Grandma on the porch so many weeks before. In the envelope was a month's wages with Rose's name written on the outside in hard-pressed black ink. They all cried that day, but this time from full hearts of joy.

When I was young, I'd ask my mom to tell me this story over and over again. I remember it verbatim. I couldn't hear it enough.

I crawl out of bed and stand by the window looking over the water. *Being here is like a leisurely dream.* I hug my waist.

Yesterday, I bought this sheer, ivory nightgown at the speciality shop a few blocks from the hotel. *My mother used to always have a drawer full of frilly negligées, and I never saw the point. They seemed so ultra-Fifties and frivolous. Yet, when I walked into the store last night, I gravitated to this particular negligee. The fabric is lustrous and when I lifted the hanger under my chin to look at myself in the mirror, my skin glowed. When I placed it back on the rack and caught my reflection, I was taken aback by how my face appeared puffy and dull. With all that crying and wailing less than an hour before, what did I expect? Yet, I couldn't reconcile the transformation moments before. How could*

I be luminous one second and sallow the next? There was no way I was leaving this gown! It made me look alive! It was meant for me!

I breathe a long sigh as I feel the soft fabric. *I should go find some breakfast. Figure out what to do next.*

As I turn, the breeze lightly catches my hem.

SIX

"Good Morning, Ma'am. Are you ready to order?"

"Thank you, but I need a few more minutes."

"Alright," nods the waiter as he leaves to help another table.

Okay, let's see. This week is about me sorting things out so let me start with my stomach. Juice instead of coffee, maybe? What juice choices do they have?

"Are you ready now, Ma'am?"

He's back! What was that? Two seconds?

I close my eyes and the menu. "Alright. I'll have a cranberry juice, veggie omelette, whole grain toast, butter on the side, with a few slices of tomato please."

Good! I've said it fast before I can change my mind.

"Would you like tea or coffee as well with your meal?"

Coffee! Say coffee!

"Yesss… Do you have mint tea?"

Mint tea? Seriously?

"Yes, we have mint tea. I'll be right back with your breakfast."

"Thank you," I hand him back the menu.

I look around the dining room, twisting my napkin in my lap. I am falling more and more in love with this hotel.

"That is a very healthy breakfast you've ordered," I hear a deep voice say beside me.

I glance to the right. *I didn't even see him there.* I laugh self-consciously. "Yes," I smile briefly rearranging my cutlery.

"You've inspired me. Waiter, can you give me the same thing this lady is having please?"

If it were possible for me to blush, a beet would have nothing over me. I clear my throat and continue to needlessly attend to my knife and fork.

"I can't tell you the last time I had mint tea," the man wonders aloud.

I look up. *Why is this man talking to me?* I try to read his eyes. They unpretentiously smile back at me. I relax a little.

"Truthfully? Most of my meals consist of coffee, coffee, and more coffee. It's been ages since I sat and ate a real breakfast," I laugh lightly.

"You fooled me! The way you ordered, I thought you ate like this all the time!"

"No, no. Today is a new day."

"Oh?"

"Yeah," I say with a sharp nod and a grin. I can feel a glow coming on again.

"What is special about today?"

"I don't know exactly," I begin.

The man puts down his napkin and leans forward. The silence won't allow me to shy away.

"I guess it's not special, special per se. Just different. Today, I decided to have something healthy for a change."

"You chose to nourish yourself," the man surmises.

I never thought of it that way.

"Nourish myself," I thought aloud.

"I'm glad you—"

The waiter, balancing two dishes on the inside of his arm, swoops between us. "Here you go, Ma'am."

I am again startled by his sudden appearance. He graces my table with a plate before turning to lay the other on the man's table. "Thank you," I say before the waiter briskly walks away.

"Sorry, I was just saying that I'm glad you decided because it motivated me to do the same. Thank you."

"Oh, please, no thanks necessary. Enjoy your meal."

"You, too."

"Thanks."

I look at my dish and it's alive with colour. My mouth waters. I consciously try to slow my chewing. The process is painful. My mind knows I have the time, but the rest of me just wants to inhale the food and run. Run where? It's anyone's guess. I force myself to count my chews.

"Are you enjoying your meal?"

Before I can think of a response I blurt out, "No. The food is good but..." *How do I say this?*

The man bites into his toast. He's oblivious to the crumbs falling on his shirt.

"I am trying to taste the food before swallowing and it's a strain." *Why did I tell him that? Why couldn't I just say, it's fine and go on with my crazy experiment? I don't know this guy from Adam.* "I'm sorry, what's your name?" I ask.

"I'm Adams," he replies, offering his hand.

I gasp, "No way!"

"Yesss," he says slowly, his hand still outstretched.

"Oh, forgive. I didn't mean to... Never mind, I'm Vivian. Viv," I give his warm hand a firm shake.

"My first name is Gabe. I've gotten into the habit of giving my last name first. It's nice to meet you."

"Likewise."

"Is your surname also Adams?"

"No, Moji. Sorry, just, just before you said your name, I was thinking—"

"Adam. I get it now. You must have high intuition," Gabe compliments.

"Excuse me?"

"Your intuition. Your ability to read situations. Project."

"I wouldn't say that about myself, at all. It was just a lucky guess," I lie, covering my mouth as I chew. I decide to give up eating slowly and just eat. The food is delicious. *Just needs more pepper.*

"I don't know what spices they used, but these eggs are incredibly tasty!"

Is he reading my mind? "Try it with the tomatoes!" I recommend. "I think they are vine-ripened."

"Oh! That's the stuff."

I giggle. We are acting like kids tasting our first lollipop.

"What brings you here, Gabe?"

"Work. Every time I have a business trip, I drive as far as possible from the branch office to give myself a sense of space. I like to think I'm making a symbolic separation from work and home."

"Hmm..."

"How about you? Here for work also?"

"In a manner of speaking." *I'm not going to tell this man all my business!*

"Alright," Gabe smiles and returns to his meal. He taps sugar into his tea and gives it a few swishes.

We continue to eat in silence.

Why am I now uncomfortable? First, I want him to shut up and now I want him to say something... "So, what do you do, exactly?" I ask.

"Well, in a way I lead a double life. I'm a financial analyst to pay the bills, but my passion is music."

I lean forward and stop eating. "Music and finance? What a strange mix!"

"Yeah, I guess. But I get a high from both." Gabe lifts his cup. "Anyway, I could track the stock market for sport. Math and business have always come easy to me."

"I wish I could say the same. I see numbers and my heart starts to palpitate."

"Is that real or is that in your mind?"

How do I answer that?

Seeing my hesitation, Gabe elaborates, "The reason I ask is that is how I first felt about my music."

"I don't follow."

"Well, numbers have always been my thing. I knew it, my friends knew it, my family knew it, my teachers. Everybody knew it so it was a no-brainer for me to pursue accounting and finance since I could master both with my eyes closed. But music—*that* was a secret," he took another sip of juice. "Like, I loved it. Felt it. But still resisted it."

"Why?"

He shrugs, "I don't know. I'd hear a jazz riff and my imagination would go wild! Like a high. A high that didn't fit with what I thought was my purpose—to make money." He leans forward. "Think about it, what's the ratio of broke musicians to wealthy musicians? A million to one? Who knows?"

"But you knew you had a passion for music. I didn't even like math."

"How many times have you told yourself you didn't like math?"

"I lost count," I admit, rolling my eyes.

"Then we are the same. I wouldn't let myself believe I could pursue music just like you may have let yourself believe that you couldn't master math."

I need to chew on that. Literally. I grab another piece of toast and start buttering. The arbitrator in me rises. "How can you make such a sweeping generalization?"

"First, do you mind if I join you?"

Without thinking, I wave him to the seat across from me. Gabe wipes his lips with his napkin before pushing his chair away from his table. He sits across from me, and we face off.

"OK, you tell me. Do you have a learning disability?"

"Awfully personal."

"Do you?"

"No, but—"

"Who told you, *you* couldn't master math?"

I took a deep breath and thought for a moment. "I don't know. I found math harder and harder to grasp once I was in high school. Before that, I don't remember having an issue."

"What changed?"

I smile and rest my back against the seat. "Are you a psychotherapist also?" I avoid.

"No, I just love a good debate. If it makes you uncomfortable though, I can—"

"No, no. I'm not uncomfortable," I defend. "Just never thought of these things for a long time. Let's see," I take a few moments to reflect. "High school, I guess, a lot of transitions for me. My parents worked double shifts, we moved a couple of times, changed schools. It was lonely. Most of my classmates didn't look like me." Again, I search his eyes for a reaction. He doesn't blink. I take another deep breath. "Math was dull to me at the time, I guess. I couldn't lose myself in it as easily as I could with other subjects. Hmm... Skipped some classes. Oh!" I tap the table remembering something, "Because it was required for university, I had to cram several math courses over a summer. I think I cried every day that semester."

"So, in other words, it wasn't that you *couldn't* master math, but that you initially *decided* not to master math. Once you made the decision, you pushed through and excelled," Gabe grins triumphantly as he takes another sip of tea.

I slyly smile back. *How irritating it is when a man thinks he's right?* "Anyway, let me remind you that we were talking about you," I redirect. "You're in your twenties, music enters the picture..."

"Right. Music was always in the picture, but I chose to ignore it," Gabe corrects. "Yeah, I was miserable. I was headhunted straight out of university. Making crazy cash—"

"Oh, poor you."

"Sorry. Let's just say I'm not doing badly, yes?"

"Continue, Sir Gabe." He laughs at my royal joke at his expense.

"OK, but it wasn't enough. My colleagues at work lived for the cash chase and I was, well, bored. So, I decided to buy a guitar. I passed this music store every day, never went inside, and there I was *buying* this expensive guitar I didn't even know how to play! I ran out of the store with it under my arm as if I stole it!" Our laughs mingled. "After that, I'd play Earnest Ranglin badly, repeatedly, trying to figure out his chords. Drove my neighbours nuts, but I was in the zone! You know?"

"I'm still trying to get over the fact you know Ranglin!" I continue to laugh.

"Viv don't let appearances fool you," Gabe says casually.

The laughter fades on my lips. *Interesting how he says my name so easily. Like we've known each other for years instead of minutes.*

"Anyway, I got to run. It was nice meeting you," he reaches for my hand.

I take it and stand slightly. "Me too, Gabe. I enjoyed our talk."

"Me, too. Take care."

I nod my thanks as he drops more than enough money to cover both our meals. He is gone before I can protest. I stare at the money for a while before picking up my fork again.

"Waiter, may I have another mint tea, please," I request as he passes.

I replay the conversation with Gabe in my mind, savouring what remains of my breakfast.

SEVEN

The voicemail kicks in. "Hi, Qu, Faith and Justin. It's Mom. I'm still alright. Just checking in to see how you are. I'll talk to you soon." I press end and calmly set down the cell. My room is filled with light. The maid already paid a visit. As it enters my mind, I hang the 'Do Not Disturb' sign on the outer doorknob. It's still early in the morning, but the bed is calling me. I lean on my elbow and stare out the balcony window.

Gabe has given me more food for thought. I chose *not to master math. I missed out on learning math the first time because I* chose *to view it as boring. I wonder how many of my students I've lost for the same reason.*

My mind rests on Todd's expression before he left class. *He told me this point-blank yet, I missed it. How can I make history relevant to him? How can I help take away the disdain of history from him? For myself? I can't give what I don't have.*

I roll onto my other side. The thought distresses me.

High school was no picnic. Being the only one in a sea of White was sometimes debilitating. Being the new one. The different one. In later years, being bussed so far from home, not having any real friends, and not having any teachers as real mentors.

Every day, I'd plot my escape only to come home and have my parents, my mother, beat the idea out of my head. She'd made me feel so ashamed. "Do you know how much we sacrificed to come here?" Do you know how hard your father and I are workin' so you can have more than us? Do you think your father likes working for fools who don't know how good he is? Working day and night? Do you think he likes it? For you to have the audacity to tell me you don't like high school! You better like high school! Who cares what those kids say to you or about you! Prove them wrong! You go and get good grades so you can be better than them! Do you hear me, Viv? No discussion!"

Time and again, I remember sitting there mute. I didn't have the voice or heart to argue with her. If Dad were in the room, I'd look over at him for support, which was always futile. She'd rail on, and he'd just stare at her, sad-like. The contrast always struck me. Until recently, Dad never said much about anything anyway, but his face would droop that much more when she yelled.

It didn't make sense.

Every morning, I'd see him get up and iron his clothes till they were crisp. He'd whisper, "Thank God for another day," while fussing with his tie in the hall mirror. He'd eat breakfast as he skimmed the papers. Grab his keys before brushing me a forehead kiss. Heading out the door, he seemed to always have an easy smile on his face. Never did a complaint cross his lips. Again, a man of few words.

Funny... I'm an adult now and I still don't have a clear sense of what his work entailed day in and day out. He'd come home in the late afternoon and rest for an hour or two before dinner. We'd eat together and he'd ask us the usual 'how was your day' fare. Sometimes, I'd give him the pat 'fine' answer, other times I'd elaborate, but the banter was fairly predictable. He'd give me brief encouragement when he thought it was necessary, but for the most part, he'd listen and nod. Dinner would end and he'd dress in his jeans and make his way to the next job. Again, no complaining. He'd just set off and I wouldn't see him until the following morning. It amazed me that for so many decades, his day job was in sales! His quiet, calm demeanour juxtaposed against the ruthless, firestorm sales persona I assumed was mandatory. It just didn't make sense. Yet I knew he must have been successful at what he did otherwise, how were we able to live in such a good neighbourhood? I had everything I ever needed.

I see my phone vibrating on the side table. *Should I pick it up?*

"Hello?"

"Viv! Where the hell are you? I've been leaving messages! We've been worried sick."

"I know."

"You know?" Qu presses. "What you mean you know and—"

"Qu, calm down."

"Don't tell me to calm down! Viv, come home now!"

I take a deep breath and close my eyes. *Whoa! He's mad.* My spirit speaks, "Qu, I can't."

"Why? What's stopping you?"

"I am." I can hear Qu breathing heavy. My heart goes out to him, but I can't back down now. "I need this time to get my head together."

"But... Wait, are you alone?"

What the? Breathe.

"Stop. Please listen. Then you can talk," I instruct. "Qu, I need this time for me. Alone. I need to sort out some things for myself and it's hard for me to do that when I'm constantly dealing with your stuff, the kids' stuff, work, volunteering, our parents. I need some space."

"Viv, what are you talkin' 'bout? You've never said anything was wrong, and now suddenly, you need *space?*"

I wait. *I'm conflicted. Part of me thinks I shouldn't have to justify myself, but the other part of me wants to console him.*

"Yes," I reply shortly.

"Fine, come home and I'll give you some space."

"I'm not ready."

"Well, when will you be ready?"

"Qu," I sigh, "I don't want to argue. I need you to trust me. I don't know how long I'll be away, but I will call you every day to let you know that I am alright."

"Tell me where you are."

I hesitate. *No tears Viv.* "No."

"Viv!"

"I can't tell you yet."

"Viv! This is crazy! I need—"

My voice catches, "Qu, know that I'm, alone. Know that I'm alright. Know that I'll call you tomorrow."

"But!"

"Bye," I press end and rest the phone. I wipe my eyes before more tears fall. For extra measure, I power off the phone.

I did it. Wow... This is a week full of firsts! I listlessly ease myself on the bed. I stare at the cell a little longer before I drift off to sleep.

I'm at the top of a white marble staircase, looking down. The bottom is black and deep. I shudder. I'm wearing my crumpled school uniform, hugging my notebook to my chest. I wonder what to do next. On the landing, there is a hallway stretched out on either side of me, both with bright lights and activity. Voices are muffled. Faces are blank. The air feels heavy. I can't figure out what is happening in either direction. My focus returns to the stillness below. The sound to the left of me grows louder as the glow of the light softens to the right of me. I let my toes press the brink of the stairs. I'm held, suspended, before falling...

I wake up in a cold sweat. *What the hell was that?* I lift the clock radio and realize the morning is almost over. *How can I allow myself to dream the day away?* I get up and splash cold water on my face.

I close the door behind me.

A walk will do me good. Clear my head. Figure out what to do next. Or not. It's my first day of leave. I don't necessarily have to have any real plans, right? Maybe it's alright to just wander.

I make my way to the lakeshore. It's beautiful out here. I had no idea how hot it was with the air conditioning cooling me all day. The sun's intense. *Good thing I brought my shades.* I lift my hands to my hair and twist my ponytail elastic tighter. I swing my arms and purposely take a deep breath. A slim woman in a baseball cap and check-marked shorts jogs towards me. She smiles as she passes by. I nod acknowledgement just in time for her to see.

I continue casually walking towards the water. My flip-flops sink with every step, filling with more sand. There is barely anyone on the beach. I take off one sandal and then the other. Mindlessly, I swish the warm grains around with my left toes. A thrill fills me. I continue towards the shore. The sound of lapping water steadies me. My heart is at peace. I walk. A memory surfaces.

I remember looking forward to breaking free from friends and family during a trip to the island. I must have been about thirteen or so. I'd bike to the outskirts of town to this mossy seawall, just me, my notepad, and a pen. I'd balance myself, tottering one foot before the other as far out as I'd dare. I'd place ripped pages down before gingerly seating myself. Cross-legged, all by myself. Enveloped in silence, spare the lapping waves, I'd look out into the expanse. There, the water was murky blue compared to the turquoise blue I'm gazing at now. The same peace that settled in me then fills me now. I'd look all the way out to where the ocean met the sky. I'd feel my tiny life widen.

Like nothing could hurt me.

Nothing was impossible.

Free to dream the what-ifs.

There is something about looking out at the water and hearing its rhythm. It brings a sense of calm. Wholeness.

I look at the sand.

I need to be here. My eyes dance on the water. The wind kisses my face. I let my mind rise and fall with the waves. *I just need to be...* My mind grows quiet. *Why did I wait so long?* The ebbing of the waves claims more sand with each retreat. *Three hours away from home. I could be here every week.* My eyes are mesmerized by the lingering white foam. *If I'd allow myself...*

I need to commit.

To myself.

My.

Self.

Droplets of water lightly spray my face. I close my eyes allowing them to wash my eyelids. *This is my time.* The froth creeps up to my toes.

My time.

My self.

Accept.

My focus returns to the distance. I will my mind to remain open.

Respect.

I inhale.

Know.

I am enough here.

I exhale.

I have all the answers.

In my spirit.

I open my eyes with a start. *What did I just say?*

I shiver and drop my knees, vigorously rubbing my arms to try to erase the goosebumps. Shifting onto my left leg, I lean on my arm. My gaze returns to the water. I rest for a few more beats.

I once heard somebody say ages ago that we all have the answers inside ourselves. Funny how that just floated back to me now! I've always found that curious. Much like déjà vu. Something happens and you've sworn you've experienced it before. At the oddest times. Swear that you've been down this old road before. Deeper than routine. Habit.

I allow my thoughts to unravel.

Justin asked me yesterday if the bickering with Faith ever got old. Yeah, it does. It's old. It's familiar. Still...

I look down as I trail long, slow tracks in the sand with my fingers.

I know what Faith is going to say, yet I react the same way every time. It never occurs to me to change my response. It's familiar. We feed off each other. Bite for bite.

Why? Why do I continue that cycle? Allow it? I'm the adult! It doesn't support us. It doesn't connect us. How does this serve us? Even Justin can read the dysfunction on the wall. I don't even see the wall.

My mind's eye goes back to the mossy seawall. I smile wryly at the mental image. The tracks in the sand spiral.

If I have the answers, then what are they? Why did it take Dour's forced leave to get me to this place? What is blocking me?

My fingers stop at the centre of the circle. I'm afraid to continue unearthing. I rest on the whys.

Why am I afraid?

More water droplets spray my face. I close my eyes. I let my mind gently rise and fall with the sound of the waves.

EIGHT

With notebook in hand, I crack open the spine and stare at the lines. Blank.

Now what?

I cross my legs underneath me on the chaise. *I haven't journaled in years.* I rock restlessly. *A blank page never scared me before. What's my problem?!*

I meticulously write the date. I carefully underline the date.

Okay, the key to journaling is to write my thoughts, uncensored. Free flow. Maybe, I can write entries like letters to myself? Or not. Maybe, I'll just make a story out of my thoughts. Maybe, I should just fill the book with affirmations instead of thoughts. Didn't I hear that suggestion on a talk show once? Why am I overthinking this? How crazy is it for me to be arguing with myself over something so simple? Okay. Just write, damn it!

Hi.

Hi? That's all I got? Don't think about it, just write. I take a couple of deep breaths, pen poised.

"Hi," I read back.

I feel the wind off the balcony blow the strands about my neck. I abruptly twist my hairband again, forcing my bun higher on my head.

I press on.

How did I end up here?

I had a strange dream today and I don't know how to begin deciphering it. The last thing I remember was this utter terror I felt as I was falling.

It was so real. It still makes me shudder. Not knowing what or if something would catch me or if the falling would ever end. I felt lost. Lifeless. I'm not sure if I'm ready to examine it right now. Maybe, I just need some time.

I spoke to Qu. He's mad and I don't blame him. I'm such a mess! I finally admit it! If he pulled on me what I just pulled on him, I would Bobbitt him so swiftly he wouldn't see the knife coming! I was so mean not telling him where I was. Yet here I am, playing the fugitive and feeling abnormally empowered.

Qu and I haven't talked about anything lately. Nothing beyond what's for dinner, check the phone messages, and who's picking up the kids. I never tell Qu what I need. To be fair, I never truly think about what I need. Yet on this historic day, I, Ms. Viv, not only told him I needed space, but I also told him I wasn't going to come home AND turned my phone off! These two days have been shocking. I haven't felt this free in.

I have never felt so free! It's like layers are slowly peeling off me.

I told Qu!

I wouldn't be surprised if he's still staring at the phone wondering if I said what I said. I hope I didn't hurt him too badly. I hope he doesn't think I'm having an affair or something just as ridiculous. Come on now, an affair with who? The only male specimen I see regularly is Dour and he may as well be a stray cat for all the attraction I feel towards him. Qu must know that.

No. I'm not going to call back just yet. I'm going to let him cool off. I'm going to let my stuff simmer. I'll reassure him tomorrow.

So yesterday, I bought this notebook to record my thoughts. I'm hoping it will help me sort out some things. That phrase seems to be perpetually tattooed on my mind ever since Dour said it to me. "A one week leave to sort whatever it is, out. It seems like you may need some time." So, I've got five and a half more days to straighten out whatever it is that is causing me to "struggle."

I have five days to be a well-adjusted worker. Five and a half days to be strong enough to explain all of this to Qu. Five more days to make it up to my kids for bolting.

I stop writing, feeling completely depressed. I reread what I wrote. I draw a line underneath the last sentence, dividing the page.

———

I think because I tend to be stubborn and, in particular, I need to write out some ground rules for myself. Here goes:

I swallow.

1. *I will write and not censor what I write.*
2. *I will write what I am feeling, thoughts I am thinking, and ideas that interest me. I will hold nothing back.*
3. *I will only tell the truth.*
4. *I will not put a time limit on anything I write. If I write for five minutes or five hours, it doesn't matter.*
5. *I will not allow myself to reread my entries until I've finished or the following day. To reread things sooner will tempt me to censor or possibly stop me from wanting to continue.*
6. *I will remember my purpose for writing. It's to vent but not to beat myself up. It is to get out of my head what I've been holding onto subconsciously or otherwise. It's not to prove anything. It's a release. At the end of the day, it may function as a true affirmation of who I am.*

I pause after number six and let it swim around my brain cells for a while.

A true affirmation of who I am...I like that!

> 7.   *I need to commit to writing something every day, even if I'm afraid of what may be revealed.*

That will be hard.

> 8.   *I need to see this exercise as a means of taking back something just for me. I need to embrace the process. It is not a punishment or something I need to fear.*

Okay, now that I'm clear I need to step back. Going back to my previous thought, I know I can't fix myself in a prescribed period of time. My... I know it takes time to get better yet ~~my prayer~~...

I want to improve a little every day for the rest of my life. I see this day as the beginning of fulfilling that for myself.

Last night one of my favourites won a Grammy for the first time and I sat here in awe. She said, in effect, that she was thankful for everything, particularly the valleys in her life because they taught her lessons and forced her to grow stronger.

I need to adopt her perspective. I need to be more thankful. More mindful. No more hiding.

Even when I must eventually face my family. I'll start with Dour. I may have resisted his imposed 'effective immediately' leave, but I'm honestly glad <u>now</u> to have this time. I never take the time. AND, I still have a job! Some bosses would never be so generous. I have a family who cares about me. Mad at me, but care, nonetheless. I'm sitting in this gorgeous room!

So, why have I been depressed for months? I never admitted this before, but it's true. Until now, I've been blaming stuff and making excus-

es. Now I need to tell the truth on myself. This state of mind and heart runs deeper than fatigue. My spirit has been drained for a long time.

The finances. The running. The little slights at work. Past hurts. My father's illness. All these things have built up and weighted my spirit. I've been hiding behind "busy" and other people's business. My weight has been yo-yoing. I've never been so unhealthy. Every time I run my fingers through my hair, the ends flutter around me like rain. It's too much! I can't continue the way I've been going. I can't keep bouncing back and forth from just enough to not enough. I can't stand looking in the mirror some days. My age is all over my face.

In the days of the seawall, I remember feeling alive. I'd be out about the island and want to dance all day, every day, just because. Me, the water, and the sun—that's all I needed to be moved to dance. Now, but a few years later—okay, maybe more than a few years later. I can't tell you the last time I felt like dancing. Instead, I want to sleep all the time. I'm not suicidal…

Why did I go to that extreme? I don't know, but there are some days when I think about how my life insurance would benefit my family.

~~Who thinks like this! I should never have let myself get to this place!~~

I have to remember, no judging.

Bottom line, It's got to stop!

If this admission isn't desperate, I don't know what is!

Today it stops!

Today is the day I unstick myself.

Today is the day I declare this lull, temporary.

Today is the day I take this valley and grow from it.

Today is the day I begin to look forward based on the keys I draw from my reflections.

Today is the day I need to let God in.

Where did that come from? How did God flow through my pen? Let me keep going.

I am hurting. I don't know where to go.

I rest my pen in the crease of my book and close it.
Wow.
I allow the tears to saturate the cover.
I'm free.
I drop my head in my arms and sob.

NINE

I have no idea what time it is. I cried an ocean and passed out.

It's all good. I feel lighter. Buying this eucalyptus bubble bath was genius. I blow the bubbles off my fingertips. *I love the scent. It's like with every breath, I'm healing. Toxins just breaking off me.* I scoff at myself.

Why do I have to go there? Next, I'll be thinking about every germ and its chemical breakdown and how they are just swimming up and around every crevice of my body, and the joy of just sitting in this decadent bath for the sake of it will disappear and I'll be towelling off. Relax, damn it! You don't have to attach meaning to every minute thing.

Just sit. Sitting in the bath doesn't have to mean anything but sitting in a bath.

You can just be.

Consider your work done.

Turn your mind off.

I laugh ironically. *I should write comedy, right? Change careers on the brink of my fortieth. Men do it all the time, why not me? Sketches about the neurosis of a working mother. Humph.*

I close my eyes and lay my head back on the scented towel. I allow my arms to float up to the top of the water. I continue to breathe in the eucalyptus.

I've been so intent on not wasting time today that I keep forgetting that it is my time to waste! I can spend it anyhow I choose. I don't have to work 24/7.

But seriously, what am I doing?

My eyes pop open.

All I know is work, so what now? In some ways this 'sorting it out' business is hard labour.

I sigh. *But how do I take a break when wherever I go, there I am?*

I slap the water. *Stop!*

Me taking a bath. I shake my head and wiggle my toes. Deep breath in.

Me taking a bath. Period.

A moan escapes me. I turn onto my other cheek. My hand moves instinctively to the pillow beside me. *Where's Qu?* I jerk up, feeling for him. It dawns on me where I am.

It's morning.

I relax and rest my head again. *Hmm, Hmm. That was the soundest sleep I've had in the longest time.* I yawn loudly and scratch my head. *What time is it?* I lift the alarm clock and will my eyes to focus. 7:12 a.m. *Fabulous.* I lay back and close my eyes, nuzzling deeper in my pillow.

I love this bed. I wonder if I could take the mattress home with me. Have a constant reminder of what luxury feels like. I shift onto my back and stretch. *Alright, time to get up and face the world.* I throw the covers off and lay there a while. The cool air off the balcony drifts over my body. "Okay, another minute," I convince myself, jerking the duvet over my head again. *I don't necessarily have to get up this second.* Another yawn escapes me as I let my mind settle.

Qu, I should call Qu. I miss his voice.

I reach for the hotel phone and dial his cell.

"Hello?"

"Morning, Qu."

"Mornin'."

I wait, confused. *What's going on? Is he still angry?*

"Are you on your way to work?"

"I just pulled up a few minutes ago."

"Oh..."

More silence. I fidget, gripping the covers to me.

"Well, I just called to see how you're doing."

"Okay."

"Talk to you later?"

"Later."

"I—"

He was gone. He hung up on me. "That was cold," I mutter, replacing the receiver. *What's up with Qu? Should I call him back?*

I swing my legs over the side of the bed, shaking my head. *Know what? No! Just like I asked him to give me some space and time, I need to give him the same. He needs this time to sort out his stuff too, right? This time apart is good for both of us. I'm not going to feel guilty about asserting myself. I'm not! Qu will get over this. It's a few more days for heaven's sake! He's a grown man. He'll get over it!*

With a sharp nod, I spring out of the bed. My nightgown billows gently behind me as I head for the washroom.

Should I write before breakfast? I pull open the side drawer. As I reach for my notebook, my eyes glance at the Bible. I lift it instead and aimlessly flip through it. My fingers stop.

"I can do all things through him who strengthens me." ~ Philippians 4:13

I read the verse. I reread the verse, slower, deliberately saying each word out loud.

I

can do

all things

through him

who strengthens...

me?

I don't get it. It's like I'm learning English for the first time. I roll the words over my tongue again. The teacher in me picks up the cell phone and searches for another translation to see if it says something different. Something that will make more sense.

I have strength for all things...

In Christ Who empowers me...

Am I the "I" in this verse? Does this apply to me? How am I empowered?

In one swoop I grab my journal, cell, and knapsack. I cross the room and drop in my chaise as I riffle through my bag for my dictionary.

Empower: to authorize.

I write the meaning in my journal and look up a moment.

"Authorize," I twist, turn, and tumble the word over my cells.

Author, the root. *The author, like what I'm doing right now with this journal. I am writing about my life. I am the author of my life. The authority.* I go back to where my finger lay.

Authority: the power to command, determine, influence or judge; an expert in a specific field.

Authorize: to justify.

Still mulling things over, I gently lay the dictionary on my lap. I reread the verse on the screen and methodically write it out in my journal.

I have strength for all things in Christ Who empowers me. (I am ready for anything and equal to anything through Him Who infuses inner strength into me; I am self-sufficient in Christ's sufficiency.) ~ Philippians 4:13, Amplified Bible Classic Edition (AMPC)

I may not fully understand or even believe this, but I claim it anyway! I could use some strength and empowerment right now.

My stomach groans, averting my attention. I close my journal.

I have strength.

I put my books away and retrieve my sandals from under the bed. *I'll write after breakfast,* I decide as I head for the door.

The restaurant is half full. The air is filled with gentle murmuring. It's a little later than I came yesterday. I scope out the room for a window table. Spotting one, I walk casually towards it.

"Vivian!"

Startled, I look around me trying to figure out who called my name.

"Over here," Gabe waves to catch my attention.

Funny, I didn't see him. I smile and walk towards him.

"Care to join me?"

"Yeah, thanks," I reply, pulling out the chair.

"How you doing? Work keeping you busy?"

"In a manner of speaking," I answer vaguely. "And you?"

"It's good. Our meetings ended a little early, so I drove around a bit."

"Is there anything, in particular, you wanted to see?"

"Not really."

"When you head back?"

"Not soon enough," he mumbles.

I look puzzled. "You aren't enjoying your trip?"

"It's a business trip and important enough. I just miss home is all."

I nod knowingly, flipping through my menu.

"Have you already ordered?"

"No. I just got here five minutes ago."

"Hmm..."

I haven't clue what I want. The old Viv would have said forget it and sufficed with a coffee. New day.

"May I take your order?"

I look up at the waiter and then across the table. "Please, Gabe, you go first," I insist hastily turning the pages.

"Okay, I'll have wheat toast, scrambled egg with onion and tomato, hash browns, and a side order of sausage."

"Would you like anything to drink?"

"A coffee and orange juice."

"And the lady?"

I snap the menu shut and hand it to the waiter. "I'll have the same. Except for no sausage, and instead of the coffee, please make it green tea."

"Thank you," the waiter acknowledges as he turns to take Gabe's menu.

"Thanks for being my brains this morning. I didn't know what I wanted."

"No problem. I didn't even bother looking. I was already craving a big breakfast."

"Speaking of a big breakfast, I want to thank you for paying for my meal yesterday! You left before I realized."

Gabe blushes and shakes his head, "Again, no big deal..."

"Well, thank you anyway. It was generous."

"You're welcome."

We sit, smiling at each other for a second. I catch myself and hastily look at my lap and pick lint off my pants.

"Are you alright?"

"Yeah, I'm fine." I sigh and look back up at him politely.

"Seems like there's a lot on your mind."

Should I tell him? "There is but it's all good."

Gabe leans forward expectantly.

Fine, what the hell. "To be honest, I am using this week as a personal retreat. The business you assumed I was on is frankly, the business of myself."

"I'm intrigued."

"Oh, it's nothing dramatic. I'm not dying or anything."

Gabe throws back his head and lets out this resonating laugh. I can't help but join in.

"I didn't think so."

"Right..." *Why do I tend to jump to extremes?* "I'm just taking some time out to clear some stuff in myself," I explain.

"I think that's great! We all need to do that, but rarely do."

That was sweet. I genuinely smile at Gabe, relieved that he understands. Catching myself staring again, I look at my empty plate and self-consciously play with my cutlery.

"So, if it's not too personal, what have you discovered?"

I glance out the window. The water is a few hundred feet away from where we sit.

"Hmm..."

"Again, if it's too personal."

"No, it's not that. I'm just trying to choose my words. It's hard, to sum up, you know?"

The waiter returns with our drinks. After thanking him, I reach for the brown sugar packet and shake it.

"I am always running. These past few days I've been bent on slowing down, but simultaneously not taking anything, particularly my time, for granted. Does that make sense?" I ask.

"I think so. It's sort of like me driving around yesterday," Gabe takes a long sip of his coffee.

"How so?"

"Well, I could have continued working or rested at the hotel, but as this is a new city for me, I wanted to get a feel for it. See what I'd see at my own pace, you know? Is that what you meant?"

"Yes and no," I stop stirring my tea and tap my spoon on the brim.

"I guess it's that this is the first time I'm purposely slowing down. It feels unnatural."

"What usually keeps you busy?"

"Well, as you can see," I point to my wedding ring, "I'm married. It's nineteen years in October."

"Congratulations!"

"Thanks," I say mildly. "My husband's Qu—he goes by Qu—though his given names are Malachi Quaid. Long story. It's a West Indian thing."

For some reason, his name keeps catching in my throat. *I hope he's alright.*

"Kay."

"Yeah, and there's Justin and Faith, my two teenagers. Two opinionated, bright, beautiful, utterly frustrating teenagers."

"I can imagine," Gabe laughs.

"I also work full-time and volunteer at a women's shelter weekly. Help our parents when I can..."

"I can see why you would need to slow down!"

"Do you? Again, this whole slowing down thing is new to me. I have mixed feelings." I play with my mug as I order my thoughts. "I know it's necessary. When I slow down, I'm more aware of things. Of lessons in things," I try to clarify. "So, I don't regret what fills up my life. I love my family, and my home and my job and the women I've connected with at the haven."

"I don't—"

"Here you go. Enjoy!" the waiter rests our plates before us.

"Thanks," Gabe says shortly before returning his attention to me.

"Sorry, I was saying I don't doubt that, but what it sounds like is somewhere in all the routine, you've lost sight of *why* you were doing it all. Got caught up in the busyness."

"Yes, but when I slow down, I also automatically feel wrong, almost idle," I complain as I butter my toast. "Yet I know it's necessary! These past few days, I've rediscovered things about myself. New thoughts, ideas."

"Okay," he encourages.

"But there's still this nagging voice inside my head questioning my decisions. If I slow down, isn't there the potential that I might be—I don't know—letting someone down? Might neglect something? Or maybe left out of the game? Not be good enough?"

Wow, that was in me all this time?

"But if you don't slow down," he counters, "isn't there also the potential of losing yourself? At the end of the day, by whose measure are you judging yourself good enough?"

I'm taken aback. Our eyes lock.

"You should look into a career in counselling. You'd be brilliant," I volley back, breaking the tension.

"Sorry if I come off like—"

I shake my head, "I'm teasing. It's this quirky little defence mechanism I have."

Gabe chuckles as he digs into his meal. "Well, as we're sharing quirks, mine is to analyze everything to death so feel free to wave the white flag if I go too far."

I whip the napkin open and spread it on my lap. "No worries. Honestly, if I held that against you, I'd be the biggest hypocrite," I hesitate. "Let's switch topics. I feel like I've been talking non-stop."

"Okay," he complies.

"I'm curious about your music. What have you discovered through it? Where has it taken you?"

"Alright. Let's see. What have I discovered..." Gabe chews and thinks a moment. "Well, I guess the first thing I've learnt is that I'm not perfect."

We both laugh at this obvious confession.

"What I mean is, just because I like music, I thought it would come easily to me, like numbers."

"But that's not the case..."

"I sucked! It took me what seemed like months to perfect three chords."

"So why did you bother?"

"Stubbornness, I guess. I couldn't let it defeat me."

My fork spirals the food around my plate as I hang on to his words. "You make it sound so adversarial."

"I guess in a way it was. I'm forever competing against myself." He lays his fork on the table. "I never shared my love of music with anyone for a long time. It was a private passion. When I impulsively bought the guitar, it was an outward admission. I couldn't turn back."

"So, you committed and fought it till you got it."

"Exactly!" Gabe grins as he stabs his sausage.

"What kept you going? Taking so long to get the chords must have been frustrating."

"All I have is time though. Just before I was ready to break the thing into pieces, I broke down instead and signed up for lessons. After learning the foundation, experimenting came easier." He takes a mouthful. "You have to remember; my life is the opposite of yours. Though I'm in a serious relationship, I don't have the responsibilities marriage and children demand, yet. I have more time to play with."

I nod in agreement. *Maybe, that's the mindset I should adopt. I have time.* "Time is all any of us have when it comes right down to it," I say aloud.

"In degrees, yeah, I guess you're right. Time and choices."

We eat in silence.

The server reappears. "Is everything alright here?"

"The food is great, thank you. In fact," I line my cutlery in the middle of my plate, "I'm finished."

The waiter bends down and removes my dish.

"And you, sir?" he turns to Gabe.

"I'm still working on this, thanks."

The waiter nods and moves to the next table.

"You barely touched your breakfast."

"I'm good," I dab the corners of my mouth. "Besides, I'm being fed more by our talk. Cheers!" I lift my orange juice to ting against his glass.

"Hmm, are you sure you're not just watching your waistline? If so, there's no need."

Caught off guard, I cough. *Wha?* "Yeah, that too, but that's an entirely separate conversation. No, honestly, I'm full." I drink in the sweetness. I can feel my ears heating up.

Gabe wipes his mouth and drops his napkin on his plate. "Well, I am too, but it tasted so good I didn't want to stop." He opens his wallet and takes out too many bills.

"No, please, let me pay for today's breakfast," I insist, as I try to locate a safe credit card to brandish.

"No, no. I've interrogated you ruthlessly first thing in the morning. The least I can do is pay for the trouble I've caused," he smiles and lays the money in the centre of the table.

I relax gratefully. "Thanks for spoiling me again, sir."

"What, spoil? Don't we deserve to eat well and enjoy engaging conversation?"

"You know, Gabe, you're a weirdo," I giggle. "Sometimes when you speak, I swear you came straight out of the Renaissance."

"As long as I've entertained you, my work here is done," he laughs, dragging his chair back from the table. "Have a great rest of the day, Vivian."

"You too, Gabe, and please call me Viv. Thanks again."

"Don't mention it, Viv."

I watch his back, swirling my orange juice around.

TEN

I throw myself on the bed and stare up at the ceiling. *I miss Qu. I miss his voice. I miss his face. I miss his warmth at night. I even miss his scent! I wonder if he's calmed down.*

Why haven't Qu and I talked? Why is it so easy to talk to a perfect stranger about stuff that's lying on my heart? This is ridiculous! Impulsively, I reach for my cell and speed dial his number. I sit on the edge of the bed waiting for him to pick up.

"Hi! You have reached Qu at…" I listen, confused for a few seconds before deciding to hang up. *It's bizarre that his voice mail kicked in. He always answers his cell.*

I step onto the balcony and sit on the chair, crossing my legs. Another gorgeous day. I look skyward as the breeze refreshes me. *Two meals and a lot of food for thought.* I replay the conversation I had with Gabe in my mind.

In degrees, all we have are time and choices.

All this time is mine. I feel like I've been gifted yet… How do I fit in everything I think is important and still "nourish myself," as Gabe put it?

I wish I could talk to Qu about this. I need someone who really knows me to help me make sense of it all.

I'm seeing time in a whole different light.

Look at my parents. They are slowing down and growing more concerned about their health as their friends are facing advanced diabetes, arthritis, heart conditions, even cancer. Hell! More of their friends are passing away! Yet despite everything, they continue to grow closer.

In the last few years, Dad has cultivated this incredible garden. Species of plants and vegetation I will never know all the names of flourish there. It's abundant and alive, as is he! When I watch him out there, there's this joy that just drips out of his every pore. He could be out there creating and tending for hours and come inside shocked that it had been more than five minutes. Ma says that when he's in the yard, he's back home in his soul. On more than one occasion, I've caught her peacefully gazing at him from the back porch, just sipping her tea and gazing at him. Far away in her eyes. The longer she sits watching him, the more inspired he seems to grow. They are so connected. One. Time stands still. I can clearly imagine them together side-by-side in the island fields, though it was a time before I was even a thought.

My kids' faces float to mind.

Watching them grow up... so fast, seemingly overnight. I look at Justin and it's hard to believe he's the same little boy who'd love to crawl up on my lap and beg me to read him a story. He's the same little boy who'd hug my neck and press his nose against mine, forcing me to focus on him as he'd ask me questions. Now, he's this lanky, handsome guy. I have to look way up to catch his eyes. I never imagined my children would be able to peer at the top of my head and ta-da! Overnight! Tall, strong, almost adults. I find myself gazing at him all the time too.

Miss Faith. She went from four to sixteen with lightning speed. My fault though. When she was younger, I expected so much from her, especially when I decided to take more courses and still work full-time. While Qu and I were working overtime—which was for the majority of our married lives—she was my hands at home. I'd come home late, and she'd rise from bed to give me the blow by blow of what I'd missed. I'd prop my head in my hands as my food hummed in the microwave and she'd rhyme off the day's triumphs and curses. I'd barely hear half of what she said, but I'd let her rattle on anyway. I loved being with her. I loved that even at a young age, she was so exhaustive and thought so deeply. I loved that she felt it her duty to fill me in on every precious detail. Everything was important to her. Everything held her interest and curiosity.

Till now, I never realized how little I appreciated the time I spent with my family. I just move as the world moves.

I've been taking on more and more.

Gabe talks about how all he has is time, but until this moment, I behaved the opposite. Like time is running out. Time is urgent. Everything has to be done <u>now</u>. I get up tired and run. There is so much to do and it's all due yesterday. Dishes to wash, meals to prepare, laundry to sort, lesson plans to prep, tests to mark, school correspondence to answer, charities to support, shifts to cover, counselling hours to complete, committees to chair, documents to file, banking to maintain, bills to pay, meetings to attend, recitals to cheer at, cars to tune-up, grass to mow, gifts to buy, classes to teach, renovations to plan, parents to drive to various appointments, schedules to align, teenagers to chase after, groceries to buy, dry cleaning to pick up—the list is never-ending!

I get home tired and plan where to sprint next.

I'm responsible for everything!

Yet...if I stop, what will happen?

If I stop, what will it mean?

For my family?

My home?

My career?

My interests?

My self?

I've stopped now. What do I imagine is happening right now? I've stopped and time still ticks on.

Again, I'm spiralling. I shiver.

If I stop, life, as I know it ceases as opposed to life, will move on, only differently.

Can I trust that?

I go inside, grab my journal, and walk back to the balcony. My thoughts keep flowing.

I miss Qu. Maybe I was too hasty to push him away. I know why I did it at the time, but couldn't I have sorted all this out with him? I need someone to talk to. Who else than the one committed to being my soul mate? When was the last time I thought of him like that?

I stop writing.

When I met Qu, I wasn't sure about him at all. He was always handsome. Slightly muscular. Nice full lips. His smile, infectious. Strong yet gentle hands with these long, beautifully shaped fingers. I've always loved his hands. Tall. A shade lighter than ebony. Light brown pool eyes, which can take you by surprise when he flashes them your way. I didn't believe I could attract someone like him. Why would someone so attractive be interested in me? A short, plain Jane. No one special. It didn't compute.

But Qu kept coming around. I'd be walking to class, there he was, getting my morning chocolate, right in line behind me. In the campus gym, focused and reeking sweat on the cross-trainer, I'd feel his hand brush my waist as he offered a hello. I'd be at the library, and there he'd appear, drawing out a chair across from me, asking me about what I was reading. It was ridiculous! I'd be talking to him, and he'd be looking at me with these intense freaking eyes! When did I get used to his eyes? Being with him now, I take for granted that he's smoking hot!

It was unsettling the way he'd slowly nod like I was spewing the most masterful analysis he'd ever heard. He made me completely nervous, and I didn't trust myself around him. To stay calm, I'd remind myself, 'He's not interested in me. He's interested in discussing bell hooks the activist. It's not about me. He was only interested in the subjects I was studying so he could use what I was sharing for his work. Get it together!' Thinking this way relaxed me. So, I continued to treat his library 'visits' like study sessions and be excessively descriptive and enthusiastic when he'd ask me questions. I even documented reference material and underlined passages for him in anticipation of his 'happening by.'

It was about two weeks before the veil was lifted from my eyes.

My pen hovers over the paper as I am transported back to the library.

I was absorbed in reading this paragraph to him when he put his hand on mine.

"Would you like to go out with me sometime?"

Would I like to go out? Whaaa? I was completely dazed. "Sorry?"

"I asked if you'd like to go out with me."

He may as well have been speaking Greek to me because I didn't understand a word he said.

"Viv, I've been watching you for some time and I like you. I'd like to take you out."

"You've been watching me?"

"Yes! Of course. You surprised?"

"Well...yeah."

"Why?" He began gently drawing circles on the back of my hand. I couldn't bring myself to draw it away.

Think of a lie Viv, think!

"I just thought you were interested in feminist theory," I replied weakly.

"No offence, but If I were interested in that, I'd sign up for the class."

"Oh." *Duh...*

"So, you don't want to go out?"

"No. I didn't say that."

Abruptly I drew my hand away and shut my book. *I hope he doesn't notice the sweat on my forehead.*

"Where did you have in mind?"

"It's your call."

My call?

"Dinner and a movie?"

"Great! Saturday at seven?"

"Alright."

"I'll meet you at your place."

"You know where I live?"

"I told you I've been watching you," he grinned. "Later."

And he was gone.

I didn't know if I should be frightened or flattered.

It turned out he lived down the hall from me. When he told me, I felt like an idiot. How could I have not known that? Qu wasn't a stalker. Just a lot like me, I came to discover. Well, deep down, anyway. I think I'm much more obvious. He'll contemplate, observe, and consider some more before delving in or making a decision, especially if he doesn't know you.

He must have known I was nervous though. Date night, I spent most of the afternoon vetoing every piece of clothing in my closet. I couldn't figure out what image I wanted to project. Trying to raise my confidence, I talked to the mirror but everything I said was stupid, and every gesture, stiff.

"So, Qu, fancy…" *Ahh! Idiot! Who says fancy?*

Another shirt flung to the ground. The idea of going out with him had me on needles. Right up until the hour, I was ready to fake Ebola. When he finally came to the door, I had already worked myself into this great frenzy. I'll never forget it. I told my roommate Lorna to get rid of him.

"Tell him I have a stomachache!"

She grabbed my face, shook it with both hands and said, "You are going on this date, damn it!"

Incredibly sobering.

The next thing I know, the door was open, and Qu stepped inside. He was so casual about it. Just sauntered in. Faded jeans and a crew neck. All, "Hi! How you doing?" All I could do was smile and nod while Lorna introduced herself.

"Nice to meet you. So, Viv, you ready?" Qu asked.

Was I ready?

"Is she ready? Of course, she's ready! See you later, Viv. You two have a good time!"

Surrogate mom, Lorna, practically pushed me into Qu's chest. My instinct was to resist, but I let her. Qu took my hand.

Qu always had an easy way about him. We ate Thai at this restaurant near the apartment.

"How did you know I loved this restaurant?"

"I have my sources," he smiled.

After a while, I relaxed, and we just talked about everything. Growing up, school, friends, teachers, working out—things just seemed to flow.

He let me choose the film. The theatre we went to seemed to have it out for me. I looked at the neon titles and realized they all made me cringe. They were either leaning toward soft porn or crash-em, kill-em flicks. But a movie was my idea so I couldn't back down now. I settled for a biopic that had subtle elements of both dreaded genres. I'd figured I'd just grit through. He bought a large popcorn tub for us to share and led me near the middle of the theatre. He lowered my seat so I could sit first, then seemed to fold himself down beside me.

The cinematography was spectacular. It didn't take long for me to forget myself and become immersed in all that opened before me. At one particularly disturbing scene, I gasped and felt Qu rub the back of my hand. My eyes went to his face. His eyes were darting across the screen, totally engrossed in the action, though his fingers never left my hand. I relaxed again. Walking home that night, we went on and on about the film's character development and the cataclysmic ending. The closer we got to the building the more my conversation dropped off. Qu continued to hold my hand and follow my lead. When we got to my door, he faced me and kissed the palm of my hand.

"I had a great time tonight."

"Me too."

"We'll do it again?"

"Yeah, I'd like that."

"Alright."

He kissed me lightly on the lips and smiled. "I'm at 425."

"Oh! You live on the same floor!" I laughed.

"Yeah," he squeezed my hand.

I didn't know it that weekend but from then on, Qu would be the only man in my life. If he wasn't in my space, I was in his. Always been that way.

We walked every day for an hour or more. Sometimes in the mornings. Sometimes after class. Just talking and discovering more of the city together. Back then, he seemed able to read me so well. He sensed I spooked easily, so he took his time. Before parting, he'd kiss me. First an open palm. Then he'd brush his lips against the inside of my wrist. My elbow. My shoulders. My neck. My chin. Below my neck. Just took his time exploring me.

A month of this and my fear rose. We were eating Chinese one Friday night on my bedroom floor, talking about some nonsense when I finally just broke down.

"Qu."

"Yeah?"

"Where do you see us?" I blurted out.

"What?"

I was mortified. It was already exposed so I couldn't take it back. I put my plate down and faced him. "I guess I just want to know what's on your mind."

"You mean what I want?"

"Yeah, I guess, I don't know."

"You can't tell?"

"I'd rather not go by what I think. I don't want to think! I just need you to tell me."

"You are so strange sometimes, Viv. Honestly."

"You mad?"

"No," Qu fidgeted, and I instantly regretted putting him on the spot.

"Know what? It's alright. You, you don't have to answer."

"Nah, nah, nah. You asked I'm gonna answer."

"Okay," I looked at my lap.

"Viv, I just like you. You're cool. I feel I can talk to you about anything. I don't feel like there's any pretence. I can just be me."

"So, you like me as a friend? Someone you can hang with. Someone—"

He grabbed my chin and kissed me deeply. "No," he breathed.

"Alright," I sighed. I willed myself to continue. "But you've never tried anything."

"I thought you weren't ready.

"I'm not!" We both began to laugh.

"I don't understand you!"

"Well, I don't understand myself."

"Viv, this is stupid. When you're ready, we'll move, but until then, I like spending time with you, kissing you and holding you. I'm good," he started stroking my knee.

"You're good?" I scoffed.

"I'm fuckin' excellent," he grinned. "And when you're ready, you'll realize just how much."

"You're such a jerk!" I aimed a pillow at his head. He caught it midair.

"Remember, excellent!" he laughed as he grabbed for me and pressed his lips against mine again.

"I love you," escaped me.

"I love you too."

"Ready."

I shook my head and let the rest of my thoughts flow through my pen.

I haven't thought about that night in a long, long time. Back then and even after the kids were born, we could talk about anything. Mind you, he's never been one to be verbally sentimental. Even on that night, before I confessed, the most I got from him was "you're cool." I wonder if he'd ever say he loved me if I didn't say it first? After all these years though, it shouldn't matter to me, right? He's been faithful. We're married, we support one another, and for the most part, we are there for each other. He can be affectionate.

Okay, this is supposed to be a journal in which I am brutally honest with myself, so I need to step back again.

It does matter. As much as I miss Qu, I needed this time for me. I won't feel ashamed over that decision.

And the sentiment? <u>YES</u>! It matters that he doesn't take the initiative occasionally and tell me that he loves me. Tell me what he's feeling. And I can tell him how I'm feeling without him shutting down.

In the last few years, we've settled, haven't we? We've entered maintenance mode. We used to think and discuss everything to the smallest detail, but recently it's been, 'we need this, get it.' 'This happened, let's fix it.' No consideration of real needs or roots or consequences or why.

For instance, we figured we need to get more degrees to make more money. Okay. Take out crazy loans, take turns, get degrees. We're in debt a decade later, after I've got the job with the degree. Yet if I thought about it, I was educating in the nonprofit sector previously without the benefit of a masters! Did the money make a big difference? Are we contributing more with the degrees?

Look at our home. I was pregnant for the second time in as many years. We needed a bigger space. One extra bedroom. Okay. We saw a house with two extra bedrooms and a bigger backyard and got starry-eyed. We rationalized: we'll manage it once we finished the degrees and then jumped into a house we couldn't afford!

We were young when we got married. Then we had the kids almost immediately! Running after house, and education, and jobs, and so-called life so early in the game, we ended up forgetting why we even came together. Why the rush? Didn't we get married because we believed we were one another's soul mate? Didn't we have children to raise them? In all the running we forgot our purposes. Bottom line—we came together to love and strengthen one another.

Remembering, I flip back a few pages and reread. I rewrite the words that inspired me in the morning.

I choose to believe this.

I have strength.

I am ready for anything.

I am equal to anything through Him Who infuses inner strength into me.

If this says anything to me now, it says that I still have a chance to reclaim time. Reclaim my purpose.

I can still be Qu's soul mate.
I can still be mindful about how I parent from this time forward.

It's not over.

I close my notebook, biting my bottom lip.

Know what? I'm going to find the gym! Get me some clothes and find me an elliptical trainer!

I smile thinking back to my university days. *How fit, healthy, active, smart I was. I was a catch and didn't even know it! That girl still lives in here... somewhere... under all of this.* I pinch my belly with a groan. *Goin' to find her again.*

Placing my journal on the side table, I bounce out the door, happy. *It's not over.*

ELEVEN

Can you believe it's already seven? What a day!

I grab a towel from the bathroom and wipe my face.

There was hardly anyone in the gym by the time I got back from the sports store. I did myself proud doing my brand of circuit training. I almost forgot how good it feels to work out. Once I deciphered the equipment, I pressed myself to go faster, increased the resistance, and tried heavier weights. There is something about moving fast and feeling strong. It's intoxicating. And then, bonus! Discovering the sauna! After working out so hard, I could feel all this tension melt off as I lay in the steam.

What a fantastic afternoon. I am so glad I thought to do it.

I peel off my robe and turn on the shower. I let the water run steady tracks down my back, close my eyes, and sigh. I hear a hesitant knock at the door. My eyes bolt open.

That can't be right. I didn't order any food, and no one knows I'm here.

I turn around and let the water splash my face, closing my eyes again. As the soap bubbles wash away, the knocking grows louder and more insistent. I turn off the tap and wrap myself in a fluffy robe.

I peer through the peephole and am startled. I tear open the door. "Qu!"

"Viv," he answers formally, looking over and around me.

"How did you know I was here?"

"Caller ID."

I stare at him, surprised. Mr. Clouseau stood before me impatiently.

"You goin' let me in?"

"Yeah, of course. I'm just surprised." I move aside to give him way. He walks into the room on a mission. He opens the door to the bathroom. The steam hits him as he forcefully pushes the shower curtain back. Satisfied, he moves into the main area scanning all corners of the room. "Can I offer you a drink or are you still casing the joint?"

"Just checking."

"Checking for what, Qu? Some ridiculous, half-naked stud to just spring out my bed?" Annoyed, I fold my arms and lean to one side. *Stupid!*

"Just thought—"

"Just thought what, Qu. When have I ever cheated on you?"

"It's been three days."

"Really?"

"You've been gone and..."

I could feel the effects of the shower evaporate.

"Look, I'm sorry. I didn't mean, I didn't mean..." He walks tentatively towards me with his hands in his pockets. "Viv, please, let's just go home."

I missed him so badly and now here he is, in the flesh. I take all of him in.

This is my knight. This is the Qu who came to my apartment and practically dragged me out on our first date. The same Qu who used to kiss me every chance he got. This is the same Qu with his hands in his pockets. This doesn't make sense.

I shake my head and walk over to the mini fridge. "Want a drink?"

"No thanks." His eyes follow me.

I open the fridge and reach for cranberry juice. I pop the top as I head for my favourite chair. *How did we get here?* I sit in the chaise and wave him to the armchair across from me. *I am not going to fight.* I continue to sip my juice.

"Did you hear what I said?"

"Yes, I heard you."

"And?"

"And I'm not ready to leave."

Qu stares at me and I can feel his temperature rising. I wait a few seconds before leaning forward. "Why is it so important to you for me to come home now? It's only two more days."

"Why do you need five days when three is enough to be away from your family?"

"Don't avoid me, Qu! Don't answer me with a question. I want you to be honest."

"What you mean? I am being honest!"

I fall back in my chair. *Don't lose it, Viv, don't lose it.* I drain my bottle and rise.

"Where are you going?"

"To put on some clothes and give you some time to think about what I mean." I grab a dress and head for the bathroom, locking the door.

Why is he acting this way?

I take my time creaming my legs and arms. I slip a dress over my head and smooth the fabric over my hips. I peer into the mirror, now dripping wet from the shower. I take a tissue and gently wipe a corner dry. I smile at myself as I grab my toothbrush.

I am not going to rush. I'm going to make him wait. I meticulously polish every tooth and even floss, which I rarely do. *My dentist would be so proud. When is my next appointment anyway? I got to check my schedule.* I can hear him pacing outside the bathroom door.

Good.

I reach for my makeup bag and start plucking my eyebrows. One hair, hmm, two hairs, ouch. Jeez. Through the pain, I keep my focus on my reflection. *That man is going to answer me before this night is out! This is my time! This is my space! Come up in here an' tell me he don't understand henglish! Whatever.* Nine hairs, um, ten hairs. *Wait, is that a grey one?! Not today, Satan!* I yank it even harder. *Good. That ought to do.* "Where's my concealer?" I mumble.

"Viv!" Qu bangs on the door. I drop my brush.

Whoa! He's mad.

"Yasss?" I sing sweetly.

"How long you gonna be in there?"

"As long as it takes."

"Come on! We're wasting time."

I abruptly open the door shocking him backwards. "Wasting what time, Qu? I have all the time in the world." I walk past him to my chaise and fold my legs under me.

"So?"

"So what?"

"Qu, I still expect an answer. Why is it important for me to come home now?"

Qu opens and shuts his hands over and over before patting his legs and sitting beside me on the chaise.

"You've been gone."

I wait.

"The kids have missed you..." He looks at me and realizes I'm not going to finish his sentences.

"I miss you and need you to come home. The place isn't the same without you." Exhausted, Qu takes my hand and strokes it. We sit in silence.

It's a start, but not nearly enough. I'm not nineteen anymore. Stroking hands isn't enough for me anymore. So sad. I get up and secure the door.

"What are you doing?"

"Locking the door," I say as I turn around. "Take off your pants."

"Are you insane? You want sex now?"

"No, no. I saw it in a film once. The woman asked her man to take off his pants so that they could talk, and he couldn't escape."

"You seriously think I'm going to run off?"

"Qu! Just do it! I'm not asking you to do anything difficult. Just take off your pants!"

"Are you going to throw them off the balcony?"

"I may throw you off the balcony if you don't get movin'!"

"Alright, alright. I'm taking them off," he smirks as he draws one leg out and then the other.

Man... focus Viv, focus. But damn, look at his legs! Has he been working out when I haven't been looking or am I just horny?

He hands me his pants.

"Satisfied?"

"Not quite." I take them quickly and throw them in the bathroom, firmly shutting the door.

"Now what?"

I push him back onto the chaise and sit cross-legged beside him. I take a deep breath.

I have strength.

"Qu, as much as I've missed you and the kids this week, I've been having these revelations. I don't know when last this happened to me. I don't know when I will ever again. So, it's important to me that I not waste what few days I have left."

"But I told you I'd give you space at home to sort things out."

When did he say that? Never mind. Just give it to him.

"Yes, and I appreciate that. But being away from what's familiar, forces me to look at myself... and us."

Qu stiffens. "What do you mean?"

"I mean that I've been thinking about my life and ours. Qu, do you realize that more than half my life has been spent with you?"

"I never thought about it."

"Exactly, neither did I till this week! We are a huge part of each other's lives, and we don't even think about it!" I pause. I can tell from his eyes his mind is ticking.

"So, what are you thinking about us?"

"You know what, Qu? It's your turn to tell me something. What do *you* think about us? About me?"

Qu rubs his palms against his thighs and looks down. "It's a bit cold, can I have a blanket?"

"No," I say shortly. "You're avoiding."

"Why do you keep saying that? I'm avoiding, I'm avoiding. I'm here, aren't I? If I were avoiding, I wouldn't even bother showing up!"

No one asked you to be here. Deep breath.

"Qu, I'm not going to fight with you. When I say, 'you're avoid-ing,' I mean you aren't answering me."

"What do you want me to say? I've already told you I miss you. What more do you want?"

Viv don't back down.

"Okay, you want to know what I want? Here's what I want. I want you to be open and honest with me. I want you to answer me with what you are feeling and not with questions. I want you not to be so defensive." I gently put my palms on the side of his face, forcing him to look me in the eyes. "I want us to talk like we used to. I used to be your best friend that you could tell anything. I want you to talk to me like you did her."

"You are still her."

"I don't get that Qu, I honestly don't." I release him.

"Viv, as much as I hear you, I need you to know I'm not avoiding you. I want you."

"Why?"

"Because…"

Even with his pants off.

"Because what, Qu?"

"Because you're mine."

Damn, it's like chipping away at stone. This is exhausting.

"Okay, let me ask you this. Are you completely happy in our marriage? When you asked me to marry you, is this how you pictured we'd turn out?"

"I don't regret marrying you, Viv. And yeah, I admit that things could be better but that's what marriage is about."

"What do you mean by that?" I wait so he can put his thoughts together. He folds one leg underneath him.

"I married you because I love you and didn't want to lose you. We had a good thing going and I didn't want it to end. I love you still."

As much as I want to rejoice that he finally said the words, I bite my tongue. I need to be quiet.

"Let's face it, Viv, what more can we expect? We have jobs, kids, a house, a car, elderly parents, and stuff to maintain. I think we are doing good."

I pause choosing my words carefully. "I guess this week I've realized that there is more that I want for us," I share. "I've decided that I can't keep running the way I've been." I let him digest that for a few moments.

"Remember when we were dating, Qu? We were still keeping our grades up, but we also took the time to explore together, have fun together and get to know one another. Every day."

"Don't you think I know you after twenty years?"

"You see, that's what I'm talking about!" I start pacing. "Take this week. You think you know me, but can you truthfully say you expected me to do this? Just take off and stay away for days at a time?"

Qu hesitates. "No, this I didn't expect at all," he concedes.

I stop mid-step. "The funny thing is, neither did I! How can you claim you know me after twenty years when I am still discovering new things about myself?" I could see in his posture that my words were penetrating. "This also makes me wonder what new things about *you* I don't know. Before 'stuff' it was only you, me, and our relationship."

Qu gets up and starts pacing. I watch him.

"There has got to be more to us than the house and the kids, right?" I press. "I've been thinking about that a lot lately. Like what's *next* for us."

"What do you suggest we do then?"

"What are *your* thoughts, Qu?" I volley back.

"Frankly?" Qu says hastily. "I didn't know what to expect. I've never known a healthy marriage. You know this. Until I met your parents, I didn't know any couple that made it past the five-year mark."

"So why marry? The question hung in the air for what seemed like an eternity.

Qu finally stopped pacing and looked at me. "As I said, I didn't want to lose you. Maybe just seeing how your parents stay, opened up the possibility."

"So, past the wedding day, you didn't envision anything else?"

Qu shifts his gaze away from me. "I guess not. I guess I just thought we'd stay together as long as we could."

I walk over to him and rub his shoulders. "But a good marriage doesn't just happen."

"You have doubts about our marriage?"

He looks like I punched him. Think Viv. Make him hear you. I swallow. "It's not that, Qu. Trust me." I keep my eyes focused on him. Qu's jaw relaxes. I exhale and let the silence rest for a while.

"If we were living in an ideal world, how would you like our married life to look?"

"Can we just stop this now?" Qu insists.

"No."

"Fine. Happy. I'd like us to be happier," he turns around and holds my waist. "How do you see it?"

I slip away and sit on the edge of the bed. I'm not letting him off the hook. "Yeah, happy, but what do you mean by happy?"

He sits beside me. "Okay," he closes his eyes for a few moments. "It would be good if we acted like we were dating again. Go see a movie once in a while. Go out for dinner, whatever. It would be good if we could get rid of the debt we've accumulated," he sighs. "That is my biggest worry these days."

"Okay."

"But our life together isn't all that bad, Viv! I mean I'm happy where I work. You're happy where you work. I'm happy that we had the kids. I think you are too," he half-smiles.

Are you sure about all that?

"We love our home," he continues. "I love sleeping beside you at night."

Oh, he's good. He's gonna try to sexy-talk me.

"You know we haven't slept apart in ages! Since I cut back on business travel, we always sleep side by side," Qu gives me a playful nudge. "This week has been brutal! I haven't had a good night's sleep since you left."

I sigh. *Oh, he meant companionship, not sex. Still, he isn't getting off this easy. Dig deeper.*

"I'm not trying to imply that our life is unbearable. I know we've got some good stuff going, but..." I gently push him away as he tries to nuzzle my ear. "Particularly in our marriage, we've kinda gone off course," I correct quickly.

"Hmm..." he slumps.

"I don't think our efforts need to be huge. In fact, I'm thinking of simplifying." *I don't want him to feel like I am blaming him.*

As we sit on the bed, I tell him about my flashbacks to when I was young, peacefully balancing on the seawall. I share how my parents grew up and ever closer, from the time they lived on the island. How they grew more mindful of one another in their older years. This is the first time I've ever shared their intimate story with Qu in such detail. Eventually, we lay facing each other on the bed as I bring the conversation back to us. I reminisce about our early days.

I yawn.

"It's funny you say you were nervous around me when from the minute I met you, I felt comfortable. You were like home."

"You never told me that before."

"I figured you knew."

"It's still good to hear."

We continue to smile, gazing at one another. Qu looks over my shoulder and jumps up suddenly. "Shoot! It's one-thirty!"

Panicked, I hold his arm. "What's wrong?"

"I came here straight from work. I didn't tell the kids where I was going," he scrambles off the bed.

"Wait! Qu! You can stay the night. We can just call the kids and let them know."

Qu stops in the passageway and looks back. "Are you sure, with this being your 'space'?"

I can't tell if he's being sarcastic or genuine. I sit up and hug my knees. "Yeah, I can make an exception," I grin as I reach for my cell.

Walking back towards the bed, he slowly unbuttons the rest of his shirt.

My eyes flutter open. The sun is hidden. I look over my shoulder and realize that it's barely 4:30 a.m. I yawn and snuggle closer into Qu's chest. I look into his face and lightly stroke his cheek. *If only we could live like this forever. I think last night was a breakthrough.* I sigh and hug him closer. Qu stirs and returns the squeeze. His palm starts rubbing circles on the small of my back. I suddenly feel self-conscious. *Shoot! I didn't mean to wake him.*

"Hmm, what time is it?" he murmurs.

"Go back to sleep. It's still early."

"Yeah, but I gotta go home and get ready for work. Besides the kids—"

"Our kids are grown and can dress themselves. You can stay a little longer."

"Don't have to tell me twice," he draws me even closer into him. Qu strokes my lip with the tip of his tongue, ever so slowly.

"I didn't mean all that," I giggle. *I don't want to start something I can't finish.*

"Why not? I won't tell your husband," he teases as he kisses my collarbone.

"Qu, you know if we do it now, I'll be high as a kite and liable to agree to anything."

"I love the way you beg!"

He's having too much fun.

"Stop playin'."

He comes up for air and leans on his elbow, fixing his eyes on me. *When was the last time he looked at me with so much desire?* I feel warmly sensuous.

"You are the same person who said a few minutes ago that we have time. Why are you pulling away now?"

I lean on my elbow and raise my face a fraction of an inch from his. "Qu, we've been at it all night. If we want some semblance of control, we should—"

"Hmm..." he moans, totally ignoring me and moving back to my neck.

I caress the back of his head and fall into the pillow. "You are so wrong...wait!" I gently push him back. He lifts his head.

"You want to do something? We could walk on the beach!"

"And leave this incredible bed? That ain't gonna happen," he traces designs on my stomach, playfully tugging the lace of my negligee with his teeth.

Oh boy... "How about we order room service? You could bathe and eat before you leave."

"Mrs. Moji, hmm, I love the sound of that," he pecks me on the cheek. "Relax. Let's just be in the moment. We can eat later. We can bathe later. But right now, I just want to be with you in this bed, under these amazing covers, touching you here, oh, and here and... here and... Hmm," he moans mischievously, raising the comforter over our heads.

"I love this hotel room," Qu says, tugging at his socks.

I'm moving the small table from the sitting area onto the balcony. The food we ordered arrived while Qu was showering. The smell of bacon, eggs and coffee linger in the air.

"I can see why you wouldn't want to leave it just yet," he sighs, grabbing the other side of the table.

"Yeah, I was just thinking, wouldn't it be amazing if we could design our bedroom like this room? Nice king size bed with not too soft, not too hard mattress. Is it memory foam? Silky linen. Beautiful chaise. A romantic oasis..."

"Ha!" Qu snorts. "As it stands, our bedroom feels more like a thrift shop!"

"Oh! Don't say that! That sounds terrible."

"Well, it's true! It's got my computer bits in one corner, your books and papers piled in another corner. We've slept on the same bed we got when we started living together, the dresser drawers are hanging on an angle—"

"Alright, alright. You win! We are living in the Salvation Army."

"But you're right, we can change that," he adds quickly.

"Yeah, we can. Thanks," I say as he pours my coffee. I uncover his breakfast and hand him a fork.

"Thank you," he returns as he caresses it from my hand.

We eat in silence for a while, enjoying our view of the beach. I tug at my robe belt a little. I didn't expect the breeze to be as cool as it is.

"Viv."

"Yeah?"

"I know you said you need the time, but after last night, I don't want to leave you here."

"Qu."

"Now hear me out. I understand you need your space. I understand it's gorgeous here and may give you a sense of freedom. But I can help! We can work it out together. We just said we can create this," he waves his hand over the room.

"I don't doubt that we can. But I committed to five days to myself and I'm not going to back down."

Qu looks at me intensely. *Don't back down Viv.*

"Being here is about me. Yes, I am part of you, but my decision to stay here is about me alone. Can you accept that?"

Qu takes a mouthful and shakes his head.

"Qu, think about it. It's two more days. We have a million more days together."

"Only a million? I expect at least three!"

"And the funnyman is back," I shake my head. "We good?"

"We're excellent," he replies, stroking my knee under the table.

"Do men always have penis on the brain?" I pull my robe tighter.

"Aah! Why you have to go there?"

"Come on, Qu! I'm talking about our relationship together, and you brought it back to the bed. Who's being base?"

Qu gently removes his hand. "That's your mind. Don't put that on me," he says matter-of-factly. "I was agreeing that we were alright. Me touching you isn't a signal that I want sex. I'm showing you I care. I love you."

How do I remove the foot from my mouth? "I'm sorry. I jumped—"

"Let's forget it," he rises and kisses my cheek. I blush as he settles back.

He says forget it, but why did I say that? Qu may not say the words, but he's always been affectionate. Another thing to throw in my consideration basket.

"What are you thinking?"

"Hmm?"

"Just now. Your eyes went all glassy. What's up?"

"Now you're stealin' my lines. What's up?" I snicker under my breath.

"Fine, don't tell me. Who's avoiding now?"

"Hey!" I throw my napkin at him.

"Just keepin' it real," he retorts as he takes another bite of his toast.

I hate when men think they're right. I kiss my teeth as I lift my cup. "Fine, I was just thinking about my reaction just now. What you said hit a nerve."

"Oh?"

"Yeah, Mr. Know-It-All, what you said got me thinking."

"What I say?"

I look at him in disbelief. "You don't remember what you said a minute ago? Are you having a senior's moment?"

"Maybe," he keeps chewing, unfazed.

"Alright," I exhale deeply. "I was just reflecting on how I'm this great ball of contradictions sometimes. I want us to be affectionate, I push you away. I want us to have a better marriage, but I don't know how. Whatever."

Qu sits quietly for a few minutes. I can see his wheels turning as he leans slightly forward. "Viv, have you ever thought that maybe, just maybe, a marriage involves two people?" he challenges. "You're thinking and thinking and... why? I am with you. Do you see me?"

Great, something more to throw in my consideration basket.

"Viv!"

Startled, I snap back, "Yeah?"

"You're doing it again! Why do you feel you need to figure this out alone? Get out of your head!"

I burst out laughing. "Qu, have you just met me? I've always lived in my head!"

"Viv, stop avoiding. I didn't say you shouldn't think. I'm saying that you don't have to carry all this stuff when I'm sitting right here and want to figure it all out with you, instead of you spinning around and around and... DAMN!" he slams his napkin on the table.

"What?"

He points his chin in the direction of the clock, "Time is in overdrive." Qu takes a quick swig of his coffee and gets up abruptly. "I got to go. Where's my jacket?"

"I think I put it in the closet earlier," I reply, trailing him.

Qu spins around, finger loaded, "I may have to run, but I'm not through with you."

I stand on my tiptoes and plant a kiss on the end of his nose. "Whatever, Mister. Go! I'll see you soon."

"You'll call me later?"

"I'll call you later."

"Alright. Have a good day," he quickly kisses me goodbye.

As we part, I realize I'm not ready. "Wait!"

"What wait? I'm late for work."

"Give me a minute," I drag on my jeans, t-shirt, and flip-flops at record speed.

"You are so strange sometimes."

"It's not strange. I just want to walk you out."

"Alright," he closes the door behind us.

We walk with our fingers entwined as we wait for the elevator. *Though it feels good, it also feels odd. Anyone passing us now may think we were having an illicit affair, him in his office attire, and me with a bandana gripping my curly hair, wearing crumpled jeans. Should I have stayed in the room? I look up at Qu and find him smiling at me. I squeeze his hand as the doors slide open.*

"Now it's my turn to ask you what you are thinking," I counter as I press the ground floor button.

"I'm just thinking how I love the way you glow, all sexy curvy in the morning—and still manage to live in your head!" he teases.

"Whatever!" I laugh.

He's so corny. God, I love him.

"True!"

"Well, whether what you say is true or not, I need you to know that I'm not hiding anything from you."

"We'll talk more."

"Agreed," I breathe as we reach the lobby doors.

"I'm glad you came, Qu."

He kisses my lips and delays. "Me too," he holds both my hands. "Bye."

"Bye."

He turns and walks towards the parking lot as I stand and watch his back. *I miss him.* He honks as he drives past me. I wave in acknowledgement. Long after he's gone, I find myself still standing there. Arms wrapped around me. Thinking.

TWELVE

I emerge from the washroom refreshed. I wring the water from my hair, sitting on the edge of the bed. Reaching for my bag, I spread out all the products beside me. Oil, curling mousse, leave-in conditioner, gel, comb, brush... why do I bother? I switch on the TV for company.

In Iraq, another suicide bomber—

Too early. I click to the next station.

They found her body—

Click.

You may want to avoid Highway 10 where they are still cleaning up the debris from a major rollover—

Click.

If you're happy and you know it—

Click.

Steroid use is suspected—

Click.

Make my day—

Click.

Warning that the following images may be disturbing for younger—

Click.

And enjoy life and have it in abundance…

Say God is good.

GOD IS GOOD!

All the time.

ALL THE TIME!

Hallelujah! Oh, amen and amen!

Now let's turn our Bibles to Romans—

Nope. Click.

… Dressed head to toe in a sequin gown she strutted the red carpet—

Click.

It is estimated that 520 passengers were killed in this latest, most horrific plane—

Click.

Just a sprinkle of thyme—

"Nope." Click.

Oh-ma-god, Tina! You sure he said that 'bout me? No—

Click.

Harvey Habber was released from jail today after serving ten years for killing his wife and—

Click.

Umm, baby, do it again, ahh, harder—

Click. *Porn this early?!*

Get out your sandals. It's going to be another gorgeous day!

Good! The weather channel I can handle! Well, unless it'll cover some part of the world where volcanoes, tsunamis, hurricanes, out-of-control forest fires or catastrophic floods are prone. Keep the remote close.

I start applying conditioner to my hair and comb it through.

No wonder depression is on the rise in this country. Everyone hears the worst and expects the worst. A second ago, I felt refreshed and alive thinking about Qu and BOOM! Ten seconds of flicking channels and my buzz is gone. How can TV have everything and nothing at the same time? In fact—

Click. The screen flashes black.

That's enough. There's always radio. Twirling the dial to my favourite old school station, I settle back on the bed.

Ring, ring! Excited, I answer the phone, "Qu!"

"No, sorry. It's Gabe. I hope you don't mind."

"Oh, Gabe! How you doing?"

"I'm good, I'm good. I noticed you didn't come down for breakfast."

"Yeah, Qu was here so we decided to have room service instead."

"Oh, that's great. Listen, I leave for home this evening and was wondering if you would like to have lunch with me this afternoon."

"Yeah! Why not? Is twelve alright?"

"Yeah, perfect. I've got a few things I want to run around and do so that should give me plenty of time to get back."

"Dining room?"

"I'm thinking lobby. Be nice to take a break from hotel food. What do you feel like eating?"

"I'm not sure. We'll decide when we meet."

"Great! I'll see you then."

"Till then. Bye."

"Bye," I hang up smiling. This is turning out to be a gorgeous day! Applying oil to my hair, I wrap it high into a ponytail.

What now? I could exercise. Spinning? Yeah, why not! I've never done it and I saw it on the schedule yesterday. If I hurry, I can make it.

Spinning class...what was I thinking? I limp to my bed rubbing what's left of my butt.

I thought they'd need to peel me off that thing. If I wasn't so stubborn, I woulda left screaming when the first pain hit me ten minutes in. Spinning class? What sadist invented that? It ain't natural to be revving up to a car speed, standing and sitting and twisting on a bike. Ooowww... To electric ZZ Top, no less! Coulda at least spared us with some Outkast. Damn! Never again!

Silver lining—still alive.

I throw myself face-first into the bed and let out an agonizing grimace. I open one eye to see what time it is. I've got two hours to pull myself together. *Viv, you can do this girl. Can't let no measly bike knock you out. You the girl! Get up! Get up now! Come on Viv. You can do this.*

My flesh is weak. Not one of my muscles will listen to my brain's weak attempt at pep talk. I drift off.

I shiver awake. *Ooohhh... gotta go! One hour.*

I drag myself off the bed and wipe the drool from my mouth with the back of my hand. I reach for the phone and dial.

"Hello, front desk," the dry voice answers.

"Hello. Can you please patch me through to Gabe Adams' room?"

"Certainly."

I rub my neck to the muse-ac. "Hello?"

"Hi, Gabe. You're there."

"Yeah, hi. I'm having a slow start. Is everything alright?"

I hesitate. *May as well tell the truth.*

"Yes and no. I found out this morning I'm old."

He laughs, "What?"

"Yes, Gabe. I'm an old broad. I took a spinning class an hour or so ago and it just about whipped my butt."

"Sorry to hear."

"No apologies necessary. I just think I need a little more time to pull myself together."

"No problem. Is one o'clock better?"

"I should be asking you that. Would that be too late for you?"

"No, I'll see you then."

"You're a doll, you know that?"

"So say the rumours. Take care."

"You too," I hang up the phone, thankful. *Bath or shower? A sauna? Shower then sauna! Things are looking up!*

I spread one of my towels and sit on the upper ledge. Someone turned the dial high, so the heat is intense. My breath catches in my throat, which startles me. Breathing evenly again, I lay on my back and close my eyes. Smooth out my towel. I am already perspiring. I feel the tension in my shoulders slowly loosen. I rest my foot against the wall, getting used to the fire on my heel. I will myself not to worry or stress. *This is my time.*

This is living. I open my eyes and watch the mellow haze float about the ceiling. This is Gabe's last day and my last day is tomorrow. Soon it will be home and work and maybe, volunteering again. *I wonder what I will be stepping into. I wonder if I'll be tempted to step into old patterns.*

Beads form on my forearm. I can't see anything but waves.

When I told Qu yesterday that I didn't want to go back, I could see fear in his eyes. I think he thought I was planning to leave him. Qu and I are different and have our differences, but I'm not going to give up on us like that! I'm glad he knows that now.

I try to wipe the mist from my eyes.

Surprisingly, with all my wish list talk, he saw right through me. Calling me out like he did when I was trying to figure out things on my own. When I don't take initiative, it seems like things don't get done or they fall apart. But is that true? What would happen if I let other people take initiative? Like now, I'm not in control of anything at home this week yet things are still being managed, right?

I need to learn to trust again. Trust that we can get things done together. It can't be all about me, living in my head, trying to make sense of the world on my own, right? I don't have to shoulder everything. I breathe in again and close my eyes.

The water drips off my legs, soaking the towel. My face is awash. *They say one shouldn't be in here too long. You know it's hot when the hairs in your nose start to prickle. Ah! I'll stay one more minute before I shower.*

I lost track of how many minutes passed. *I think I've reached my limit.* I roll over to my side and attempt to push myself up. Wow! The room is bleary and sways slightly. That 'one more minute' cost me my balance.

"Dizzy?"

Though I hear the voice, I have no idea where it came from. I try to focus through the fog.

"Yeah. I just got up and my head started spinning."

"That happens sometimes. Put your head between your legs a second and see if the dizziness passes. Sometimes if you get up too fast, you lose equilibrium."

I do as I am told. After a few seconds, my head clears. Feeling stronger, eyes wide, I take my time sitting upright.

"Thank you... Hello?" The room is empty. *Strange.*

I climb down carefully and open the door. The cold air rushes in, sending shivers throughout my body. Hugging both wet towels to me, I make my way to the stalls.

I'm wearing a new peach-coloured dress I bought on impulse the first day I got here. Light and airy, it sports an empire waistline and grazes my knees. Paired with jewelled sandals, and a hint of makeup, I feel refreshed. *It was fun getting ready for lunch today. Why can't I feel like this every day? As it's on my mind, I should make a list of all the small changes I want to make when I go home. I could start with taking an inventory of my wardrobe. Throw out everything that doesn't make me feel gorgeous. Come to think of it, that would be half my wardrobe. Hmph.*

Second, take my time to dress in the morning. I usually slap on whatever my hand hits before running out the door. I groan as I haul my creaky leg over my opposite knee, thinking about my pending transformation.

"Ahh, Viv, you're already here."

"Yeah, but only by a few minutes," I reply, painstakingly unfolding myself. "You look good!"

"Thanks. Old school dies hard. I don't like wearing jeans or anything too casual when I'm going to the airport. Too formal?"

I check Gabe over from top to bottom. "No, business casual is fine. The purple looks good on you."

"Well, thank you. Have you decided what you'd like to eat?"

"No, but I have decided that wherever we go, it has to have a patio so we can sit outside."

"Okay, we'll just drive around then till we find a patio," he smiles. "After you."

"Thank you," I say walking past him. I push through the rotating doors.

"I'm parked just over here," he gestures.

"Sweet ride!"

Gabe blushes, "Yeah, the perks of working in finance." He opens the door wide for me to step inside.

"Thanks," I say, backing my sore behind into the leather seat.

Gabe sparks the car, "So, what direction?"

"How about west along the lakeshore?" I grin as I fasten my seatbelt.

"Kay!"

The traffic is unusually light as we cruise along the boulevard.

"So, was your business trip successful?"

"For the most part, yes. My biggest reason for coming was to get us on the same page. We were able to iron out some numbers and come to some agreements, so yeah, it was successful."

"That's great," I peer out the window enjoying the drive along the water.

"How about you?"

"Excuse me?"

"Your trip. Any discoveries since we last spoke?"

I continue to look out the window as Qu floods my mind. Sighing, I turn and look at Gabe's profile. "Do you remember what we last talked about?"

"Let's see," he muses as he manoeuvres a turn. "I think our famous last words were time and choices."

"Ah, the famous time and choices. Well," I look ahead, "I think I took our conclusion to heart."

"How so?"

"Later in the day, Qu showed up and—"

"How 'bout that place?" Gabe points up the street at a gigantic façade of a fluorescent sombrero.

"Why not?"

"Sorry, you were saying?" Gabe apologizes as he turns onto a side street to park.

"No, I was just saying that Qu came by unexpectedly and we got to talk. Like *really* talk."

"Hold that thought. I have to feed the meter."

"Alright," I swing my feet onto the curb. Awkwardly, I raise myself by pushing on the back of the seat. The rays hit my face, causing me to squint. I search for my sunglasses as Gabe returns with the ticket.

"You alright?"

"Yeah, the sun's just brighter than I thought. Couldn't tell with tinted windows."

"Oh," he says, clearly sceptical.

"Let's go!" I say, holding up my glasses in triumph. We stroll easily towards the restaurant.

The guitar music grows more inviting as we near the oversize umbrellas. Gabe motions to the server as we sit outside.

"Here you go. Can I offer you a drink to start?"

Gabe looks at me and smiles, "After you."

"I'd love an iced tea with extra lemon."

"And for you?"

"A cola, please."

"Alright, I'll be right back."

We settle in and browse the menus. I put it down abruptly.

"What?"

"I'm not a Mexican food connoisseur, but I do know what I crave. Nachos!"

"You can have anything on the menu, and you want—"

"A big honking plate of nachos dripping with beef, peppers, cheese -- all that!"

"And you call me strange."

"You still are strange. Strange is good!" I declare, hitting the table.

"Nachos it is!"

"Great! What you having?"

"I'm gonna ask the server to bring me the special and hope for the best."

"Fabulous!" I grin as we both shift the menus to the side.

"So, Qu came over yesterday and it was good."

"Gabe, it was beyond good— Oh, thank you," I say, looking up as the server rests the drinks in front of us. As I sip my drink, Gabe gives the waiter our orders before returning his attention to me.

"Sounds like fireworks."

"Depending on what you mean by fireworks. It started rocky and a bit... hmm... confrontational. Me, leaving like I did hurt him, so it seemed he came ready for a fight. It took a little chipping away at both of our egos for us to get to talking."

"Oh..."

"What's oh?"

"Nothing, it's just interesting."

"How so?"

"Well, with me and Jules, we've known each other for years, but just started dating about a few months ago. When we are together, all I want to do is talk with her. Be with her."

I stare at him awhile, thinking. "I've never heard a man say that before."

Gabe blushes, lifting his glass. "Funny, I didn't expect to say that either."

"Sorry, I didn't mean to embarrass you."

We both laugh.

"Have you told her that you feel this way?"

"No, it's pretty obvious. When I'm away, I call every chance I get. I try to always be with her when I'm home."

"So? Still, tell her!"

Gabe laughs, "Nah, we're fine."

"Yeah, whatever, I still say *tell her*. There is something powerful about saying the words. Like I was telling you about Qu and me. We've been together, what, twenty-three years, nineteen married? We are always with each other. We love each other. But yesterday, saying the three little words out loud, sparked something. Am I making any sense?"

"I'm not sure."

"Alright, let's take it out of the context of intimacy. Let's take it to parent and child."

"Alright," he folds his arms and leans on the table.

"So, I've been thinking about this lately about my daughter, so it's good for me to use you as a sounding board."

"Go ahead."

"Well, Faith and I have fallen into this pattern that in some ways mirrors my mom and me." I pause and take a sip of my iced tea. Its tartness takes me off guard. "Wow!"

"Not good?"

"No. I like sour. I just didn't expect the taste to be so strong. Anyway, back to what I was saying," I take another sip.

"I love Faith with my whole heart, but I never tell her. Do you know what she *does* hear me say a lot? Did you do your homework? Is the table set? Why did you slap Justin? Can't you stop complaining? Your skirt's too short. When are you ever going to...? You can fill in the blanks. That's our entire relationship!" I let out a deep sigh. *Feels good to confess even if I sound like the world's worst mother.*

"That may be your experience, but Jules and I rarely argue."

"It doesn't matter. You can hug her to bits every waking second, but trust me, we need to hear the words too. Both are important."

"So that's what last night was for you and Qu, telling and showing—"

"And showing and showing some more!" I laugh and fan myself with my napkin, mimicking a southern belle.

Our laughter tumbles over one another till tears run down my cheeks. "You're crazy. Wait, when did the food arrive?" I scan the plates in front of us as I catch my breath.

"I don't know, but they're huge! Please take some nachos. They don't taste good unless they're shared."

"Alright, only if you do the same with this I-can't-pronounce-its-name-special."

"You're daring, aren't you?"

"I like living on the edge."

"Deal!"

We both angle our plates to the middle of the table and dig in.

"Well, you've convinced me. As soon as I land, I'm going to tell her I love her and want to marry her."

The food dangles out of my mouth as I stare at him. "What?"

"I'm going to tell her I love her and want to marry her. Tell and show."

"That's great, Gabe. Congratulations and all, but be clear, I was just suggesting you tell her you love her. Marriage is a whole different ball game."

"But here you are, married to a man you just showed and showed and showed some more," he teases. "Who you've loved for nineteen years of holy matrimony, and you don't think I want the same?"

"Let's step back a moment and forget the recent showing," I wave no in the air. "Gabe."

"Hmm..."

"You're a lovely man and Jules would be lucky to have you."

"I feel a 'but' coming on."

"And I don't want to talk you out of marriage—"

"But..." he rushes.

"Marriage can be wonderful."

"Viv, spit it out already," he chomps on his nacho.

I hold back as I try to balance just the right mix of beans, cheese, and meat on my chips.

"Viv!" Startled, the chips collapse and I'm left re-scooping.

"Gabe, twenty-three years didn't just happen. Okay, it did, and that's my point. Wait, let me back up," I give up on the chip and look him in the eyes. "If you don't want to have all these years for years' sake, it takes work."

"And you think that I'm afraid of work? I love Jules."

"Love, love, love, love, love," I chant sarcastically. "Gabe, give me a break! How old are you anyway?"

"How old are you?"

"You never ask a lady her age!" I smirk.

"Aha! After years of burning bras and women taking back the night, I still can't ask a woman her age?"

"Yes!" I declare adamantly.

"Fine. I'm thirty-nine."

The food drops out of my mouth.

"Whoa! Here," he hands me a stack of napkins as he starts to wipe the table.

I don't know what he's talking about.

"Thirty-nine?"

"Yeah, thirty-nine. Why? Is that so hard to believe?" he says, amused as he settles back in his seat.

"Frankly, yes! All this time I've been thinking you're twenty-something and you're around the same age as me! I need a drink," I motion for the server.

Gabe chuckles.

"Yes, please, can you bring me a *Long Island* iced tea? Thanks," I dab my napkin in my ice water and try to salvage my dress.

"I don't know what the big deal is. So, we're the same age."

"You're right, what's the big deal…" I let my words trail off. "But—"

"But you're so young, Gabe! It's like the fountain of youth quenches your thirst every day. It's disarming."

"You're exaggerating," he smirks.

"Am I? Gabe, you play the guitar. You're an artist. You own your own home. Make crazy cash in an industry I barely understand. Travel. In love like it's your first time."

Gabe sobers, "And none of that happened overnight!" he leans forward.

There's a long pause between us as I stare at him. I shake out of my trance and look at our messy plates.

"Well, look at you!" he breaks the silence. "Beautiful woman in one of the hardest professions in the world. Raising teenagers in a society that eats teenagers for breakfast. Married to the love of your life, with a home."

Did he say beautiful?

"Exactly, we are different."

"Not really. Yeah, our lives have taken different paths, but we are still living full lives, on the right track. Still believe in love."

I hold up my hand to cover my mouth as I chew.

"Forget what I was saying. Marry this woman."

"Why the about-face?"

"You're thirty-nine, not twenty-five. You know yourself. Marry her."

"There is that age assumption again. What makes you think I didn't know myself at twenty-five? You were married before twenty-five."

"My point exactly! I had a husband and children by the time I was in my mid-twenties and barely knew my name! I thought, get married. It's time. You are thirty-nine and have been around the block."

"Hey, now. You make me sound like a gigolo!"

"You are old," I mock. "Seriously, who says gigolo anymore? Repeat after me: P-L-A-Y-A."

"Right," he snorts. "Like playa's any better!"

We both giggle like teenagers. "You're right. I'm sorry," I shake my head. *I need to backpedal and quick.*

"Viv, I've always felt age was just a number. I'm not going to stop living or learning just because the calendar keeps running. It's supposed to run! I'm blessed to be growing older. We are both blessed. Know how many people would die, have died, wishing they were us?"

I sit in silence, mechanically munching. *Gabe has this uncanny way of humbling me.*

The server hands me this humongous, tacky, pineapple-shaped glass of Long Island tea. I start sucking it back like water.

"You alright?"

He's asked me that a lot today. I unintentionally slam the glass with a bang.

"Yeah. As usual, you've given me more food for thought. Knock it off!" I take another sip. "No, seriously, I've talked all this time about word power and here my words are full of assumptions," I move the salsa around with my chip as I continue. "You say growing, I say old. I say love, you jump to marriage," I rhyme off.

"So? Even if you didn't say it, I know you believe love and marriage are linked."

"Yeah, you're right," I hedge. "But back then I also saw marriage as expectation. Then, somehow it morphed into a contract, you know, where we agree to do this and that to move x forward."

"I think you are being a bit harsh. I see the look in your eyes when you say Qu's name."

I pause. *I was always in love with Qu from the beginning. But getting married...*

"Yes, but I've been thinking about my marriage more this week... and then when Qu came over, we were able to start to explore it some more, together."

"That's good, right?"

"Of course. I guess I've been projecting on you what marriage was for me at a younger age," I shake my head. "You said it yourself, you love Jules, so you are going to ask her to marry you. You made this simple yet profound declaration."

Gabe shakes his head in response, "It is simple. It's like connecting the dots."

"Hmm…"

Gabe wipes his mouth. "I don't know about you, but I am stuffed."

"Funny, I feel like I'm just getting started."

Gabe smiles as he rests his napkin neatly in front of him. "Then don't let me stop you. Keep eating. Waiter? Could I have a coffee please?" The server nods his acknowledgement.

"Would you like another drink?"

I continue to pick at my nachos.

"No, I'm good."

"It seems like I've upset you somehow."

I look up quickly and give him a weak smile. "No, you haven't. It's just…this week has been heavy with lessons," I sigh. "Here I thought I'd be sharing this incredible revelation with you, and instead you turn around and teach me triple what I came to the table with."

"Why do you think I enjoy having meals with you? It's like we talk, and you bring up stuff that reminds me of something or teaches me something," he smiles. "You know how long I've been thinking about marrying Jules? Too long! And the funny thing is we already seem married! I'm waiting for nothing! She's always been the one."

"She's always been the one," I repeat, playing with my food.

"Always."

"Qu, too. I may have rushed into marriage, being so young, but I've never regretted choosing Qu. He's mine."

"Have you told him?"

"No, but I will!"

"Yeah, we both will."

I take one last scoop. "I think I am now officially stuffed."

"Did you want a coffee or dessert?"

"Hmm... I'd like to walk a while. The food was heavy. Do you mind?"

"No, I've got time."

"Alright then. If I see something along the way, then maybe—"

"No problem, I'll just pay inside."

"Oh, come on, Gabe! I can cover this."

"Let my old man ways die hard. I want to treat you," he winks.

"Thank you, yet again," I blush.

"My pleasure... again."

I lean back and take in the shore across from me. *Gabe is right. I have a lot to be thankful for. These old bones are only as old as I think they are.* I close my eyes and listen.

"Ready to go?"

"Yeah," I say opening my eyes and stretching. *Whoa! That felt good.* Pushing my chair back, I yawn into the back of my hand.

Gabe briefly holds my elbow for balance.

"The food is heavy. I could sleep right here."

"Hopefully, the walk will revive us."

I love being near the water. We cross the street to walk along the boardwalk. *Ah! I can't let it go!*

"So, you've been thinking about marrying Jules for a while..."

"Yeah."

"What took you so long to ask?"

"She's my best friend. I was afraid that if we married, things might change between us. Why fix what's not broken right?"

"Hmm..."

We stroll in silence, both lost in our thoughts.

"What changed for you? I mean, what about our conversation changed your mind?"

"Well, as I said, I've been thinking about it a long time. Being away from her more frequently because of work, meeting you and hearing about your life... I've just been doing a lot of soul-searching about what I want. What's important."

"Me too," I take a deep breath and swing my purse. We look over the water in silence. Gabe."

"Yeah."

"I have to thank you."

"I told you, I wanted to pay for lunch."

"No, not that, though, thanks for feeding me again," I giggle.

"Then what?"

"For challenging me and not letting me get away with anything."

Gabe laughs out loud. "Really?"

"Oh, you'd be surprised! As a teacher, I have this innate ability to ward off anybody from challenging me on my stuff. I've been getting away with murder for years."

"You're not serious," he continues to laugh.

"A little. But breaking down this week..."

Gabe stops mid-stride and stares at me. "You had a breakdown?"

"I didn't tell you?"

"No!"

"It's not important—"

"How can you say it's not—"

Oh, boy. I pick up the pace. Gabe trails a step behind me, still determined. "I can say it's not important because it had to happen eventually. I was a pressure cooker ready to explode, and everyone seemed to know it, except me."

"Wow."

"Yeah, wow," I laugh dryly to myself. I flash him a half-smile.

"I'm going to miss you, Gabe. You just met me, yet here you are talking to me like we're old friends."

"We are old friends. Spirit's eternal."

"What?"

"It was something my mother used to always say. Spirit's eternal. Us being here in the body is temporary, but our spirits live on for eternity."

I look at him, unconvinced.

"Our thoughts and ways of being have lived for centuries," he concludes.

This time I stop in my tracks. "How deep is that?"

Gabe chuckles, "Well, think about it. Nothing's new, just framed differently through us."

"Hmm, if you're talking about reincarnation, I don't—"

"No, not reincarnation. Just how we are all connected by spirits that live forever," Gabe sighs. "You would have loved my mother. She was a modern-day philosopher. Incredibly faithful."

"Past tense?"

"Yeah, she passed away about five years ago."

"So young?"

"Yeah, she got ill and left us early."

He says that so simply. There are so many layers to him. I've barely scratched the surface.

"We keep stopping. You want to sit awhile?" He motions to a nearby bench.

"Yeah, sure. I'm sorry about your mother," I add quickly before leaning back against the bench. We sit in silence.

I truly enjoy talking to him.

"Gabe?"

"Yeah?"

"I know you need to catch a plane soon. Do you mind if I see you off? You know, at the airport."

"It's not too much trouble?"

"No, I have time. I have a car."

"That would be great."

"Great."

I rest my head back looking up at the clouds. "Spirit's eternal."

"Spirit's eternal."

"Hmm..." I close my eyes and hug my purse to my chest.

"So, when are you going back home?" he asks.

"Tomorrow. I decided tomorrow's the day, but now I'm thinking maybe tonight."

"Are you ready to face the music?"

"Will I ever be ready to face the music?" I laugh softly to myself.

"I'm sure you are."

I lift my head and reposition myself on the bench. "Honestly? I'm not sure I'm ready to face the music but I know that it's time. I miss my kids. I'm excited about seeing them again. Telling them what I've discovered being away from them."

"Where to start..."

"I guess I'll start by telling them exactly what happened, why I left in the first place. I'll probably have to reassure them that I won't do it again."

"Why would you do that?"

"They're kids. I've always been there for them. And taking off like that? They must have felt abandoned somehow."

"But you just said, not even thirty seconds ago, that doing what you did, leaving like you did, was necessary. Who's to say that getting away in the future, perhaps before you 'break down,' won't be necessary again?"

"What are you suggesting?"

"I'm saying don't make promises you may not be able to keep."

"But I have to be responsible—"

"And being responsible means doing what's necessary to keep your mind, body and soul together. For all you know, you may need to get away every four months just to keep things in perspective and to relax."

"Oh boy."

"Yeah, oh boy," Gabe laughs.

"Yet, on some level, it makes me feel..." *Like a bad parent.*

"What?"

"Never mind," I fold one of my legs underneath me and sit taller. "I haven't given returning home much thought. I'm not sure I'm prepared to face some stuff with them."

"Well, you can take another day and think about it. You can cut yourself some slack."

"Hmm..."

"You're thinking about it right now, aren't you?"

"Can't help it?"

"What's on your mind?"

I muse before replying. "Well, having this space this week to myself has made it easy to indulge in rest, exploring, stretching. I crave more of that."

"Alright."

"I don't want to go backwards. I don't want to be the woman that I was."

"What specifically?"

"I can be controlling," I say softly, picking my thumbnail. "You know, routine. Strict. Stubborn."

"I know the definition. Sounds like now you know what you want to change," he smiles at me.

"Great."

"Yeah, great! Can't change what you don't know."

I close my eyes. *I want to go back to sleep.*

"There is so much for me to do! Staying in the hotel another day or twenty sounds tempting," I grimace.

"Do you have something to write with in your purse?"

"I should," I open the clasp and start digging around. I rip out a page and poise my pen ready for instructions.

"Okay."

"So, go ahead."

"Go ahead and what?" I look puzzled.

"Years ago, my therapist suggested I do this whenever I feel stuck. I find it helps. Just write the first fears that come to mind about facing your family."

He takes the pen and paper away from me. I feel flustered. He takes a long look at me and puts them down.

"Too much?"

"Yeah, I don't want to write anything right now."

"Okay."

We let the silence return.

"Why do you think you are controlling, by the way?"

I shrug, "I guess because there are so many things to keep track of."

"And?"

"It's become habit. If everything is under control and I've made it through the day with most things accomplished, it's been a good day."

"But does it work for you?"

"Well, yes and no. I fail more times than I win."

I can feel my breathing become laboured. *What is that?* "Yes, because if I know I am in control, then I know it will get done, and if it doesn't, blaming myself is easier than having to deal with anyone else's failure."

Wow... Keep breathing.

"And now, since it keeps some people, particularly my daughter, at arm's length... Sometimes, I wish Qu would take the lead on some things so that I could just be responsible for just 'being' for a change. It's stressful."

"So, what's next then?" He leans back.

"Not be controlling, obviously." My eyes begin to dart as I laugh nervously.

"How?"

"How?"

"How?"

"Right, how..." I rub my temples.

"Do you always do this?"

"Do what?"

"Become this huge knot. Look at you? We start to talk about your life and family and you're sweating buckets!"

"Gabe, it's summer. It's hot."

"Viv, it's not the temperature, it's your reaction. You are so stressed *now*."

"I'm fine. I just need a few minutes to think about how to change my entire life. Is that so much to ask?"

Gabe throws back his head and laughs. "Viv, give yourself a break! We are just brainstorming. That's it! We couldn't possibly draw up the blueprints for the rest of your life in the next eight minutes." He looks at his watch.

"Well, how about in half an hour?" I tease as I knead my shoulder. *Why is he always right?*

"Well, in that case, let's solve the cure for cancer while we're at it."

"Yeah, piece of cake," I smile, letting my shoulders droop.

"You alright?"

"You've asked me that a lot today."

"Hmm..."

"Hmm..."

"Well?"

"Yeah, but the more we talk, the more I realize I'm not ready, at least emotionally, to go back home. Bit frightened."

We sit in silence, watching the waves.

"What do you think will happen?"

"I think that this week and all its revelations may be lost when I step back into the past."

"You don't think that's a little melodramatic?"

"I always had a flare."

"Well, you have the power to expect the worst and you have the power to expect the best."

"The power..."

"Yes, superwoman, the power."

I have power.

"Fine, but enough about me. What about you, Mister! How are you going to propose?"

"Honestly, I don't know. What do you think? Candlelight dinner?"

"You could do that."

"By that you mean no. By the lake?"

"Maybe."

"Got suggestions?"

"I don't know Julia. It's Julia, right?"

"Jules is for Juliet."

"Tell me about her."

"Well, she's beautiful. Originally from Tortola..."

Interesting.

"But lived in Santa Cruz for most of her life. She has this clear, rich laugh that grabs me every time. She comes from a big family. Loves to cook and plays the piano. Her musical style is jazz all the way, though she has a general appreciation for all music. She's a nurse and midwife by profession. Teaches salsa on the weekends."

"Wow."

"Hmm?"

"No, just she's a female. Well... you! A little bit of this. A little bit of that."

"No, she's more than me. Being around her makes me feel, well, more."

"You're beaming just talking about her so I can imagine."

"Yeah. She's it for me."

"Well, you have plenty of themes to choose from, so pick! She's into jazz so take her to a club. Let the MC dedicate something to her for you or better yet, play something you composed for her. And as you are dancing cheek to cheek, whisper your proposal into her ear. Or..." I'm on a roll now, "Take her to one of those make-your-supper-outside-the-house trendy joints and have the ring cooked into something and served to her. I mean there are a million things you could do to make her feel special."

"Have a ring cooked into food? How many rom-coms have you watched?"

"Let's just say a million and counting," I blush. "It's about the surprise, the specialness of it all. It's important."

"I don't know... What's wrong with just asking her while we're watching TV?"

"You're kidding me, right?"

"No. Listen, we've been friends for years. She knows I love her. It's about asking her to spend the rest of my life with her, not the style in which I ask her."

"Gabe, stop being such a man. Of course, it's about the style!"

Why are we going around this mountain again? I mutter to myself.

"What?"

Did I say that out loud?

"I'm talking about what we were talking about before: the words AND the actions. Make her feel special, Gabe. This is the moment you are telling her you love her so much, you can't live without her. Don't you think that should be set up in a way that doesn't involve a rerun of Friends?"

"No offence, but I hate Friends."

"Fine, Seinfeld."

"Worse."

"Who friggin' cares Gabe! TV isn't going to cut it. Got it?"

"Fine."

"Good." I'm exhausted.

"We gotta move. I want to be early," he rises abruptly.

"You're not upset, are you?"

"Are you kidding? I love sparring with you," he grins.

"Now I know you're weird."

"No more than you."

"Touché."

"Shall we?" he extends his hand to help me up.

He must have noticed I am still a bit sore. "We shall," I reply, taking his hand.

As we are walking, I push my finger into his forearm. "You will make a fantastic Mr. Jules."

"Why thank you, Madame," Gabe laughs as we quicken our pace.

THIRTEEN

I'll change my dress and freshen up a bit. I close my door and race about the room. I choose another light summer dress that swirls out, grazing my ankles this time. *I like wearing my jewelled thong sandals though, so I'll wear them again.* With octopus' skills, I brush my teeth, my hair, sponge myself and powder my face in five seconds flat. *Ready! Got gloss?* I double-check my purse. *Got gloss, keys, little cash... I'm outta here!* The door slams behind me.

Swishing slowly through the lobby, I look around, making a beeline for the reception.

"Hi, have you seen a man, yea tall with sandy—?"

"Viv, over here! I've already checked out!"

I wave at Gabe before patting the desk. "Thank you," I say hurriedly to the receptionist before meeting him at the revolving door.

"Ready, I see."

"More than ready. Anxious."

"Alright, then. Let's put your luggage in my car and I'll follow you to the car rental."

"That's alright. I called and asked one of the managers to take care of the return. Her assistant will come by later and manage the details. I thought it would save us some time."

"Smart! Alright. I'm the pearly beige car over there," I press my fob and the car greets us with a sharp chirp. "Great," I pop the trunk so he can lift his bag inside. I slam it shut and amble around to the driver's side. "It's open," I say before lowering myself into my seat.

"Right," Gabe replies as he does the same.

After keying in my GPS, I rev the engine. "We're off!" I exclaim as he clicks his belt in place.

Even when I'm clearly going nowhere, I love going to the airport and just being there.

"You look positively gleeful."

"I am. I love the airport."

"Me too."

"Really?"

"Yeah, I love to fly. I do it as often as I can, even if the distance is short."

"Hmm..."

"The speed, being in the clouds... you know."

"I was thinking of the building itself. Travellers going to all points all over the world. Different purposes, different experiences, different tastes. I feel like it's a slice of the globe. It's exciting."

"I wasn't thinking about that."

"I know."

"You're right though. There is an energy in airports—"

"Some of it's anxious, some of it's hopeful..."

"Even after the tightening of security these past few years."

"Now that you mention it..." I let my words trail off as I merge onto the highway. The traffic flows at a steady clip.

"Pardon?"

"Sorry, I was just about to say that stress at airports has increased."

"Where were you when the planes hit?" Gabe asks casually.

It's odd how something so tragic has become normalized in our collective conscious.

"I was walking down the hallway at school. There was some murmuring as I was walking towards the cafeteria. I remember walking in, and the TV seemed unusually loud. A few teachers mesmerized by this news report I couldn't seem to wrap my head around. It played out like an action-adventure, crime drama..." I lost my train of thought for a moment. Quickly, I blink and refocus on the road to manoeuvre a lane change. "It didn't dawn on me that it was real," I continue, "until later in the day when I was preparing to go home. Do you remember where you were?"

"Yeah, I was also at work. It came to me like a rumour. Then it didn't matter what radio station or TV channel you tuned into; it was everywhere. No escaping the cries or the explosions."

"It was all-consuming."

"Yeah."

"And now, so many years later, it's imprinted. The fear..."

"Hmm..."

"Years ago, we weren't suspicious about a water bottle being taken on board. Wouldn't scrutinize the heel of my shoes. The discriminatory pat-downs? Normalized masks, more security guards and dogs on duty..."

"Point made. Thanks."

"Sorry, didn't mean to depress. Just thinking aloud," I sigh as I execute a sharp turn. "Despite all that, I love the airport! The anticipation of the possible. Look at you! About to be reunited with Jules."

"Yeah," Gabe blushes.

"Let's focus on that instead," I grin.

"Sure, but seriously, when are you going to take a trip somewhere?"

"I don't know. Right now, I'm living vicariously through you."

"That's not enough."

"But I'm content for now," I lower my window to grab the ticket from the parking machine. The arm slowly rises as I inch forward. The digital tracker above the rows glows the number of available spaces left to park. Satisfied, I swing between two vans a few feet from one of the entrances. I lift the button releasing the trunk.

"Thank you. We made it in record time."

"It pays to know these parts," I brag, sliding out of my seat.

Gabe slams the door and fiddles with his carry-on, apprehensively. "Pretty sure the GPS had something to do with it," Gabe counters.

He got me.

"You alright?"

"Yeah, just nerves. Want to check my documents one more time before I reach the counter."

"Okay."

We walk to the moving sidewalk silently and wait for it to deliver us to the other side. The terminal is abuzz. Flurry. People racing in every direction. Worn jeans, colourful dresses, backward baseball caps, heels clicking, exposed jewelled belly buttons, pieces of conversation wrapping around one another in a general din. Cell phones sounding, bags being hoisted, tossed, swung, just missing contact with the masses. White lines drawn from ears to tunes, teardrop plugs glowing in ears answering to head nods, people staring tearfully into the windows of loved ones' eyes. Concrete dome hovers overhead. Different languages and nuances co-mingling. Counters flash enticing bright neon signs. Dropped bags and joyfully eager embraces.

I feel at peace.

"Oh, I'm over here," Gabe points.

"Right," I reply, following his lead.

"Gabe?"

"Yeah?"

"Do you mind if I sit over there and just wait for you?" I nod in the direction of a row of stiff faux leather chairs.

"Okay. I shouldn't be long."

"Alright," I smile as I casually make my way.

Crossing my legs, I take it all in again. I glance up at the electronic schedule and dream. Jamaica, Italy, Brussels, Amsterdam, Montreal, Arizona, London... *From this one place, I can travel the entire world. Meet new people. Discover places I didn't know existed. It's breathtaking.*

"Ready?"

Startled, I see Gabe beaming beside me.

"Did you fly through the line?"

"Pretty much. The family before me was in the wrong line so..." he starts to explain as he follows my eye line to the electronic board. We sit for a few moments watching the board flash upwards.

"So, do you have enough time for a coffee before you board?"

"Yeah, we don't prepare to board for just over an hour or so. I also wanted to pick up a magazine to waste time."

"Fine. Let's go!"

Gabe swings his carry-on over his shoulder, and we head over to the food court.

"It's amazing how airports worldwide have transformed into mini-malls."

"Consumerism is a force."

"So is debt."

"It's scary how we've accustomed ourselves to it though, isn't it?"

"Do you even know anyone without a credit card or a credit line?"

"No. That would be virtual suicide. The whole economy is based on a borrower mentality. Even if you have the money, companies encourage credit."

"It's serious. Take hotels! You can't even book a room without a credit card."

"And choice! Remember growing up and the only real choice you had were jeans, more jeans and maybe a pair of khakis?" Gabe laughs as we pass the window of a famous American designer. The window mannequins sport matching elaborate sequin ensembles with prominent logos sewn to their chests and furry sleeves.

"I don't think it's even a choice, Gabe! Can you imagine showing up at work in that?" I point.

"Maybe I'll propose in that. All flashy and chic! That'd be special," he drawls dryly, glancing at me.

Our laughter explodes. It's hard to catch my breath.

"You do and you will be a bachelor for life!"

"That's mean."

"Truth hurts."

"OK. I won't."

"Like you were seriously considering it!"

"Exactly!"

We catch our breath as we continue walking through the terminal.

"You're right though. There is so much choice now. Is it all necessary?"

"I just think we take things for granted. What are you going to have?" Gabe asks as we sidle up to the counter.

"I'll have a low fat-decaf latte-extra foam-with cinnamon sprinkles-no-sugar," I rhyme off in one breath. Gabe stares at me incredulously.

"Well," I say with my hands on my hip, "don't want to take choice for granted now, do I?"

Gabe chuckles and shakes his head. "Alright then, and a large regular coffee," he orders. "You are too much sometimes, you know?"

"Yep, gotta be me," I grin as I hand the server a few bills before Gabe has a chance.

"Thank you," he says as he closes his wallet.

"You're welcome."

"Well, here's to a safe and comfortable trip home. Clink!" I tap my paper cup against his own.

"Thank you. And here's to the rest of our lives and the freedom we will have," he replies with another tap.

"Now, that's even more! That deserves a double-tap and sip! Clink, clink!" I nearly scald myself in my declaration.

"Careful! The steam alone can peel skin."

"I should know better. Too anxious."

"Napkin?"

"Umm... this is yummy," I say as I wave him a no.

"Not bad."

"How much more time we got?"

"Hmm... twenty, thirty minutes, maybe."

"Okay."

"Strange, isn't it?"

"How?"

"It's only been a few days since we met—"

"Oh! Before I forget, here's my card," I hand it to him. "I wrote my home info on the back."

"We do think alike," he reaches inside his shirt pocket and hands me his card. I smile as I slip it into my thin wallet.

"Will you call?"

I involuntarily hesitate before looking him in the eyes. "Probably not."

"What? Why?"

"Because I hate the phone. I only use it when I absolutely must."

"Oh, you prefer texting. That's fine."

"Nah, I'm strange. I prefer snail mail, and email."

"Both are fine. I can't wait to hear how things go when you talk to your kids."

"Seriously," I sigh.

"Look, I think I better head over to the waiting area."

"Alright," I say softly walking beside him towards the gate.

"So…"

"So…"

"Goodbyes suck, don't they?" he comments.

"Only if you think of this as a goodbye."

"Touché!"

"I love when I'm right!" I grin.

"Okay, I wouldn't go that far," he retorts.

"Gotta tease, gotta tease," I snap my fingers playfully.

"I gathered as much. Well Viv, take care of yourself, alright?" Gabe gives me a big hug.

My breath catches. *No tears Viv.* I roughly pull away, immediately embarrassed by my reaction. "I'm sorry, Gabe. Sorry. I guess I do suck at this."

"You were right the first time, Viv. Remember, not a goodbye."

"No goodbyes, yet explain why I miss you already?" I think aloud.

"Because now marks the end of the retreat and the beginning of—"

"Reality. I get it."

"Not just you!"

"Go! Go quickly before I sink into mushdom!" I push him towards the frosted sliding doors.

"All right, Viv. Till next time?"

"Till next time. Safe journey."

"Be well."

"Thanks, you too."

And with a wave, he is gone.

I stand and watch. *How can I be standing here missing someone I just met a few days ago??*

Long after he's gone, I find myself still standing there. Arms wrapped around me.

Thinking.

Buzzing. People racing in every direction. Worn jeans, colourful dresses, backward baseball caps, heels clicking, pieces of conversation wrapping around one another in a general din. Cell phones sounding, bags being hoisted, tossed, swung, just missing contact with the masses. White lines drawn from ears to tunes, teardrop plugs glowing in ears answering to head nods, people staring tearfully into the windows of loved ones' eyes. Rods floating around bodies trying to detect steel, finding only cloth and flesh. Concrete dome hovers overhead. Different languages and nuances co-mingling.

I am at peace. Strangely engaged. Quiet.

FOURTEEN

I drop my bag on the bed and run my fingers through my hair, massaging my scalp. Glancing at the clock, I realize it's now after 5:00 p.m. Where did the day go? Should I order some food? I yawn. Too lazy. Think I'll just skip it. I kick off my shoes and throw myself on the bed beside my purse. Stretching, I jump at the ring of the phone.

"Hello?"

"Where've you been? I've been trying to reach you all day."

"Huh? Is everything alright?"

"I should be asking you that."

"Of course. I just stepped in."

"Oh, back from dinner?"

I hesitate. *Not ready.* "Not important. How's your day?" *Why did I do that?*

"Work was alright. Kept thinking about last night and well, I missed you."

"Hmm... that's nice to hear."

"Not surprising though, right?"

"Yeah, it is. When was the last time you called me to say you missed me?"

"Well, if you have to ask the question then the answer is obviously, too long ago."

"More food for thought," I giggle.

"So, did you miss me?"

"Tremendously."

"Should I come over?"

I pause, as I glance at the bed. "No. I'm going to come home." *What?*

"You serious?"

"Yeah," I say shortly.

"Well, alright then. Good!"

"Hmm..." I hesitate again.

"What's gotten into you?"

"Well, you, of course."

"Come again?"

I can sense him blushing. "You! We got so much out in the open yesterday that I just don't want to lose momentum, you know."

"You are taking what I said seriously."

"And why not? I take what WE said seriously."

"Hmmm..."

"Viv..."

"Yeah."

"I don't want to lose you."

What?

"Viv? I..." he begins to repeat.

"You are not losing me, Qu. Didn't I just say I was coming home? I've only been gone a couple of days."

"I just need you to know that."

I hold the phone with both hands and close my eyes. "I hear you."

"Love you."

"Me too."

"Later?"

"Yes."

"Bye."

"Hmm," I moan as a tear rolls down my cheek. I gently return the phone to the cradle. Flopping on my pillow, I cry, releasing the emotions of the day.

The salt dried on my face. My mouth feels like parchment. I lift the clock. 5:50. Ooh. I raise my aching body to the washroom and slowly peel my crumpled dress off. I feel gross and empty. *I don't want my last night here to feel like a hangover. All this indulgent living is catching up to me in spades.* I roughly dislodge the crust from the corners of my eyes only to have an eyelash fall in. I quickly flick the faucet on, creating a pool in my cupped palm. The stinging subsides as I open and close my eye in the cool water. I tighten the lever and decide to take a warm shower before preparing to leave.

Water rushes over me. I close my eyes and will myself not to think. It's no use though. The pending days ahead stretch out like a series of questions and wonders in my imagination. I have no idea where to start.

If only I could just stay here and live like the ridiculously rich without a care in the world! How easy it would be. Sip margaritas. Stroll the beach. Be pampered with hot stone massages, mud baths, and indulge in caviar—not that I even know what caviar tastes like. Frequent hot tub soaks, saunas whenever I want. To live completely free, to do what I want when I want.

But...I know it doesn't make sense, avoiding the inevitable.

I sigh again, continually lapping water over my face.

I don't know what I'm going to say to Faith and Justin. 'I've had an amazing time without you.' Probably not the way to go. 'I've missed you but needed time apart.' Then the never-ending whys would follow. How about, 'Faith, Mom had to leave to sort things out.' Why am I talking in the third person? Faith is not a child. She's a teenager. A young woman. A woman. Maybe I just need to tell her what's been happening to me for some time now. Is 'to me' the right words? What has been happening? What I've allowed to happen. Does it matter? Just be straight up and direct! But how direct? How 'straight up' will she be open to hearing? Would it be better to call a family meeting or talk to them individually? Maybe I should wait a couple of days...

I'm getting a headache. Stop thinking Viv. Just feel the water flow over my skin.

I have some time to figure out this mess. Besides, my mind is still foggy.

I want to wail!

I massage my damp scalp with a vengeance. I'm on the edge of bawling and I don't want to succumb.

After all this, I can't fall apart now. How do I release this... this... Unease? This shower isn't the answer.

I snap the water off and step out of the bath. The cold air hits me as I grab my robe.

I've already told him I was coming home, or I'd just go back to bed. Ugh, forget it. If I shut my eyes for ten minutes, it won't hurt.

I'm at the top of a white marble staircase looking down. The bottom is black and deep. I shudder. I'm wearing my crumpled school uniform, hugging my notebook to my chest. What do I do next? On the landing, there is a hallway stretched into the distance on either side of me. Both hallways have bright lights and faint voices at the end. Muffled voices. Sounds of movement. The air feels heavy. I can't figure out what is happening in either direction. The sound to the left of me grows louder as the glow of the light softens to the right of me. I confidently turn to the right. The light grows brighter. I am filled with bliss as the noise grows fainter and fainter.

I stir and nestle deeper into my pillow. The glow behind my eyelids startles me awake. I fall back against the pillow. *Who would want to leave the comfort of paradise? Who am I fooling? I love it here. Just one more hour. One more hour of rest and forgetfulness. One more hour before I face the drive ahead and myself.* I swing one foot to the floor. *No turning back now.*

What was I dreaming about?

I rise, racking my brain, trying to conjure up the image, but it's gone. All I am left with is warmth. *It's enough. I'll take it with open arms.*

I must find a way to recreate this space at home. No more room for room's sake. No more utility and storage depot. I need to find a way to reclaim our bedroom as a retreat. A comfort zone. Was it ever a comfort zone? Come to think of it...

Know what? Stop! It doesn't matter. The past is gone. The future is mine to embrace. The present is mine to revel in. Every moment is sacred. Time and choices.

Overwhelmed, I flop back onto my pillow.

Knowing and doing are two distinctly different things.

I turn my head and let my eyes rest on the phone. *Could I stay another night? Call up Qu and tell him I changed my mind and need more time? I shake myself. No. I have to face the music. Besides, everyone is expecting me home tonight. I have to report to work in a couple of days. I can't let everyone down. Myself down. Stop being such a coward.*

Dinner. Let me get some food. Everything will seem more manageable after I feed myself. Now if I could just catapult myself out of this bed, life would be awesome.

Reluctantly, I poke my big toe out from underneath the duvet. The frigid air forces it back under the covers. My inner voice shames me. *You are being a baby. Get up!* I throw back the covers in one toss and half jump out of the bed onto unsteady feet. *Good! The first battle won. Now go get ready. Hmm... drill sergeant works! Now get out of resistance. You need to get moving and face the music.*

I trudge to the bathroom as my inner sergeant continues to crack the whip.

The dining room is deserted. It's strange not seeing Gabe anywhere. I miss my eating partner. Drawing out a seat in the middle of the room, I purposely try to take my time leafing through the menu. Everything looks good, yet everything isn't what I want. Undecided, again, I frustrate myself by the second. *Just pick something. Anything!*

"Waiter?"

"Yes, Ma'am."

"I'm having difficulty deciding. Could you recommend something?"

"Well, the chef's shrimp fritters are very tasty. I also like the grilled red pepper and onions that he serves with it."

I grimace. It seems too heavy. I glance back at the pages. "Thank you, but on second thought, I think I'm going to have a snack. Could you bring me some sweet potato fries and a cup of warm water with lemon? Thank you," I hand him back the menu.

"Are you sure that will be all?" the waiter asks, removing my menu.

I nod. "Yes, that's all."

"I'll be right back."

Sighing, I look around the dining room, wondering. It's strange how empty it is. As much as I wouldn't normally strike up a conversation with a total stranger, having so few people in the place is lonely. Now is when I really miss Qu.

I stare at my plate and fidget.

What am I doing? Change!

"Waiter!" I yell.

He spins around, "Yes?"

"I'm sorry. I've changed my mind. Please bring me some brown toast, no butter, a small fruit plate and a mint tea."

"In addition to—"

"Instead of."

"Yes, Ma'am."

I settle deeper into my seat. *I can't afford to go backwards. I need to face...*

"Viv!"

"Qu?"

"Hi," he leans low and kisses me. I feel a thrill race through me.

"What are you doing here?"

"What? You don't believe I missed you?" he fakes shock.

"I just didn't expect you. Sit, sit." My face breaks out into sunshine as he settles in.

"I thought I'd surprise you."

"How did you know?"

"I took a chance after realizing you weren't in your room."

"Wonders never cease, Mr. Moji."

"May they never, Mrs. Moji."

I turn red despite myself. He brushes my hand as he signals for the waiter.

"Yes, sir?"

He turns to me. "What did you order?"

"Brown toast, a small fruit plate and mint tea."

He stares at me like I'm an alien. "That's it?"

"Yep. That's it."

He shakes his head. "Do you serve espresso?"

"Yes, sir."

"I'll have that and a plate of sweet potato fries, thank you."

No, he didn't...

"Thank you," the waiter turns as he continues to scribble on his pad.

Qu returns his attention to me, "How are you?"

Talk to him, Viv.

"Honestly. My nerves have been jumping."

"Why?"

"I don't know how to face you and the kids."

"What do you mean face me and the kids? You are just coming home."

"But I left so badly."

"Yeah, but home is home. You just need to talk to them like you talked to me."

"Without the sex, of course."

"Obviously," he laughs. "Seriously, Viv. We made headway. It wasn't about the sex."

I slowly take in his face. Relaxed. Earnest. *I love his eyes. Big, deep brown worlds framed by those thick black lashes. He's beautiful...*

"Viv."

"Sorry?"

"Where did you go just now?" Qu asks, casually.

I giggle self-consciously. I look up, acknowledging the waiter as he rests our meals before us.

"Thank you," I say under my breath. I pick my toast apart.

"I was just thinking that once upon a time I thought it was all about sex with you."

"Why?"

"Just my stereotype of men in general that I stamped onto you somehow."

Seductively, he leans in towards me. "Well, as much as making love to you is one of my favourite things, just sitting here with you..." he rests his hands on mine.

I choke on my toast. He hands me a glass of water. I push it away.

"Okay! What's gotten into you? Scared?"

"Hmm..."

"Why," he smirks, enjoying my embarrassment.

I grab my tea to soften the bread lodged in my throat.

"Back to tonight, it's not complicated," he picks up a fry and uses it to punctuate his words. "One: you come home, and we'll talk as a family about whatever is on our minds. No script. No plan. Two: I'm your partner and I love you. I'm in this with you. The end. Now," he motions at my plate with his fry, "are you sure you don't want any more food? Even squirrels eat more."

I scoff. *Everything comes so simply to Qu.*

"No, I'm watching my weight."

He wrinkles his eyebrows and shakes his head. "Here," he spoons half of his fries from his plate onto mine. "Eat," he grins as he continues to chew.

A tear threatens to roll down my cheek as I look at the fries. *Doesn't he see my girlish figure is long, long gone?*

"Are you flirting with me, Mr. Moji?"

"Just loving you," he grins.

I lift the napkin to my face and let the tear fall. I feel his hand rub my thigh.

"Viv, there's nothing to be sad about."

"Who said I'm sad?"

Qu takes his napkin and slowly dabs the moistness from my cheeks.

"Me loving you should be a given."

"Still, it's good to hear."

I sniff back and fan my face with my hands. *I don't know what got into me.*

"Better?"

"Much," I laugh lightly.

"You know we've been together for nearly—"

"Shut up and eat. You'll ruin the moment," I retort more sharply than I intended.

He settles back in his seat. Looking down, he smiles as he chews. His hand hasn't stopped stroking my thigh.

I love this man.

My gaze returns to his face.

Thoughts float in and out of the crevices of my mind.

I can do all things through Him Who strengthens me. I am ready for anything.

"Eat. Eat! Stop thinking," he says without looking up.

I giggle as I reach for the ketchup.

We walk to the lobby doors, hand in hand.

"Do you want me to follow you home?"

"No. I'll be alright. I'm going to meander. I'll see you at home."

"Alright. Well," Qu swings my arm as he faces me, "I'll see you then?"

"Yes," I rise on my toes as he bends to kiss me. "Qu, thanks for coming."

"I wanted to be here. Later then."

"Later."

He pecks me one last time before rushing through the doors towards his car.

I am still standing there long after he has left.

I slowly put the last item in my backpack. I close my eyes.

Did I dream this? Did my husband, my Malachi Quaid Moji, drive several hundred miles out of his way to eat with me? Pour mounds of honey sentiments all over me?

I shake my head.

This week has been rife with surprises! Last week I could barely get Qu out of bed in the morning and today, bam! He hits the highway to see me when he'll see me in a few hours anyway. It's mind-blowing. What's even more mind-blowing is the very second I yearned for someone to spend time with, he's at my table! Unreal! My Qu... After all these years... coming to me like fresh water.

A shiver runs down my back.

I don't know why I overthink everything... Trust! Just trust that everything will be alright. Qu, Justin, Faith, and I will talk and figure it out together. I'm not alone. Admittedly, I've never been alone. Somehow, I've lost sight of that.

I have to remember to send Dour a bouquet. That man—again with the men in my life!—knew I needed time and gave it to me. He looked past my bitterness. I can be so blind. I resented him when he was doing me a favour! Dour. Imagine... I need to apologize to him. I also must remember to call him Etienne. Apologies are useless if I keep calling him by his last name. He hates that. I laugh to myself.

I may as well rest. I have a long drive ahead and have to prep for work when I go home. Family meeting, cleaning, on and on and on.

Pace yourself, Viv. I am just going to relax and enjoy the ride. What needs to be taken care of later will be taken care of later. Right now, I need to chillax. I am dating myself. What song was that from? Fresh? DJ Maestro? Who knows. Let's move.

"Did you enjoy your stay?"

Do I have everything? I rummage through my bag to make sure.

"Ma'am?"

"Sorry?"

"I was just asking if you enjoyed your stay."

"Yes! It was amazing, thank you. Here is my key," I hand her the door card as I lean against the counter.

"Room 212. Excellent. Everything has been paid in full."

"Excuse me?"

"Your balance is clear. Thanks for staying with—"

"How is that possible?"

The receptionist looks at me, puzzled, as she angles the screen for me to see. She points at the balance line. My eyes travel over the screen as she rattles on.

Credit Cardholder: Gabriel Adams

I don't believe it!

"Thank you, thanks, Tracy, is it?" I read her name tag.

"Yes! You're welcome. We hope to see you again soon," she smiles as she repositions her terminal.

I lift my baggage in a daze.

"And here is your receipt. Goodbye," she hands me the paper over the counter before returning to the screen.

I take one last sweeping look around the lobby.

This place has been such a blessing. I slowly walk to the revolving doors and push.

Note to self: buy TWO huge bouquets! Look at Gabe! He just met me and is generous to a fault. That's so rare.

I sit in the driver's seat and wait. Impulsively, I reach for my cell and dial.

"Hello?"

"Hi, it's me."

"Hi, me," Qu replies.

"Hi. Listen, I just thought I'd call to let you know I'm on my way."

"Great! You taking the highway?"

I hate taking the highway. "I'll see how it goes."

"Well, I'll have a real dinner waiting for you, alright?"

"Don't you think it's too late?"

"Just in case."

"Alright, thanks."

"Drive safe, kay?"

"Will do."

"Love you."
"I wanted to say that first!" I tease him.
"Next time."
"Alright, bye."
"Bye."
I click off and firmly turn the ignition.

FIFTEEN

I fix my sight far down the road, ignoring the on-ramp to the highway. *I don't need to rush. Not just yet. I'll take a ramp further along the way. I don't want to flash past neighbourhoods. I want to savour them.*

I take in more as I drive further north. *I don't recognize most of these buildings. Trendy facades on some of the older buildings. Amazing how people can make art out of crumbling walls.* The structures that have been restored and maintained draw my eye. Similarly, the coffee culture is apparent as I pass numerous bistros and cafes. I continue my journey, not faintly tempted to stop for java or sweets.

I drive mindfully. I pass hamburger joints, Italian restaurants, and Indian cuisine. Nothing entices me to stop. Despite the mild rumbling, I keep on driving. *Nothing seems good enough for me to stop. Not when I know I have a hot dinner waiting at home. Nothing seems as good.*

Being in control of the wheel is soothing. I'm not ready to give up the drive. One community merges into another. Houses to lofts, to malls to high-rises, I pass them all on my journey. The sounds float past me in droves. Car radio buzz, pieces of conversation, cell ringtones, dogs barking, laughter, and storefront Latin beats float in and out my car windows with every passing block. Time slips from me.

I love music. Jazz, R&B, even the choir music in Faith's school move me. I rack my brain. *When was the last time I've even turned on the radio other than for the news, traffic, or weather report? I think it was at the hotel! It's been a long time since I played music in the house. When was the last time I danced? Not just absently nod my head, but sway with abandon. I remember going to spots with Qu when we were dating. Even if he just wanted to be cool and drink at the table, if the right beat filled the air, I'd be gone. I didn't care who was around me. I didn't care if I had a partner or not. The music was playing, and it was calling me! It was never about the drinking. I just needed the beat!*

I smile at the memory.

My mind gently floats to the beach.

Memories of the island take me back.

I went home for holidays, with Qu, earlier in our marriage. It was important to me. Though I didn't grow up on the island, my heart is there. Coming from island people, it doesn't matter where in the world you grew up. The island is in every expression, thought, gesture, and parental chide, so by osmosis you may as well claim citizenship and declare, "Yes! I am also from the island."

Qu is very Western, but he tries. His generations have been on this side for what seems like centuries, so those homeland memories have long been beaten into submission. It was important to me that he knew me through the lens of where I come from. Now that we were committed to one another, I wanted him to be intimately entwined with my roots.

When I go home, my pressure goes way, way down. Food tastes richer. Water is sweeter. My skin glows. The humidity in the air twists and curls my hair to the point I don't even bother fighting it. Morning come, and I'd lovingly band a cloth around it and let my naps just reach in whichever direction. My gate swings. My tongue loosens. The dialect flows. It's the strangest thing. At first, I didn't even recognize it about myself. Then I caught him. Qu... looking at me with those eyes. His stare seemed to silently whisper, "What just happened?"

I'd laugh at him and tell him to relax. "We are home and it's time to trade in our loafers for flip flops, khakis for the lightest cotton shorts and muscle tees! Just be free! Listen. You are with me! You are with my people. We are home!"

It was incredible how many kitchens we sat in that first week. My aunts and cousins just wanted to devour him. Nosy questions and little needling to see if his sense of humour and self were sound. That is when I'd sit back and watch. Not so much because I cared what they thought of Qu. He's mine. My choice. It was more out of curiosity, like seeing the unfolding of a drama. I'd watch him laugh and question them right back like he was playing a fierce verbal ping pong tourney. Smooth swings. No offences. Just for the sport of it. I remember smiling realizing he was easily one of us.

One night, one of my cousins swung round and took us to a wedding reception. I didn't know where we were going, but it was an excuse to dress and see something new, so I was up and ready before the invitation was fully out of his mouth. Qu was cool. Them days, anything I wanted was, by definition, what he wanted. Without a word, he was up and ready too. We bounced down this dirt road in the pitch black in the back of Cousin Reenie's wagon. I must have split a gut laughing at Qu's expression. Where we come from, that car would have been pulled off the road and shot in an alley, but here, on this night, it was our chariot. We held hands, wide-eyed, happy.

We got there and the street was pulsating. Music. There is nothing like a beat that just envelops an entire people. It wasn't the volume. It's hard to explain. We got there and it was like the music was in our very veins. It was palpable. Virtually intoxicating. I stretched my legs out and slowly rose from the seat. My feet were jumping in time. Skin to skin, Qu slid behind me, holding my waist. I could feel his heart. Smell him. The heat of the night and...

Let me pull back.

The village was modest, but everyone was dressed in what was their finery. The bride was this voluptuous white-sequined flower, with thickly painted red rose lips and stiff, high-bunned hair with little wavy ringlets stretched and plastered to her forehead and cheeks. Now that I think about it, she was too far over the top to be deemed exquisite, yet at that moment I was so happy for her and happy for us for being able to share her moment; she was divine. The groom was slightly shorter than her with an equally rosy, baby potbelly. He was enamoured. His eyes never left hers. Their eyes never left each other. They could have been there all alone and still...

The reception hall was a club at the bottom of a home. The house was two stories above ground, so the club was on the main floor. The lights were dim, but the fluorescent paint on the walls reflected a glow that echoed off any speck of white on the revellers' clothes. There were a few tables pushed to the corners, holding refreshments. Bottles of cola and sweets. We had missed dinner, so the room was now transformed into a dance hall. The whole community came out. Inside the hall and on the street, people were grinding, mingling, electric!

From the time we left Rennie's wagon, Qu and I were vibrating. We were one with the music and each other. DJ'd spin oldie after oldie, familiar riffs mixed in with some new... it was all-consuming. We knew each other's motions by heart. We danced until we sweat and then danced some more until we soaked. Completely swept up. He'd pull some new moves. Instinctively, I went with him. A beat would carry me. Instinctively, he went with me—me, who usually feels comfortable dancing in the middle of the floor all by my lonely, was dancing as one with my man. Connected. Totally in sync. Lost in it. I was so caught up in Qu that everyone else fell away. I fell in love with Qu over and over and over that night. I never wanted it to end.

We danced till we slept the next morning. My cousin found us curled up into each other in the corner of the dancehall and convinced us to come upstairs and refresh.

I will never forget that night. Decades later, I still remember it as the most sensual, miraculous, captivating night of my life. Period.

That night, I floated.

My mind was still island-bound before I realized I was minutes away from home.

Wait!

I turn into a familiar juice bar and turn off the ignition. I'm so hot. *A mango drink would hit the spot right now.* Counting my change, I step to the counter and order the biggest size. Thanking the cashier, I stroll back to my car, satisfied. Sipping my memories behind the wheel, I notice a neon yellow flyer waving at me from under my wiper. I open the door, reach around, and bring it inside.

Family Christian Church

You will find our worship is informal and natural.

We are energized as we publicly honour the Lord.

Our prayer today is for you to be stimulated and empowered by God's love and presence.

It would be our privilege to become your new church family if you don't have a church home and are looking for one.

Join us this Sunday for an uplifting session led by our Pastor, Cher Fields. This week's theme is Appreciating Divine Grace.

Time: 10:30 a.m.

Location: 30 Main Street

For more information, please call...

I stop reading and crumple up the paper. *Cher Fields. That's interesting. Rare to find women preachers. Hmm...* I toss the paper ball onto the passenger seat. I take another drag on my straw. *This thing is so sweet. Okay, I'm ready now.* Putting the cup in the holder, I spark the car, peer into my rearview mirror and reverse. *Home, here I come!*

The lights are on. Out of habit, I reverse into my parking space before switching the car off. Looking in my side mirror, I see the front door open. Qu stands there smiling. *It is a new day. When was the last time Qu greeted me as I came home? I could get used to this.* I watch him as he walks to the car and opens my door.

"You alright?"

"Yeah, the drive was smooth."

"Highway?"

"No, I decided to take the scenic route."

"Oh, okay. Pop the trunk and I'll grab your bag."

"No need. The bag is in the backseat. Where the kids?"

"Inside. They already ate so they're just finishing homework."

"This late?"

"No worries. I waited. We can eat together."

Still seated, with my feet on the driveway, I watch Qu, loving me. A thrill runs down my spine watching him also swing my purse over his shoulder.

"You say something?" he asks, slamming the door shut.

"No, nothing... I..."

He offers his hand to help me rise. "Come on. A little dinner may do you good."

Remembering my drink, I lift it out of the holder before accepting his hand. "Thank you."

He squeezes my hand and kisses my cheek, "Ready?"

"Yes."

We walk inside.

I step softly. The kids are back in their rooms, so the house appears still. Qu shuts the door behind us and carries my few bags towards the bedroom. I stand in the foyer awhile. *The house is... clean?* I bend and unwrap my sandals. I gently lay them, toes touching the wall. I rise and stare at them. *Where did that suspicious habit come from? Spirits walk in our shoes if the heels touch the wall.* Rebelliously, I kick the shoes out of place with my foot.

"Viv!"

Startled, I look up. "Yeah?"

"You coming in?"

"Of course," I say, shaking my head. Grabbing my purse from the side table, I move towards the kitchen. As I draw closer, I realize Faith is leaning on the counter.

"Faith!" I drop my bag and embrace her. I feel her tense and release.

"Hi, Mom."

"Hi."

Qu intercedes. "Let's talk later. Right now, Mom needs to settle. Alright?"

"Sure," Faith answers shortly before leaving.

I'm frozen. "Whoa. That was a cold breeze."

"She's tired... She'll warm up," Qu says encircling me. He kisses me on the forehead.

I relax in his arms.

"She's angry."

"Yeah, that too," Qu lifts my chin. "It will pass."

I linger against him.

"When did you get so insightful," I look at him, "and attentive?"

"You like?"

"I love!"

"Let's just say this week has given both of us time to think."

"I hear."

He starts rubbing my back, warming me up. "Okay. Enough of this. Let's eat!"

"Great!"

Taking my last mouthful, I sit back and watch Qu sip his wine. He spared no detail. A little Merlot, silk tablecloth, golden candles, all this rich West Indian food I love. A little jazz, volume turned low. Succulent chocolate cheesecake with raspberry sauce on the side. *How'd he pull all this off in a few hours? No way he cooked all this.* I was fully sated.

"You keep staring at me."

"Sorry," I avert my eyes.

"What gives?"

"Just in awe, I guess."

"I don't take my promise lightly."

"Sorry?"

"My promise."

You could hear the wind whistling in my head. He smiles at my blankness.

"I'm going to take care of you."

I wait for the punchline.

"What?" he asks.

"I thought you were going to say something else."

"Like what?"

"I don't know. I just didn't expect you to say, well, that."

"What were you expecting?"

I fold my napkin trying to piece my answer together. *Viv, tell the truth. Tell the truth!*

"Qu."

"Yeah?"

"The dinner was delicious."

"Oh no! You are not changing the subject!"

"What?"

"You know what! Say what's on your mind."

"Alright," I close my eyes and take a deep breath.

"Where's Justin?"

"Viv!"

"No, I'm serious. Where is he? I've been home an hour at least and haven't seen him."

"He probably fell asleep. You can check on him later. Now—"

"Mom? You're home!"

Qu leans back and folds his arms, dumbfounded.

I rise and hug my son. "Justin, it's good to see you!"

"Yeah, we missed you. You, okay?"

I couldn't love this boy, I mean man, more. Look at him. I swear he looks like he shot up another foot!

"I'm great. It's really good to be home."

Justin flinches after catching Qu's expression. "Wah, well, I think I'm going back to my room," he says, backing away, thumb pointing towards the archway.

"You don't have to."

"Okay, son, we'll see you later," Qu responds quickly.

"Alright," he grins knowingly as he turns and sprints up the stairs.

"What did you do that for?"

"Stop avoiding."

"Here we go…"

"Yeah, here we go! You didn't let me off the hook the other day, so why should I? What gives?"

"Nothing gives."

"Viv!"

"Alright, alright," I twist my napkin nervously. "I'm just wondering when the other shoe is going to drop."

"Meaning?"

"Meaning, I love all this and all, but it's new, right."

"Yeah."

"I'm just wondering how long it will last."

"A lifetime. I don't intend to revert back."

"Oh."

"Yeah," Qu looked slightly hurt. "What did you think? I'd wine and dine you now and next week forget what I said?"

Foot. In. Mouth.

Qu folds his arms.

"Unwrinkle your forehead, Qu. Don't be angry."

He sighs deeply and rubs his face. "What do I have to do to make you—"

"Qu," I reach for him. He unfolds his arms.

"Qu, it's not you." *How do I explain this?*

"In the hotel, I could be anybody. Change was easy. But now I'm back and...and I... um, find myself fighting myself."

He's motionless. *Go on Viv.*

"I came with the expectation that things would be the same. And then look at you! Way ahead of the game, already putting in the effort. Already changing. You blow me away."

"Viv, it's dinner."

"Yeah, but I'm grateful for the thought you put into it."

"Thank you. I'm trying."

"You're welcome and I can see that," I rub my belly and smile.

We sit a while, listening to the music. He gets up to clear the table.

"Qu, don't worry about the dishes."

"I just want to get them out the way."

"Okay," I push my chair back and head for the couch to lie down. I am feeling groggy. Qu comes back into the room and sits by my feet.

"Tired?"

"Yeah, suddenly the day just caught up with me. I could fall asleep right here."

"Why don't we leave our talk till tomorrow so you can rest?"

"Sounds like a plan," I yawn and let my eyelids fall.

I feel his hands kneading my feet in time to the tempo. I don't know when I drift off.

I am at peace.

SIXTEEN

I wake with a start.

That dream again... Falling... Haunting... Falling... Maybe I should talk to the kids... Faith... It's been days without explaining anything to them... Justin... What kind of mother... Screams... Falling... Hole...

Where am I?! Out of breath, I bolt up, scanning the room frantically.

"You alright?"

"What?!"

"You're sweating. You have a nightmare?"

"Yeah, I think... I don't know."

Qu shifts in the bed and rises onto his elbows. I rub my eyes, trying to adjust them to the dark.

"Qu..."

"Hmmm..."

"Nothing. Go back to sleep. I'm fine."

"Sure?"

"Yeah, I got spooked, but I'm alright."

"Hmm..." he yawns, moaning. He trails his finger down my back before caressing it with a kiss. Before I can turn and react, he slumps into the pillow, asleep. *How do men do that?* Awed, I watch his chest rise. And fall. And rise. Gently, I place my palm over his heart. Strong beat. I lay beside him facing him. My hand is fused to his chest. Bump... bump...bump...bump... I snuggle in deeper. The comforter partially covers my face. I fall back asleep still touching his heart.

I stir. I stretch. I open my eyes and find my head completely covered by the comforter. It's like a warm cocoon. My fingers are empty. Alone in the bed, I detect some light on the other side of the comforter but I'm too warm here to greet it. *Not just yet. Let the light stay where it is and me where I am. Savouring has become a cherished art form for me these days.*

"Sleepy..."

I grin but pretend to still be fast asleep.

"Viv..."

The game continues.

"Viv, I know you are awake."

I see his leg slide under the covers. My face is exposed. I can't help giggling.

"Well, so much for that."

"Good morning."

"Good morning. But I don't want to get up yet," I whine.

"So, don't. It's still your day."

"You gettin' ready for work?"

"I was, then I changed my mind."

"Changed your mind? Who are you and what have you done with my Qu?"

"I'm right here and I'm staying. Hybrid day. I brought some work home so I can deal with that later," he balances on his elbow, looking down on me. His eyes unnerve me. I back away slightly. He inches toward me.

"You are going to work from home?" I repeat.

"In a manner of speaking."

"Qu?"

"I'll tell them I'm working from home. But my being here totally has to do with you."

"You don't have to do that."

"I want to do this."

"I'm not going anywhere, Qu."

"Neither am I."

"I don't get it."

"What's to get?"

"I'm going back to sleep," I turn around gently and cover my head again. I feel his arm encircle my waist. He rests his head in my hair and inhales. My body blushes to my very soles. I breathe with him.

"Ahh...Dad? Mom?"

I jerk up to see Justin filling the doorframe. *Seriously, it's like he grew overnight.*

"Morning," I greet.

"Morning. Faith and I got breakfast already, but we were wondering about a lift to school?"

"Are you ready to go?"

"Yeah, pretty much."

"Good. Meet me at the car in ten," Qu says, throwing off the covers.

"Great. See you later, Mom," Justin says, already striding through the hallway.

"Later, have a good day," I yell after him. *Hmm, how I love my bed.* I hug the pillow tighter.

"I'll be back soon," Qu throws over his shoulder.

"Don't worry about me. I'll be here," I say with a grin, "sleeping." A yawn escapes as my eyes gently close.

Ring.

Hmm...

Riinngg!

Oh! I scold myself as I roll over to the side table. "Hi! Hello?"

"Viv? You alright?"

"Yes, yes. Ma? How you doing?" I sniff, sitting up straight, smoothing out my hair.

Interesting how I want to look good for my mother even over the phone.

"I'm good, sweetheart. Just been thinking about you. Qu told me about your little hiatus."

Great...

"Aha."

"So, are you feeling better?"

"Yes, Ma. All better."

"You sure? You sound tired."

"I got up not too long ago." *Sort of,* I clear my throat. "Say Ma, I wanted to come by the house later this afternoon. Would that be alright?"

"We'd love that. We'll be around."

"Good, I'll just finish up some things around here and head on over."

"Sounds good."

"Great. I love you, Ma."

"Well," she says slowly, "I love you too, Dear. See you soon."

"Alright," I click off the phone and swing my legs over the side of the bed. I look at my toes.

"Hey, hey, hey, getting up so soon?"

I giggle as I watch Qu try to wrangle out his pants.

"Too late! I'm on a mission," I tease as I bounce up and walk slowly towards the door.

"Where you going?" Qu grabs at me as I swerve past him.

"Ma just called, and I realized that there is stuff I want to get done before Monday kicks in."

"What happened to change? No more rat race?"

"Tell you this much, no rat race isn't synonymous with comatose. I'm still going to get things done."

"OK, OK, what are we doing? What's the agenda?"

We? Agenda? Whoa, I hadn't thought... I pause before the bathroom. "Why don't you join me in the tub while we figure that out?" I feign seduction, clumsily banging into the doorjamb. Streaking past me, I laugh hysterically as he pulls me in.

"I see you started transforming our Goodwill."

"You noticed?"

"Yeah. The mattress feels strangely like the mattress at the hotel."

"Perceptive."

"And your equipment?"

"In the garage till I can figure out something."

"And my papers?"

"Come, I'll show you."

He takes my hand and leads me down the flight of stairs to the basement.

Our basement needs a serious update. Wood panelling and shag carpeting are so 1900s! If only I could figure out how to get on one of those inspiring home makeover shows, I'd be in seventh heaven. Maybe I'll look into some fresh lighting in the summer. Qu flicks the switch.

Wow...

"It's not much, but after our talk, I went into overdrive trying to figure out what I could do to create a space for you. It's not much but given the time I had to pull it all together, I think it's workable," he stands back sheepishly so I can take it all in.

My heart stops as I look around. Behind an old folding bamboo partition is a nearly new teak desk with three drawers. The old computer I had been using is replaced with a newer laptop. Against the wall lies an inviting loveseat with autumn-hued throw pillows. *He knows the colours I like.* A picture I had long forgotten about hangs with care above the desk. A small, burgundy area rug is placed before the loveseat. My exercise equipment is arranged against the opposite wall.

"How?"

"You like?"

"It's fantastic, but how? How did you…?"

"Relax. Sit."

Shocked, I obey.

"First, I knew they were replacing some of the furniture and equipment at work so I asked if I could take a few things. They said, whatever, so I was in and out with this desk, swivel chair, and computer before they could change their minds."

I smiled.

"Then I checked online and found your two-seater on sale. I remember you telling me you liked it some time ago when we were at the mall, so I jumped when I realized they still had it available."

I let my fingers run softly over the velvety fabric.

He points, "Carpet from a liquidator in the same mall. The desk lamp, partition and that picture we had in the garage already."

"Seriously! I didn't even recognize it! Who knew we had a lamp?" *Note to self: clean out the garage.*

"Do you recognize the picture?"

I look at the picture above my desk. It was taken the year we were on the island. Someone had caught us in an all-consuming frenzy, wrapped around one another. We had the image blown up in a sepia hue. The pureness of it takes my breath away.

"How could I forget the night of the wedding! It was incredible!"

"How about the other one?" I get up to stare at the picture above the couch.

"It's familiar, but no..." I continue gawking at the waves and horizon. I am mesmerized by the calm it emotes.

"I wanted to surprise you. I took it near the hotel. Blew it up and framed it."

"Wow." Absently, I swipe a tear from my cheek.

"I take it you like it."

I nod before falling back on the chair.

"Good," he exhales.

We sit beside each other in silence. *I feel overwhelmed. I'm sitting in my room filled with things that bring me joy and peace and I didn't have to work for it! I didn't even ask.*

"Viv."

"Yeah," I wipe my cheek again and smile at Qu.

"Please don't leave me again."

"Wha...Oh, come on Qu! We've been over this," I reach for his hand.

"Viv."

I swallow. Waiting. He measures his words. "I went to the police station. I laid here the first night and didn't know where you were..."

"OK," I answer as I stroke his arm.

We sit a while longer, lost in our thoughts.

"Qu, I want you to go to work."

"What? Why?"

"It would be good if I could be in the house alone for a while."

"But I don't want to go," he playfully snuggles my neck.

"Listen, I'm going to see Ma and Dad later on, but I thought if I had this day to just get myself together, by myself, sort out my next steps, by myself, I'd be ready to have that talk with the kids later."

"I can give you space to do that."

I grab Qu's head. "I'm not going anywhere. I just want to be alone. Kay?"

"I don't want to," he sulks.

I kiss him tenderly on his left cheek, his right cheek, his lips...

I run my fingers over the kitchen counter. I stop and listen to the stillness. *No time like the present.* I switch on the faucet as I search for the washcloth. I squeeze and rub the liquid into the rag until thick bubbles cover my hands. I set it aside and start scraping and submerging each plate and cup into the sink. I hum a song I don't recognize.

I have no idea what I'm doing today. Convincing Qu to leave seems like more than enough work. I smile.

No matter how mad or completely crazy I may be, leaving Qu was never an option. Leaving myself on the other hand... I let the thought linger.

No, it's a new day, remember? A new day. It's going to be alright. I have strength for all things. Remember that.

I pause.

Strength for all things...

Strength for all things... through Christ... who empowers me... Hmm...

I look at the cross over the kitchen archway.

It's amazing how things just pop into my mind without me knowing where they come from. I thought I had forgotten that verse and POP! There it is! I'm about to doubt myself and POP! I remember.

I lean my hip against the cabinet and continue to rub circles over each dish before setting it aside for the next. I look out the window to the backyard.

Yikes! When was the last time I planted anything? Or even picked up the lawnmower? Maybe I'll get Justin to do it... maybe, I'll do it myself. I ought to make myself a list.

Seeing Ma

Do yard work.

What's going on with the laundry? I wonder if anyone remembered to run the machine.

Groceries.

I glance at the fridge.

I got to check that.

Oh! I never did call the haven to tell them I was away. I wonder if I can switch shifts.

Ma, Dad.

I think I said that already.

I sigh. I'd better sit downstairs and just write it out. *If only I could spend the day doing absolutely nothing. How selfishly wonderful that would be!*

I smile impishly.

Selfish... And wonderful.

S T O P!

Okay, I should call Dour this afternoon and find out what I missed and need to cover in the lesson plan. I have to remember to send Gabe some flowers. Dour too. Can't forget Dour. Pack my work bag, check my emails... There are so many people I need to catch up with. I wonder how Trech is doing. I haven't spoken to her in a long time. Baby shower?

A glass shatters. I startle myself.

S T O P!

Shaking my hands free of suds, I step back from the counter and remember to breathe.

Clean up this mess. Sit down and remember I didn't build Rome in a day. Or at all...

I have too much on my mind.

Finish the dishes.

Stop worrying about what's next.

With that, I dry my hands and find a bag to dispose of the shards.

"He remembered my couch," I murmur to myself, letting my fingers travel over the cushions. I wrap a blanket around my shoulders and fold my legs underneath me. I reach for my pen.

Good Morning Vietnam!

Why that line came into my head, I have no idea, but I love the rules of this journal. No judgement.

Mine is not to question why just to let it flow. I found myself wrapped up in my thoughts and worries upstairs so bolted down here to clear my mind. Get my thoughts out of my head so I could be free of the noise. Amazingly, I can be in this empty house, totally by myself, and there is still this constant buzz in my head that prevents me from enjoying the silence. It's like I can't turn myself off even for a minute! That can't be healthy. That can't be good if I'm serious about not taking backwards steps.

I'm staring at my exercise equipment right now. Qu put my dumb-bells, mat, and bands by the wall of my new 'Viv space.' Dumbbells ... Why call them dumb? They should be called world bone-crushing muscle exploders or something equally hallelujah to make people want to pick 'em up and train like wild beasts.

I digress.

Seriously, until I went to the hotel, I forgot how I used to enjoy working out. I'd love to push myself. In my mind, back then, no sweat meant I hadn't trained. My twenty-something self loved the rush of pushing my limits. Seeing the calorie burn rack up. Hitting the shower, already soaking wet. Knowing I'd done all I could to knock myself out was a high! I don't know why I stopped. I wonder where my DVDs are. It's not an A-1 gym here, but if I could discipline myself to do a few reps every day, maybe in the mornings, it would be a start, right? Or even stretch. I used to have some pretty good Pilates tapes some time ago. Seriously, what year is it? I got a laptop and internet. What do I need DVDs for? I could easily improve this space with a little effort. I could move our little bedroom TV to this room. I'll have to add that to my list. Speaking of that, let me start one now before I forget.

I rip a sheet from my notebook and start brainstorming. *Okay...*

~ *Ma, Dad*
~ *Mow lawn*
~ *Groceries*
~ *Send flowers to Dour and Gabe*
~ *Call Dour for update*
~ *Work on lesson plan*
~ *Pack work bag*
~ *Clean out garage*
~ *Call haven, rearrange schedule*
~ *Start dinner*
~ *~~Shop for new exercise DVDs~~*
~ *Move TV downstairs*
~ *Gas car for Monday*
~ *Check emails, voice mail*

I reread the list. *Most of it is job-related. I'm still on hiatus, as Ma puts it, and yet my mind is back at work. This list is devastatingly un-fun. Well, maybe the grocery shopping...* I set the list aside. *Oh!* I pick it up again and write:

~ *Call Trech.*

I added some fun. I smile and return to my journal.

Well, for what it's worth, I drafted my list. If I had to say what I'd like to do though, first it would be looking after the house stuff. Okay, I'm lying. If it were up to me, I'd go back to bed. I could sleep another hour or two easily. I don't know why I'm so tired. I don't think I'm coming down with a cold or anything. I also can't use the jet lag excuse. I think it may be because I'm thinking about all I should be doing, and it feels overwhelming. The thinking is wearing me out.

Now that's stupid. And that's judging, so let me back up. This "changing my life" thing is wiping me out! It's amazing! I'm tired if I don't change. I'm tired if I do change. Thinking about changing is draining. Where do I go from here?

I throw my head back and close my eyes. The pen drops from my fingers, and I wait.

Okay, inspiration. Hit me and hit me hard because I have no idea where to start or how.

I enjoy the quiet as I rest on my new couch. I hear the phone ring upstairs. I slowly open my eyes and wonder if I should race to get it or not. *Just go, Viv!* I bully myself as I creak up the stairs two at a time.

"Hello?"

"Viv?"

"Yes, this is Viv."

"Hey, it's Carol. We were wondering about you!"

"Oh, Carol, hi. I had you on my list to call."

"Everything alright?"

"Yes. I just took a few days to..." *(What? What am I going to say?)* "get some things done."

"Oh."

"Yeah, nothing to worry about. I'm sorry I didn't call to let you know I couldn't do this

week's shift."

"That's fine though it would have been better if you called to let us know. We've been really short."

"Yes." Dead air fills the space as I try to figure out what to say next. 'Yes', seemed hollow, but it was all I could think to say without apologizing again.

"Carol."

"Hmm."

"I'd like to take a couple months' leave from the haven."

I would?

"A couple of months? But we need you! Are you sure everything is alright?"

"I'm just trying to make some changes and could use the time."

"Is there anything we can do to help?"

I pause. *I shouldn't do this. I can keep the haven and still change, right? It's important work.* My mouth opens.

"No. No. It's stuff I need to do on my own."

"I see."

Really? I barely see.

"It will only be a couple of months," I try to sound reassuring.

"Well, the women here will miss you. You have this easy way of engaging with them. You also give them a lot of hope and ideas. You make a real difference."

My voice catches. *I don't know how to respond to that other than to say...*

"Thank you."

"You'll keep in touch, right?"

"Yes, I'll call. Do you need me to sign anything?"

"No, I'll just pass the message on to Sue. Viv, let's talk soon alright?"

That sounds final.

"Yes. Thanks again, Carol."

"Don't mention it. Bye."

"Bye," I press the red icon and lean against the counter.

I can't believe I just did that! I quit the haven! Well, I took a leave, but I may as well have quit because I <u>never</u> take a leave from anything. I love the women at the haven! I love being a part of that work. The counselling. The mediation. The workshops. Talking and laughing with the women. Running food drives. Even reception! Why would I quit? Out of the blue? That doesn't make any sense!

I check the wall. 10:27.

Know what, I AM going to bed. Sometimes when I open my mouth, I have no idea what I'm going to say. Who am I? Quitting the shelter... what kind of irresponsible, idiotic...

I continue to berate myself all the way up the stairs, gripping my cell.

I flop into bed and tug the covers roughly over my head. *What am I doing? It's 10:30 and all I want to do is sleep. Is it about sleep or hiding from the world? At this point they are synonymous.*

I groan and force myself deeper into the mattress. *Qu bought me my mattress. The mattress.* I frown. *I wonder how much it cost. Stop. It was a gift. Move on.*

I turn over.

I've got to get up. Too much to do. The list is downstairs still, I think. Maybe it won't seem so brutal if I space the tasks out. Aaaggghhh!

I throw the covers off and reach for the mobile. I dial the number by heart before pulling in my knees. I wait.

"This is Mr. Dour speaking. May I help you?"

Ever the professional.

"Hi D..." *why can't I ever remember his name?* "Etienne! It's Viv."

"How are you, Viv?"

"Well, thank you. I wanted to call you for an update before I return to class on Monday."

"Was the week enough time?"

What a strange question.

"Yes, of course. I'm eager to come back to work."

Better not think of dumping my ass.

"Yes, I was just wondering if you had adequate time to rest, think..."

"Yes, all of that Etienne. Good as new. Now, about Monday's prep."

"Well, Millie was available to substitute for us again."

That airhead! My poor class.

"She had your class this week. I've asked her to leave her notes with me to hand over."

Will I be able to decipher them?

"I can scan them if you want to review them over the weekend."

Millie Smythe, oh no.

"Viv, are you there?"

I catch myself.

"Sorry, Etienne. Yes, scanning. Yes, that would be very helpful, thanks."

"Is there anything else you would like to discuss...?" he trails off.

"No, that should do." Another thought surfaces.

"Actually..."

"Yes?"

"I'd like to set some time aside to talk with you on Monday. Maybe fifteen, twenty minutes?"

"That should be easy to arrange. I'll have Beth get back to you with a time."

"Thanks again Etienne, for everything. I truly needed this week to reflect."

"I'm glad," he sighs. "Have a good weekend, Viv."

"You too, Etienne. Bye." I gently replace the phone on the side table and roll onto my back.

"Damn!" I slap my forehead. *So much for telling him thanks. And about Todd.*

I pull on the sheets. *Ah, who am I foolin'?*

Shaking myself, I head to the basement again with Gabe's business card in hand.

Before I forget, I sit at my new desk and type a quick email to Dour and order, online, two arrangements for both him and Gabe. Satisfied, I close my laptop.

Snatching my list and pen, I alter my tasks.

~ *Ma, Dad*
~ ~~*Mow lawn*~~
~ *Groceries*
~ ~~*Send flowers to Dour and Gabe*~~
~ ~~*Call Dour for update*~~
~ *Work on lesson plan*
~ ~~*Pack work bag*~~
~ *Clean out garage*
~ ~~*Call haven, rearrange schedule*~~
~ ~~*Start dinner*~~
~ ~~*Shop for new exercise DVDs*~~
~ ~~*Move TV downstairs*~~
~ *Gas car for Monday*
~ ~~*Check emails, voice mail*~~
~ *Call Trech*
~ *Talk with kids*

Okay, seven more things! Can I handle seven things? Do I want to handle seven things?

I take a deep breath. I randomly scratch out four more things and tuck the list in my pocket before I can change my mind. I climb the steps two at a time back to the bedroom.

Next: find something comfortable to wear to Ma's.

"Viv!"

"Ma! How are you?" I say into her hair, giving her a squeeze.

"Good, Dear. Come in, come in."

"Thanks," I say stepping inside.

The house is always so inviting and pulled together. Though a lot of things, nothing out of place. Neutral core with punches of colour here and there. Love the lilies! I walk through the foyer towards the family room.

"Would you like a drink?"

"Maybe later, I'm fine for now."

"Well, I was going to make myself a cup of tea so let's go sit in the kitchen."

"Okay," I reply, redirecting my steps towards the dining area. I peer out the patio doors.

"Where's Dad?"

"You don't see him?" she chuckles as she casually points her chin in the direction of a hunched figure in the yard. Dad tears a second fertilizer bag open with relish. I tap the glass to get his attention to no avail.

"What would Dad do without his garden?" I sigh.

"Beats me. You sure you don't want anything?" she asks as she pours hot water into her favourite stoneware mug.

I reconsider. "Well, alright. Do you have any green tea?"

"Do I have green tea?!" Ma scoffs as she dramatically swings open her cabinet. "Earl Grey with Lavender, Sencha, Dragon Well, Citrus Green, Angi, decaf, Kabusecha…"

"Kabuwhatcha? Ma, please surprise me. I'm sure it's all good," I laugh.

"I'll let you try the Dragon Well. It's quite invigorating. It'll wake you up," she smiles as she busies herself.

I look tired? Deep breath. Don't react. Let it go.

"Whatever you say, Ma," I reply calculatedly.

"I hope you are using a tempered steel tea accessory at home, Dear. The steel bulbs are terrible! They leave such a bad aftertaste."

"I'm a bag woman all the way, Ma. I don't own a tea steep."

"What?"

"Nope."

"I'll have to get you one then. It makes teatime seem so much more extravagant," she grins as she presents me with a perfect cup in her best china. I blush.

"Thank you, Ma," I take the cup in both hands and drop it suddenly.

"Careful, Dear. Cup's hot."

Right, you'd think the steam would have tipped me off. I rub my hands on my lap as I blow into the cup.

"So, I see," I mumble.

"So, what brings you to these parts?"

I shrug, "Nothing just wanted to see you and Dad."

"Hmm," Ma takes a sip of her tea as she crosses her legs.

We sit in silence a while, alternating between tastes and watching the vapour drift from our brews.

"Are you surprised I wanted to see you?"

"No, no, it just seems like it's been a while since you've wanted to visit."

"Well, you know, I've been busy."

"Yes, I know, Dear. Busy."

"Yes, busy, Ma... you know... with the kids and their drama, work and whatnot."

"So, how are my babies?"

"If you are referring to the too-grown-for-their-britches teenagers running my house, they're fine," I smile despite myself.

"So, what are they up to?"

"Well," I took a moment to think. *What are they up to?*

"The usual, I guess. Faith is..." I stop self-consciously.

"Faith is what?"

"Sorry, I..." I fidget.

Silence envelops us again. I wipe an invisible spot off my pants. Ma gently replaces her cup on her saucer and sits back, looking at me intently.

"What's going on with you?"

I look up at her. My throat constricts. "I'm sorry," I say, reaching for my cup.

"What do you have to be sorry about?"

"You know what, Ma? I don't know anything," I sniff. "I was about to complain about Faith and Justin when I realize, what am I complaining about? Complaining that they are normal teenagers trying to find their way like every other teenager? I mean, I'm not a teenager and I'm still trying to find my way!"

"What are you talking about, chile?" Ma settles in, amused by my revelation.

I lean in, "How is it that you and Dad make being in this world seem so easy? He's out in your garden, and you're in here sipping tea in this perfectly manicured house. Everything seems so relaxed, peaceful, and in order."

"Ha! How short is your memory?" she chuckles. "Coming to and being in this country has been no bed of roses. I'm just now getting time to spend and enjoy with your father," she smiles into her cup as if they were sharing a joke. "All those decades of him slaving at all those ridiculous jobs... think back!"

I impatiently tap my cup with my fingernail. "Can I have a biscuit?"

"Sure, of course," she rises to check her supply.

I watch her back as I try to figure out how to better explain myself. *Ma and Dad have this connection. When I think of Ma, it's like she's welded to Dad's side. They are inseparable in mind and heart. Besides that, I don't remember any hard times coming to this country. I was born into all of this!*

"Ma, honestly, I don't know what you are talking about."

She takes her time selecting two boxes of cookies before gently closing the cabinet doors. "Well, you know we left the island when we were fairly young."

"Yeah."

"And we came here with a few dollars, not knowing anyone."

"Hmm..."

"Well, think about what it would mean for you to start over in a place that doesn't see you as anybody because of who you are naturally. You're nothing because you have no reputation. Know nobody. Look like nobody. Think about what it means for a man to not be able to provide for his new bride months after promising his mother-in-law that he would care for she *and* the dawta!"

She is rolling now. *You always know when Ma feels passionate about something or is about to blow when her mother tongue takes over.*

"Imagine coming to a country that doesn't see you as person... not deservin' of anything but scraps. You can't 'magin. When we landed, we knew nobody. Nobody was for us."

I dip into the box and lay the ginger snaps onto the plate Ma hands to me. Her eyes soften looking out the glass patio doors.

"We came here all romantic and in love. Girl, your Dad was ten feet tall in my eyes," she smiles at his back. "He sacrificed so much for me and stood up to my mom! You don't find men like that in this day n' age," her face shines with the memory. "I could tell the pressure of not finding work and not being able to establish a home for us right away was piercing your dad's heart, but you see how your dad stay? He don't talk his pain. Always been that way. He loved me hard n' didn't say a word 'bout 'im stresses." She gulps, "Me on the other han'—ha! Always with the lip! Always with the yammerin'. I think the more I talk, the more 'im retreat. It took me years to understand that words are as deadly as a machete. Seeing I wasn't getting any reaction from him, I left him 'lone."

"You never left me alone," I mutter. I feel her laser eyes burning me now. I hang my head in shame for talking back.

"I guess not," she says, shortly.

"I didn't realize it was hard for you, coming here," I half apologize. "All these years I just remember us living well."

She clears her throat. "Who in their right mind is going to show or tell a child they're poor and life's a burden?"

You must not watch the news. I bite my lip.

"We always wanted the best for you, for us," she shrugs. "I think it worked out alright."

"It did, Ma. It did," I sigh as I dunk my snap in my tea. She glares at me disapprovingly.

"Why you do that?"

"Do what?" I look mystified as soggy crumbs drop from the side of my mouth.

"Defile a perfectly good cup of tea with mushy cookies," she tisks.

I giggle despite myself. *The drama queen is alive and well!* "Defile, Ma? Really," I wipe my chin, still enjoying the bits of sugar swimming about my mouth. She settles against her seat.

"Tea is supposed to be enjoyed without dunking food in it."

"But does it matter how I enjoy the tea as long as I do?"

"Hmm, whatever girl."

I lift another biscuit and poise it in the offending position above my cup. I smile as I watch her angrily divert her eyes.

"So, I'm sorry, I still don't get it," I munch.

"What's to get?"

"I mean about you and Dad. Are you saying you faked it till you made it?"

"I never thought about it."

"Well, think about it. I'm curious."

"Why?"

"Why? Well," I break from chewing, "faking it till I make it isn't working for me, apparently. Frankly, I feel so overwhelmed by all that I have to change, I end up just wanting to crawl into bed."

"Oh, come on, I'm sure you're exaggerating," she chides matter-of-factly.

"No Ma, I'm not," I object. "I had a breakdown a few days ago."

"No, you didn't."

"Ma, I'm telling you—"

"No Dear, you were just tired and needed some well-needed rest."

"Ma," I moan.

She can't be seriously telling me what I experienced? How come she doesn't hear me? I'm telling her one thing and she's insisting on another and it's about me! I'm a grown-ass woman. I don't know breakdown from fatigue?

Irritated, I crush crumbs with my index finger and flick them into the saucer. "Ma, I had a breakdown. Yes, part of it may have been fatigue, but that's not it. I've been out of control. Overworked. Out of step with the kids. Finances are tight. I've been... unhappy."

"Dear, we all have those times. Life is full of ups and downs. It will all work out."

I stop eating and look at her. My mother. *She still doesn't hear me.* I shake my head. *I'm done.* "Sure," I rise to clear the table. "Where's your washcloth?"

"Oh, leave them there on the counta. I'll wash up layta."

"Okay, I'll go say hi to Dad."

"Alright."

I wipe my hands on a napkin and head for the patio doors. I slide the glass gently. I don't want to disturb his sanctuary. *When Dad's in the zone, nothing else exists. It's him, the ground and sky.*

"Hi Dad," I say as I walk toward him.

"Oh, hi Dear," he looks up, shielding his eyes.

I drag a lawn chair over and sit watching him tackle the earth.

I absolutely hate gardening. I just don't get it; maybe that's more accurate than saying I outright hate it. I don't get why anyone would want to be knee-deep in dung, with mess caked under their fingernails. The smell of manure fertilizer on you, the constant need to water blooms and yank out crabgrass. Damn it! Why does he look so happy?

Pivot.

"Beautiful day."

"Yeah," he wipes his brow with the back of his wrist, barely skipping a beat.

I lean back and look at the sky. *I can understand wanting to stay outside on days like today.* I close my eyes and smile at the rays.

The digging stops. I hear Dad move.

I've got so much to do. Where did I put my list - I remember I was to call Trech... was that today or tomorrow? Mow the lawn? I don't feel like doing that. See if I can shift that to Justin. Groceries! Got to get food for next week. I'll do that when I leave here... and work...

"Girl, you alright?"

"Sure."

"For someone sunning herself, you sure seem restless," Dad chuckles returning with a trowel.

"How you mean?" I sit up.

"Sittin' there, eyes popping under your lids."

"You exaggerate. I'm fine. Just thinking is all."

"Oh, 'bout what?"

"To-do list stuff, nothing exciting."

"That's why you come here? We were on your to-do list?" Dad pauses, smiling mischievously at me.

He's good. "Of course not," I lie. "It's been a while, so I wanted to come and see you before things get hectic again."

"Why they need to get hectic? You have your family, you have your job, little entertainment, that's all you need. What's hectic about that?"

I stare at the man posing as my father. *This same man who worked umpteen jobs simultaneously for decades. The man I barely saw growing up telling <u>me</u> what's hectic. I need to let it go... yet...*

"Talk about the pot calling the kettle..." I blurt out.

He digs the trowel into the earth and sits back on his heels, gently jabbing the air at me with his gloved hand.

"What I'm saying is, don't follow this old fool. It took me fifty years to figure out I don't have to shoulder the world," he grins and grabs the tool again, starting another row.

"Whatever you say, Dad."

"Whatever nothin'. I'm talkin' troot."

"No, you ain't. One, you aren't an old fool, and two, just because you aren't doing a gazillion and one paid jobs, you're still up and around town, in the garden and whatnot 24/7."

"Yeah, that's called P-L-E-A-S-U-R-E, my girl. Not to-do lists and hectic. Pure, unadulterated pleasure. You should try it sometime," he smirks as he playfully tosses dirt on my shoe.

"Ew, Daddy! Why ya go do that? Nasty."

"Listen, city girl. This is earth. Nothing nasty 'bout it."

"Now I'm going to smell like manure," I whine.

"Good, then you have no excuse not to help me."

"I ain't going anywhere near—" I start to mumble just as I feel another clump hit my shin. "Hey!"

"Well?"

I laugh despite myself. "Dad, you know I hate gardening."

"What's to hate? Look at this rich earth," he squeezes a clump of soil and attempts to place some in my hand. I shrink away.

"Please Daddy, stop."

"Girl, this is gold. How you gonna refuse gold? Soil cradles beauty. Food. Trees, minerals, gems. Lord, soil is the key to prosperity. Have you seen the price of gold lately? Diamonds? Straight from the earth! You better recognize."

I secretly love it when he tries to talk street.

"Hmph, it's all dung to me," I say unconvinced. "I'm only here to see you. I have no intentions getting down on all fours to hoe or dig or any other crazy gardening thing you want to enlist me in. You, Dad. I came to see you."

"Fine, be all ornery about it. You have no idea what you are missing."

"Yeah, I do," I scoff.

"No Dear, you don't."

I so don't want to argue with this old man. I swipe at my leg.

"Go ahead and tell me about all this other pleasure you're lapping up."

"Well," he drawls, "pleasure for me these days is coming and going as I please, eating what I want, staying out here until my skin's crispy, and kissing your mother till she screams uncle," he chuckles. "That's my favourite."

"Hmm," I smile.

"I hope you're still watching what you eat."

"Hush now, I just told you, I'm doing what I like!"

"Still Daddy, you know food is like drugs—some are medicine, others pure poison."

"I'll take my chances," he wipes his brow again. "Say, hand me that glass over there by the door."

I turn to get him his water, exaggerating my sigh of disapproval. "Fine, be that way."

"That's right! I am living the life! In fact, I say EVERYONE should retire. We'd all have a happier universe!"

I giggle, watching him down his drink with gusto. "I don't doubt it." I sit, mulling the prospect over. *Retire-er-ment...*

"Now, what's on your mind?"

I shake myself. "Everything's good, Dad. Everything's good. Just got me thinking about retirement. Your pleasure sounds good and all, but I've got so much busyness, I don't know if I will ever retire. How can anyone realistically retire?"

"You stay there with your busy. God didn't put me, or you for that matter, on this green earth to work ourselves like dogs and die. I know YOU have enough sense to know that."

"I know, but—"

"What's going on with you? Why you so busy?"

"Daddy, I have responsibilities—"

"And?"

"School."

"And?"

"Volunteering..." *Sort of.*

"And?" he keeps digging and patting his earth.

"Viv, the kids—"

"Viv and kids? Don't you mean Qu?"

"Yeah, I meant Qu. Whatever. Chores!" I start counting on my fingers.

"Anything else?"

"Yeah, Dad. Papers to mark, meetings to attend, commuting, bills to pay. Life's busy!"

"Says who? It's as busy as you make it."

I'm dumbfounded. "What kind of logic—"

"Quit breathing hard and listen," he plunges the hand shovel into the ground. "How is busy serving you? You come over here all to-do listy, I ain't gonna garden, life's busy, woe-is-me. Life ain't hard! You make it hard for no other reason than to say that life's hard."

Say what? "You're wrong."

"Really?"

Staunch faced, I fold my arms ready to fight this old man.

"Okay," he replies lightly, turning back to digging his patch.

Say what??

"Okay? That's all you got?"

"Yup."

"Unbelievable."

"Not really. Proving you wrong gives me no pleasure, and I'm all about being the

pleasure machine, girl!" he laughs out loud. "I'm the pleasure machine!"

"Right Dad, you the man."

"Got that right!"

I laugh right along with him. *It's impossible to stay mad at him—ever.* I lean back in my seat again, soaking up some of his pleasure. Dipping my head back, I look up at the sky again.

"Where you been?"

"One guess," I say exhausted, dumping the heavy grocery bags on the table. Justin starts rifling through. I teasingly slap his hand.

"No emptying the car, no eat! Get moving!"

"Ahh," he fake limps towards the door.

I smile at his back with my hands poised over the bag. As soon as he's out of sight, I grab and jam the Chocolate Fudge Chunk Delight to the back of the freezer. Before I can slam the fridge door shut, I feel someone behind me.

"Hiding something?"

"Who me?" I jab Qu in the ribs.

"Caught!"

"Whatever, where's Miss Faith? She could be helping Justin with the groceries."

"She said that she was going to hang by Kara's for a bit, so we'll see her around dinner I guess," he shrugs as he reaches for an apple.

"Why you do that?"

"Do what?" Juice drips from the corner of his lips.

"You're going to spoil your appetite for dinner," I look disgusted as I continue unpacking.

"Did you just meet me? This apple is like a drop of water in this stomach. I'll eat anything you throw down..." he hesitates. "What are you throwing down?"

I stop and stare at the wall. "I don't know... actually... hey! That's not the point." *It's the principle.*

"Well, in that case, I'll take my chances ruining our phantom dinner," he laughs, juggling the bread and hummus.

"You know better."

"Viv, seriously, let it go."

"Let what go?" Justin chimes in, carrying what seems like a truckload of food. *Skinny and strong. We all should be so blessed.*

"Never mind," I mumble.

"Your mom doesn't want me to ruin my appetite for dinner, yet she doesn't even know what we're having for dinner."

"Yeah, what are we having?"

"Did it ever occur to you macho men that you could make dinner?"

You could hear a pin drop. I look up and find them staring at each other in mock shock.

"We're eating out!" They shout in unison, high-fiving each other.

"You both are ridiculous, cavemen."

Justin puts his arm around me. "Ahh, don't be like that, Mom. We just want to celebrate you coming back home and thought going out would be fun for you."

"I eat out all week and you think taking me out to eat will be a change of pace for me?" Hand on hip, I'm ready to rumble.

"Right," Justin pats Qu on the shoulder, "take it away, Dad."

"Viv, no one wants to cook, so we're going out or ordering in. What do you want to eat?" He crumbles the plastic bag and stuffs it in a drawer.

"Going out. Thai," I say resigned. *I don't want to wash dishes either.*

"Good, Thai it is. We'll call Faith, pick her up, life is good," Qu smiles as he pecks me on the cheek.

"Not so fast! How you let Faith go to Kara's before first coming home and getting her
homework done?"

"It's Friday, Viv."

"Work before play."

Qu stops, head hung.

"What gives? You are totally stressing over nothing."

I put away the last confection and slam the cupboard door shut. Justin slinks out of the room, almost unnoticed. *I'm not going to let him off the hook.*

"We're the parents, Qu. The kids need to know that they work first and *then* they can hang out or party or whatever."

"It's Friday, Viv. Did you 'work' before you 'played' today?"

"I never play." *What? That sounds so righteous.*

"Now I know you're cracked!"

"What?"

"C-R-A-C-K-E-D."

"If you are not going to take me seriously, just forget it," I turn to leave.

"Okay, I'm sorry. I'm sorry, okay," he grabs my waist, kissing my neck.

"Beggin's not sexy," I half-joke, trying to wriggle free.

"You love it, you know you love it," he ignores me.

"Work then play, Qu!" I say, picking up the bunch of broccoli as if to throw it.

"Play all day long Viv."

"I can't talk to you."

"Fine," he releases me.

"Fine."

"Fine."

What just happened?

"You win," Qu states, throwing his hands in the air.

"I what?"

"You wanted to win, and you won. Do what you want."

"I didn't mean..." *What?*

Qu is halfway up the stairs.

I can't breathe. What just happened?

"I'm sorry!" I yell after him, dropping the broccoli.

Everything's still. *Did I just apologize? I apologized! Check me out.*

"What?!" he stops mid-step.

Lord, he's going to make me say it again. I hurriedly pick up the veggie and spin around trying to busy myself. I hear him bound back into the kitchen. *Caught.*

"What'd you say?" he repeats.

Shoot. "You heard me."

"No, I don't think I did."

Deep breaths, girl, deep breaths.

"I said, I'm sorry."

"Whoa! Where's the pen? I need to mark the calendar."

"Oh, shut up, Qu!"

He's laughing uncontrollably now. *I may have to shoot him for real.*

"Mom has said SHE'S SORRY!" he shouts, cupping his hands over his lips like a megaphone.

"Don't let me be sorry for saying sorry to your sorry ass." Now, we are both laughing like hyenas. I'm bent over trying not to choke.

"What is wrong with the two of you?"

I didn't even see Justin come back into the room. "Nothing, your dad's just making fun of me again," I say, gasping for air.

"Whatever, when we leaving?"

"Soon as we pull ourselves together, I guess," Qu replies, wiping his eye with the back of his hand, and reaching for me with the other. I'm still shaking with giggles.

"Thank you," Qu whispers in my ear as he tries to compose himself.

"I'm sorry," I swallow as he kisses my cheek. Justin rolls his eyes as he reaches for a bag.

"What's up? Where we heading?" Faith drops into the back seat, slamming the door behind her.

"We decided to go out for dinner," I reply, still staring out the window. *Man, they know how to landscape. I should find out who Kara's mom uses as...*

"Well?"

"Well, what?"

"Didn't you hear what I asked? Figures," she says under her breath.

"Let's try this again. Hi Faith. How are you? How was your day?" I dramatize.

"Whatever."

"Faith, watch how you talk to your mother," says Qu.

"She doesn't watch how she talks to me," she kisses her teeth.

All of us veer left as Qu slams into the shoulder and shuts off the car. "This ends now," he slams the steering wheel.

I look back at Faith. Her arms are crossed as she glares out the passenger window.

"Talk to your wife," she retorts.

"No, I'm talking to you. You don't talk to your mother like she's nothing. Apologize."

"Yeah, right," she sneers.

I'm looking at Qu intensely now. *Wow, check out my man. If the kids weren't around, I'd jump him right now. Focus Viv, focus.* I clear my throat.

"Okay, what's really going on with you, Faith?"

"Never mind," she grumbles.

I reach and firmly grab Qu's arm before he can react.

"I'm sorry I didn't hear what you said before."

Wow, this sorry thing is just flowing today. "My mind was elsewhere, but I don't understand why that has made you so angry."

"Who says I'm angry?"

"Ah, your folded arms and bitchy attitude to start," I throw back.

"Hmph," she sinks deeper into her seat.

Great, now she REALLY gonna make me work for this. I just had to say bitchy.

I wait. I look at Qu and make a slight 'no' motion with my head as I continue to squeeze his arm.

Justin fidgets uncomfortably. He looks anxiously at Faith before leaning forward.

"Look Mom, she just wanted to know if you saw her note at home. There, can we go now?"

"What note?"

"The note I left by your lamp on the nightstand."

"No, I didn't go upstairs when I got home. What did it say?"

"Let's talk about it later."

"Is that it? Are you angry at me because I didn't hear your question, didn't get your note or is there something else?"

"It doesn't matter. Let's just go. We're all hungry."

"So what? First, you accuse me of not listening and now you won't talk to me so I can listen?"

"We can talk about it later."

"Will we?"

"Yes, so let's just go."

I look bewildered at Qu.

"Fun, fun, fun," he chants sarcastically as he restarts the engine.

I have to cut my hair. I'm tired of product after product and curling irons. I hold out my hair and pull at my dry ends. *Straw. Crazy-ass straw for hair.* I pick up the comb and declare war on my tangles. *Split ends, your days are numbered.*

"You're beautiful."

I snort and drag my hair through the plastic teeth with a vengeance.

"I mean it. You are beautiful."

"Thank you," I grunt back.

"What's going on with you, Viv?" Qu shifts on the bed, staring at me.

"Why does anything have to be going on?"

"Why do you have to answer a question with a question?"

"Nothing is going on with me. I'm just tired, I guess," I sigh.

"Cop out."

"Call it whatever."

"Okay, a total cop-out."

"You realize the more you say cop-out, the more you age decades before my eyes?"

"I'm serious."

"What—"

"DON'T SAY WHATEVER!"

"Are we fighting?" I stop combing and look at him.

His head thuds back on the mattress. "I repeat, what's going on with you?" he rubs his eyes.

I rest the comb and think. *What is up with me?*

"I don't know." I turn around and lean against the dresser. "I snap, right, and I find myself by the seashore nearly selling seashells and everything's nirvana. I'm clear, I'm alive, I'm ready to start life fresh. And then, BANG!" I hit my fist in my palm. "I'm back and I feel... overwhelmed. I don't know how to talk to you. The kids. I still haven't talked to the kids... again. It's like I'm being pulled back to the way things were before I snapped."

Long silence. I'm still looking at Qu, eyes closed and motionless. *Should I check if he's breathing? I take a step towards...*

"And?" he demands.

Lord, he startled me! I clear my throat.

"Aaannnddd... It's my fault. I thought I'd take a time out, be clear and come back, still clear."

Another long silence. I wait. *Really, Qu?* I turn back and inspect myself in the mirror.

"And..." I hear him say more softly behind me.

"And that's it."

"No, that's not it, there's more."

"Then please, oh wise one, tell me what 'and' is. I'm intrigued."

"Sarcasm doesn't become you."

"Qu, you are giving me a headache."

"Well then, finish your thought."

"I could just deck you right now."

"You want to go there? Don't let me pin your skinny ass," he jokes.

"You think I'm skinny?" I blush as I give my belly a pinch. *Wow.*

He laughs. *I love the sound of his laughter.*

"I'm not letting you go, Viv."

"Was I going anywhere?"

"Only around this crazy mountain."

"My brain can't decipher metaphors right now. Give me a clue."

He grabs for me. "Come here, I'm pinning you down."

I playfully swerve in time. *It's hard to be serious with this dude.*

"I mean it," he tries again.

"Yeah. Whoa!" I yelp as he throws me. The next thing I know, I'm bouncing on our mattress, staring up into Qu's eyes. They are no longer laughing.

"What am I going to do with you?" he asks.

"Love me?" I pucker up as I grab his face. He moves his head out of my hands.

"Viv, we need to deal with this."

This. Is. Exhausting.

"Deal with what? You asked me what was going on in my head. I told you. Now, either you let me comb my hair, make love to me, or let me sleep, but there's not much else we can do in this position."

"We could talk about why you feel overwhelmed and how we can work through this, so you don't feel you need to be away from us to get cl—"

"It's fine, Qu. I'll figure it out." *I want to stop talking already.*

"Viv!"

"Ugghhh, forget I said anything! I'm going to bed. Get off me," I start to wriggle.

"No."

"What?"

"No."

I try to push him off. *Damn his buff, firm, tall, dark... don't go there, girl! Focus. At least look mad. Why the hell is he so sexy? Stay mad girl.*

"Get off." *That even sounded weak to me.*

He settles in and stares at me. *All warm and glistening skin. Damn! I'm dead.* "Didn't I already tell you I'm not leaving?" I plead.

"I want you to *talk* to me, Viv."

"I. Don't. Know. How."

He rolls off me. "You are the most bizarre brotha I know," I accuse, not moving.

"Good, that doesn't bother me. Get to talkin', sis."

"Don't call me that, it's cringy." We both laugh again.

I grow serious.

"You know what it is, Qu? Not knowing how to change. It's not about you. You know I love you. You are my best friend," I smile as I lean on my elbows. "It's me. This unsettled, this unclear, this worry in the pit of my stomach. It's not knowing what to do, or how to be... different. Better."

"And?"

"Okay, say 'and' one more time, I dare you!" I roll on top of him menacingly.

"And..." he breathes as he kisses me lightly on the lips. "We are making progress."

"Hmmm." *Whatever you say, man.* I reach over and click off the lights.

Tomorrow is another day.

SEVENTEEN

I can't sleep. How can he just lay there, snoring without a care in the world and I'm just laying here… tossing… all up in my thoughts…? It's only been one day back, and I feel like…

I wipe a tear from my cheek, panicking.

God, what am I doing? I can't even pinpoint why I feel… Is it hot in here? Damn my skin's itchy!

I throw off the covers and scratch my inner thighs till they're raw.

I've got to stop. I'm driving myself crazy for absolutely noth—

"Hmm," Qu rolls over and flings his arm over my lap. I turn to see the light in his eyes.

Nothing.

"Qu?" I half-whisper, not knowing if I want him to answer or not. "Quuu?" I mouth for effect. He doesn't stir.

I swear this man is gifted. No matter what—fight, tornado, flood—this man can and will sleep through it.

I look at him with intense envy. Crossing my arms, I curse myself for not being able to do what any baby can. Close their eyes.

Sighing, I let my thoughts float back to the hotel. *Maybe if I empty my mind on the page…*

"Man, I just need some rest!" I whimper pathetically.

I stare at the rise and fall of Qu's chest. I slide in a fraction closer until our noses are almost touching. I hold my breath. I feel Qu's air graze my lips. *I remember doing this with the kids. I'd wait until they were completely in la-la land, then bend until I was low enough between the crib bars. I'd reach through and place my palm on their little chests and then instinctively stop breathing. For a few precious moments, I'd let them, these tiny souls, breathe for the both of us. It was only for a few seconds. A few seconds and I'd just forget myself. I loved it.*

He lets out a snort and it jolts me into a giggle.

That's Qu. He may sleep like a baby, but he doesn't sound like one. I smile despite myself.

Where did I put that journal? I hum "There's a steam train a-comin'" in time to his snoring as I search.

I have no idea what to write.

My eyes trace the ceiling corners.

All I keep thinking is why I can't sleep! Why am I so restless? Why am I not different after being away? All these questions and no answers. I was supposed to come back refreshed, and instead… I'm back where I started.

I chew the nib of my pen. *Let's retrace.*

In the hotel, I told myself I would write all my thoughts. No judgement.

I remember reading a verse too. What was that verse? I could just look back, but I want to remember.

I let the pen rest, and I lay my head against the headboard.

'I can do all things' floats back to me. I start to write.

It's amazing that when I was growing up, I could rhyme off a million verses without thinking twice. I could even call out all the books of the Bible like they were all the names of my family, yet now, here I am grappling for something as simple as 'I can do all things.'

Life changes, hmm? My life just seemed to speed up and take on all these turns, and I forgot things along the way. Parenting, working, moving, teaching, volunteering—all the 'ings' took over except remember-ing. Know-ing. Be-ing. I forgot how to be.

Hmm. I sit with that thought a spell.

Let me flip through it again.

I reach inside the side table and lift out the brown leather book. I trace the embossed letters with my finger.

I can't remember when I bought this… maybe eight years ago? At first sight, the book looks no more than a day old. Not a crack. Not a crease. I fan it out from front to back. In the glow of the lamp, I watch the dust float gently out of its pages.

I am spirit.

I hesitate.

Try.

I lift my pen and write, slowly and deliberately.

I am spirit.

This body is all I've been concerned about all these years. Where am I, this body, going now? What do I need to do now? How do I look? Look how flabby I have become.

Am I good enough?

All this time, I've substituted "I" for my body instead of "I" for the real, genuine me. My spirit.

I've forgotten who "I" am.

Simple revelations sometimes can be the most profound.

On the beach gazing at the water, I thought about the relation-ships that have helped shape the real me. But now I'm thinking that I didn't do the real work. I ate well, I exercised, and I rested my body. But I didn't reconcile that my true "I" was still being neglected. How could I lose sight of that??

Right. No judgement. No criticism.

Shaking my head, I randomly open the Bible to think about something else.

I write,

The Lord said to Moses, Go in, tell Pharaoh King of Egypt to let the Israelites go out of his land... (Exodus 6:10-11)

'Go tell Pharaoh,' what's that got to do with me?

Let's see.

The 'said' implies God speaks. Really? When was the last time I heard God's rich baritone Freeman voice boom from above, "Oh my child, Vivian, do the laundry, and do such an' such?"

Yeah, right.

Do I think God speaks to anyone? The crack of thunder, streak of lightning God?

Not likely. But...

Why did I open the Bible in the first place?

What did I expect?

The Bible isn't a magic eight ball, yet haven't I been calling on God all night to tell me something, anything? Like... How can I expect something and disbelieve something at the same time?

I am one huge ball of confusion.

I pause on that, slamming the book shut. In a huff, I start to rationalize.

I'm not a stupid woman!

I know things. I have my degrees and taught thousands of young people. People rely on me. I usually give other people advice about everything under the sun. So, what would I say to someone who is feeling like I am right now? Someone who on the outside seems to be fine, but inside is... struggling?

Well, maybe I'd tell them to reflect, get counselling, exercise, slow down, not take themselves so seriously, things will look better in time, take it a step at a time, and any other cliché I could cook up at the moment.

I'd let them know it would be alright.

I stop writing and take a deep breath.
"Viv, it's going to be alright," I say, loud enough not to stir Qu.
Do I feel better? I pause. No. Man, my advice sucks. Why do people come to me when I know as much as a bubble gum wrapper?
"Viv?"
I jump and wipe a bead of sweat from my forehead, self-consciously.
"Yeah, love."
He encircles my waist, "Why's the light on?"
"I felt like reading."
"Hmm."
"Does it bother you? I can go downstairs."
"No, no," he draws me closer, "it's alright." He snores.
I shouldn't be jealous of him, but how the hell does he just fall asleep at a drop of a pin like that? It's mocking. Mid-sentence and poof! He's gone! Ahh! Where was I?
Right. I start chewing my pen again, searching for answers when Dad, in his garden, comes into focus.

Growing up, I admired my dad so much. He always had my back. I loved that he was a believer and lived his beliefs. Unlike Ma though, he didn't speak much about anything. For every fifty words my mom used, he may have snuck in two. He would sooner go to the den and pick up his Bible than duke it out with Ma, me or whatever.

I have no idea what he was reading, specifically. I felt that was none of my business at the time. Dad worked two jobs, so as a child when he went into that room, I was to leave him alone. That was his time so he mustn't be disturbed. That was the unwritten rule I created for myself.

I love my dad so much. Even when he's irritating, like he was yesterday, I could never fall out of love with him.

I wish I knew what he was reading. Maybe I'll ask him.

According to my dad, God is the "ultimate, perfect Father." Coming from a blended family and not knowing his biological father, I wonder if that meant something deeper for him. Like he belonged to someone bigger than Ma, me, and his work. Someone who protected him and had his back like a father should.

~~But even if~~

~~There's no reason~~

What do you do when you want to know something? You take action. You study. You find a role model and follow their example. I know my dad is wise. Who better to follow than my dad? He has the very qualities I wish I'd inherited. This quiet dignity. Even though he's more upbeat now that he's retired, there's still this humble assuredness about him that I've always admired.

I should tell him.

I rest the pen. Absentmindedly, I flip through the pages again. Hugging the Word to my breast, I lay back on the pillow, relieved. Qu snuggles me even tighter in his sleep as if to affirm all will be alright.

"Viv," I feel someone gently nudge me in my dreams. I roll onto my side.

"Viv!" *The voice means business.*

"Yes?" I answer the phantom voice.

"It's time to get up."

Oh, not so phantom anymore. I now recognize Qu's voice.

"Ten more minutes."

"You sure?"

Why does he have to question me? I crack open one eye and spy the blurry clock. *What day is it today? What do I need to do today anyway? Nothing seems more important than this bed right now. I burrow in deeper.*

"Fifteen more minutes," I decide.

"Why are you clutchin' the Bible?"

Am I? "I was reading last night."

"You want me to put it away for you?"

Clutching it to my bosom seems strangely comforting.

"No, it's alright. I'll put it down in a sec."

"Sure?" he says, stroking my hip.

"I'm trying to sleep and yes, I'm sure."

Silence.

"Ok."

I feel him shift and the covers bunch my back. *I'm not opening my eyes.*

I have no idea what I'm doing today. I know I have that to-do list somewhere, but honestly; I need to rethink it. I'm tired of doing and doing and getting nowhere. If only staying in bed all day was a valid to-do. Just lie here. Reflect, dream, sleep in one continuous never-ending cycle.

Wait... My eyes bolt open.

That kind of sounds like death.

I jerk up into a seated position. No! I'm being silly. Of course, I need to be on purpose. Of course, I have so much to do before I return to work in two days. Of course, I have to be responsible.

I squint at the clock. The red indicates 6:43 a.m.

"Really, Qu?" I sigh to myself.

I could afford fifteen more minutes of languish time.

I drop back onto my pillow with a grin. I rest the Bible on the side table and stare at it.

What was I thinking before I fell asleep? I close my eyes and let out a huge yawn. *No idea. Let's see. Hmm... Right! I was going to ask Dad what passages he studied when I was growing up. Knowing him, he may say all of them just to annoy me. Should I stop by today? Can you imagine the look on his face to see me twice in two days, back-to-back? Usually, it takes me a month to visit them twice. I guess I could call instead.*

I pause. Another yawn escapes me.

Nah, it's not the same. I'm just going to show up. Maybe the kids would like to come with me. They haven't seen their grandparents in such a long time. Yeah, I'll ask them... in a few minutes. I smile and drift past my thoughts into rest.

"Finally," Faith snorts as she stirs her herbal tea.

I tell this girl, don't add sugar to her tea, but no... the exasperation seeps through my pupils. She backs off.

"You good?" Qu kisses my forehead before raising my chin to search my eyes.

"For heaven's sake people, I slept in. I wasn't in a coma."

"Same thing," Justin says matter-of-factly. "You never sleep in."

Why bother answering. I scratch my side, wondering what I should eat.

"I just made some toast and scrambled eggs for the kids. Little onions, pepper, tomato. You want some?"

That sounds so good! "No, toast is fine. Thanks."

Justin shifts over and pulls out a chair for me with his free hand. I plop onto it, unceremoniously releasing my umpteenth yawn.

"Mom, I'm going to the mall after with Julie. Can I have twenty bucks?"

"I was thinking instead we could all visit Grandma and Grandpa today."

"We who?"

Sometimes this child... "We all, y'all," I gesture. "Justin and... Qu, did you want to come with us?"

"Why do we have to go, but Dad gets a choice?"

"You make it sound like I'm forcing you to get a root canal. Faith, they are your grandparents."

"So? I have plans!"

"The mall! Really, Faith? The mall isn't going anywhere."

"Neither are Grandma and Grandpa," she snorts.

"Look Mom, sure. I'll go with you. Faith can go shop till she drops, whatever," Justin takes another bite as he absentmindedly flips pages.

"Great! Now Justin will go, and they will think that I don't care! Ah! I hate this!" She stomps out of the room like only a drama queen can. *Where does she get that from?*

I stare at Qu not trusting myself to talk. He shakes his head and continues to flip the eggs.

"Didn't you just see your parents yesterday?" Qu says over his shoulder.

"Yaa, but I just feel like seeing them again. I have some things I wanna ask my dad."

"Hmm," he lays a plate of toast, eggs and all the fixings before me. I smile.

"I said only toast."

"Because you knew it was easier and you didn't want me to bother."

My heart smiles. "Thank you," I kiss his cheek.

"You guys need a room?"

"Oh, I'm sorry, my little boy feels left out?" I grab his squirmy face and plant a big juicy one on him.

"Ah, Mom, gross!" Justin jerks up wiping his cheek. "Just let me know when you're ready to go." He shoves the magazine under his arm and retreats out of the room.

I spend too much time watching the backs of my children leaving.

"So, why again today?"

"As I said... just want to see my dad again is all," I sigh, placing the egg between my toast. "You coming?"

"Nah, there's a few things I want to get done around here," he points his chin towards the front yard.

"Yeah, the grass is getting long," I chew.

"Hmm."

"What about your parents, Qu? When was the last time you spoke to them?"

An uncomfortable silence falls on us. His eyes never leave his plate.

"It's been a while, but I'm sure they're alright. What else are you doing today?"

He thinks he's slick throwing it back in my court. Whatever.

"I have no idea," I admit.

His fork drops. "Are you sure you're alright? Since when don't you have a long list of things to do?"

Am I that predictable? Wow. Try not to be defensive, Viv. I clear my throat. "It's my last weekend before I have to return to work, and I have a lot on my mind. I just want to stay close to home and take it easy," I try feigning a breezy smile. "No worries, I'll whip out my list on Monday."

"Nah," he rises and gives me another kiss on my forehead. "I was just surprised is all."

I rest my eyes on him. *What is it about men, Qu in particular? The older they get, the hotter they get! All muscular forearms... soft lips... slight grey at temples... Keep chewing girl. Damn, I can't help it.*

"Oh, so you just can't keep your lips off me, can you?" I teasingly wink at him as I tear my sandwich in half. "Don't start something you can't fini—"

"Oh, yeah," he rushes me, lifting me.

"What are you doing?" Faith stands in the doorway, deer-in-headlights written all over her face.

Bread hits the ground. *What is it about my kids' timing?* I pat Qu's arm and he lowers me back on the seat.

"Nothing, we were just playing," I blush.

"Ew! You guys know you're old, right?"

I stare incredulously at the chair in front of me, shaking my head. *I can't believe this girl.*

"You, on the other hand, are not too old for me to..." I start. *We haven't hit our kids in years, and I don't want to go back.* Before I can finish my sentence, I'm in the air and Qu's tongue is exploring my mouth. Goosebumps.

"Ew!" Faith turns her back. "Look Mom, I just wanted to know if I could go to the mall first," she peeks cautiously. "Ah! Whatever, forget it!" Horrified, she darts from the room.

I barely notice. I'm in my sweet spot.

"You never cease to amaze me," I smile against his lips.

"She was getting on my nerves, and besides," he winks, "any excuse to kiss you is a good excuse."

"Faith!" Ma squeals as she swings the door wide open. "Hon! You'll never believe who's here! Hon!" she yells over her shoulder, warmly stroking our sleeves as we walk inside.

"How wonderful to see you all. Why didn't you call? I would have made you all something. I...," she busies herself fluffing the cushions.

"Oh, Grandma please," Justin reaches for Ma and rocks her in a big bear hug.

"Look at this tall, handsome boy, Viv," she looks over at me, love dripping from her eyes.

"And you, young lady," Ma turns, reaching for Faith.

"Hi Grandma," she drawls, lacklustre. Ma embraces her, vigorously patting her on the back.

How can you give birth to two children with the same man and have them come out so vastly different? I roll my eyes at the irony. I watch as Faith taps lightly on Ma's back. Her face contorts uncomfortably. *What is wrong with this child?*

"Viv, everything alright?" Dad saunters into the room in his undershirt and pyjama bottoms, rubbing his eye.

"Yes, Dad. We're good. Just wanted to see you again, is all."

"Hon, where's your robe?" Ma asks. Her annoyance is thinly veiled.

"It's hot and it's our house," he pecks her on the cheek and makes his rounds.

"Oh, Dad," I grin as his stubble grazes my cheek.

"Please sit, sit," he motions.

"Can I make you some tea? Love, do we still have those English biscuits?" he asks, already walking towards the kitchen.

"Hmm, look in the cabinet. I can't remember," she smiles looking into Justin's eyes. "And your robe is hanging on the downstairs bathroom door," she shoots over her shoulder for good measure. "Lord, look how tall you've grown."

Justin looks at the carpet shyly. "Yeah, I'm a few inches taller than Dad now."

She nods in agreement. "And you, Miss Faith," she pats her knees. "Look how you have filled out. The boys must be beating down your door!"

"Grandma!" Faith crosses her arms over her chest to Justin's amusement.

"Faith? Boys?" he laughs.

"Shut up!" Faith shoots back.

"Faith," I warn.

"Oh, I meant no harm sweetie," Ma tweaks her chin. "Just commenting on how mature you've grown. Now," she says rising, "I'm going to see if I can help Granddad rustle up some munchies." She strides away.

As soon as I think she's out of earshot, I glare at the kids, "What is wrong with the two of you?"

"He started it!" Faith protests.

"Are you serious?" Justin scoffs.

"Keep it together, do you hear me? Or..." I threaten.

"How you want your tea, Viv?" Ma yells.

"Black is fine, Ma," I yell back sweetly.

I sink back into the couch and rub my eyes. *Breathe. What am I stressing out about? The kids are the kids.* I let my hand drop to my lap. *Feels good to just sit here.*

"Hmm," I exhale.

"Everything alright, Dear?" Ma gently taps my knee.

"Yes, Ma. Everything is fine," I keep my eyes closed and rest my arms stiffly by my sides. "Your couch is so comfortable."

"This couch is so old!" she sighs, turning her attention to the kids. "So, what you kids up to lately?"

I could hear them shuffling. My eyes spring open. Knowing my mouth was going to follow, I quickly squeeze my eyelids shut again. *I can't keep talking for them. They have to learn to swim and rescue themselves.*

"Nothing much, you know," Justin spits out awkwardly.

"I don't believe that!" She persists, "What's going on in school?"

"Everything's good. Calculus is a challenge, but I'm holding my own in the other subjects I guess," he offers.

I can hear the teacups clinking.

"What about you, Faith? Anything interesting?"

"No, not really."

What am I going to do with this girl?

"Why don't you tell Grandma about the filmmaking," I prompt behind closed lids.

"Oh, that's new, Grandma. Not much to tell yet," I can hear the bite in her voice directed at me. *I give up. Let her drown.*

"Well, I got some news," Ma announces. "Your Grandpa bought me a laptop!"

"A what?" we all exclaim incredulously.

She chuckles, "Yes, you know those machines that are several steps above a typewriter?"

"A what?" Faith and Justin stare at her even more confused.

I don't know what got into me. I couldn't help but burst into laughter. *This two-second conversation has aged me. Hold it together, girl.* I take a sip to calm myself.

"That's great, Ma. What project are you going to work on?"

"Right now, the only project at hand is to figure out how to turn it on!" she continues to giggle. "Granddad thought it would be good to video call my sisters back home. I can't wait to see them come summer but, in the meantime..."

"Come on Grandma," Justin jumps up and swats his sister. "Show us where this thing is an' Faith and I will hook you up."

"Good! It's in the next room," she says clumsily, resting her porcelain. I carefully take my napkin and sop up her spill.

"Where's everyone rushing off to?" Dad asks. He rests a tray of treats on the coffee table in front of me. Everything looks delicious and way too rich for my blood. I grab a chocolate éclair anyway.

"Nowhere, Daddy, sit," I garble with a full mouth. "They just went to figure out the laptop."

"Now, I told your mother I was going to get around to it," he sighs.

"Yeah, well, the kids heard 'computer' and flew out of here, so it's just as well," I answer as I swallow the last morsel. *Chocolate is love.*

"Well, alright then. They'd probably figure it out before me anyway."

"It was like they were born with consoles glued to their fingers."

He chuckles, "It would seem so, yes."

I never realized how my dad laughs so much like my mother.

I sit forward, wiping my hand in another napkin. "It's all good anyhow. I wanted to talk to you about something."

"Sounds serious," he replies, sipping his tea.

"Nothing earth-shattering."

"Okay, shoot."

"Right," a pregnant pause follows as I search for the words.

"Okay?" he looks at me questioningly.

"Okay," I gulp. *What is my problem anyway?* "It's about your Bible."

"You want my Bible?"

"No, heavens, no." *Heavens, no? Okay Blanche, what's gotten into you? Just say it!*

"Let me start again," I cover his hand with mine. "I love you, Dad."

"I love you too, Dear," he says hesitantly. "Is there something wrong?"

"No, not at all. I've just been thinking about a lot of stuff which is part of the reason I came back to see you again."

"Viv, just tell me. You're worrying me now."

"Oh, sorry, I don't mean to. I just don't know how to begin."

"Begin at the beginning."

I smile and look at our hands. "In the beginning was you, Dad."

"Hmm?"

"You always took care of us. You were always steady and quiet. It's only recently you've become this take-no-prisoners voice in my head."

Laughter rocks him. "Take no prisoners," he repeats.

"Yes! The dad I remember was steady. I never heard you raise your voice or get angry. It's like that was Ma's firecracker role. You were easygoing. The more Ma would fly off, you would set yourself in that chair," I motioned with my chin, "and just pour over the Word."

"I still do. The Word is life."

"You always say that. What does that even mean?"

"Well, it means it's my solace, my guide. God speaks to me through His promises, the more I believe and stay in the Word," he sits back in his chair and lets his head rest. He doesn't say anything more. The silence is deafening.

"That's it?" I ask. "You read. God talks. You're comforted?"

"I'm not sure I understand what you're asking?"

"Daddy," I plead weakly. *How can he only give me two sentences and think that's enough?*

He waits.

"You make it sound so simple, but it's not! If it were, then Ma and I would be steady and calm as the breeze like you are, well, most of the time."

He can't help but laugh at me again. "It is that simple."

"I don't believe you," I sulk.

"Listen," he raises his index finger and crosses to the bookcase. He pats the volume as he returns to his recliner. "I'll show you how easy it is."

"That's not your Bible," I comment referring to the newer, crisper, burgundy-covered book.

"Oh, you mean Old Faithful?" he motions to the side table. "The pages have been so heavy laden with highlighter and pen, the paper was disintegrating," he smiled. "I got this one a few years back. Sometimes Pastor reads from the Amplified, so I got me one."

"I thought you'd never abandon Old Faithful," I sigh. *My dad still finds ways to surprise me.*

"Me? Abandon? Never! I just enjoy them both!" He leafs through the pages and stops at Psalm 103. He traces each word gently. "Now listen to this," he reads.

"Bless (affectionately, gratefully praise) the Lord, O my soul and forget not one of all His benefits..." he pauses and smiles into my eyes. "What do you think that means?"

I have no clue. I clear my throat.

"Sorry, let me read it again," I gently take the Bible from his hands and mouth the words. "I'm still not sure. Maybe it's saying that God has a lot in store for us if we praise Him?"

I shrug and give him my best, puzzled look. He doesn't buy it.

"Read on, Viv. Maybe it will become clearer."

I look back at the page and float my eyes over the words.

Who forgives [every one of] all your iniquities.

Who heals [each one of] all your diseases.

Who redeems your life from the pit and corruption.

Who beautifies, dignifies, and crowns you with loving kindness and tender mercy.

"Hmm, verses 3 and 4," I exhale as I close the book and hand it back. "Well, it's poetic. Quite beautiful. I can see how the sweet words might be soothing."

He stares at me. *I can't read his expression. I can't tell if he's amused, miffed, or resigned.*

"Sweet?" he repeats, poker face intact.

"I'm sorry, Dad, did I say something wrong?"

He opened to the Psalms again. He stabs the book with his finger. "This isn't a piece of English literature, Viv. That 'sweet' passage was God's promise to you. Think about that."

He meticulously rereads all the verses aloud and pauses before lifting his eyes. This time, I mindfully listen. I try to listen like my dad was talking to me. He closes the Scriptures and waits. I don't know what to say. He takes my hand and tries to explain.

"Knowing God's got me, makes fear and anger seem foolish. Who can truly hurt me? Even if this world tries to kill me, and on some days, I think it is, my spirit is eternal! My Eden, praise God, awaits me." He kisses the back of my hand.

That sounds familiar.

"Nothing in this world can kill you, Dad. You'll outlive us all," I kiss his hand back. *Why are his eyes moist?*

"I just want you to understand."

I lean into his shoulder, "I want to." I speak as if reciting a rote to-do list, "So, study the Word and think of it as God speaking directly to me."

"Yes, Ms. Formulaic," he teases. "The bottom line is that you need to believe God is speaking truth to you. To your spirit."

"Believe," I repeat lifting my head to look into my daddy's eyes. *I love him so much.*

EIGHTEEN

"Mom? Can you drop me by the mall?"

Breathe. "Why?"

"I told Shawna I'd meet her there."

"What? I thought you were going with Julie?"

She snorts, "See. Again! You never listen to me!"

I roll my eyes, "Why do you need to go to the mall?"

"We got to get stuff," Faith says shortly.

"What stuff?"

"I don't know… lipstick, conditioner, notebook."

We got all that and then some in the house. She just met me? I buy everything in bulk and on sale.

"Which is it?"

"Mom!"

"Girl, we got everything at home. Do you even have any money?"

"Right… Can I have twenty?"

I jerk the car to a stop at the light. Seeing my 'whatever' gaze, she crosses her arms and spins her head around.

"You never let me go anywhere."

"That's right. That's why all your clothes are orange and there's a padlock on our door, Princess."

Justin leans forward and hands Faith ten dollars. I see her mouth 'I owe you one' from the corner of my eye.

"I got money. Can I go now?"

"Justin," I sigh. "Why do you keep rescuing this girl?"

"Not rescuing," he shrugs, returning to his book.

"Fine," I resign manoeuvring into the parking lot. "Before the stores close and you get your tail home, you hear me?"

"Yeah, Mom, fine," she hastens to snap off her belt.

I watch her disappear through the revolving doors. I pat the seat beside me. "You want to ride shotgun?"

"Nah, I'm cool," he says indifferently.

"What are you reading?"

"Some book I found in the den by that feminist you're always quoting."

"Melanie?"

"Yeah."

"What do you think?"

"Haven't gotten too far yet," he rustles the pages. "I almost finished the fifth chapter."

"That's enough pages to form an opinion," I press.

"It's not so much that I want to form an opinion."

"What?"

"I'm just readin'."

"Why?"

"Mom! Can I just read?" He quells his anger just below the surface.

I didn't take the hint. "Everyone has an opinion—"

"And then there are some of us who just want to sit, read in silence and keep an open mind," he shoots back. "Drop it already!"

For the rest of the ride, all I can hear is the hum of the car. For some strange reason, my cheeks are wet. I clear my throat as I turn the corner.

"How are your parents?"

"Fine," I say abruptly, taking the stairs two at a time.

I softly close the door behind me and lean against it.

Whoo... I'm sobbing and can't seem to reign it in. What is wrong with me?

I roughly swipe my cheek with the back of my hand.

How many times have I cried this week alone? This is crazy! Keep it together for God's sake.

I peel off my shoes and one after the other, throw them at the wall. I stare at them lying there, forlorn. I deliberately inhale and force the air out. I try it again, this time more deeply.

No more sobbing, Viv. There's nothing to cry about. He told you to stop. You blew him off. He had a right to get angry. Open your ears!

The sobbing intensifies. "Ah! Stop it already!" I roughly chide myself. I lay my hand over my heart and start breathing intentionally again. I let my eyes close as I inhale. Runny salt drips over my lips. *Disgusting.* Looking around, I head toward the tissue box just as Qu peeks in. *How long has he been on the other side of the door?*

"You want to talk about it?"

"Nope."

"Viv, come—"

"I said no, damn it!" I glare at him. He seems unaffected. I dab my face and turn away.

He sighs, "When you're ready, I'm downstairs."

"Hmm." The bite is still in my voice.

"Maybe later we could go for a walk or hit a bookstore."

What is he talking about? "When since you like bookstores?"

My eyes take him in this time. *Look at him loving me. So sad. I'm terrible.* I look away.

"I'll be downstairs if you need me."

Standing alone in the room, I'm not sure what to do with myself. *I am so mean to him. He's just trying. How can I slap him down for trying?*

Wait! Justin got it from me! Slapdown—like mother, like son. Aw!

I fall back on the bed dramatically. *I need to get out of this funk, number one. Number two, I need to apologize to Mr. Sweetness. Now! This thing is draining. I'm tired of feeling like crap! I'm supposed to be better, and ready to deal with all of this. What's the matter with me?*

I keep wiping my face as I stare at the ceiling. *I got to fix this. Why can't I move?* I feel the warm blanket beneath me. I feel the tears run down the slope of my face into my ears. *I need to go, yet I want to stay. Safe.*

"Hi."

"Hi," Qu unfurls the cord with a snap.

"I'm sorry for talking to you like that."

"Kay."

"Kay," I turn to retreat. I can feel him watching my back.

"Are you still interested in taking that walk?"

"Sure," I pause briefly.

"When I finish with the grass I'll come and get you."

I nod, not breaking stride or turning back. *He must think I'm the oddest thing. I wish I could blame this angst on hormones. Then I wouldn't have to explain myself.*

I reach for any book off the shelf to distract myself as I wait. *One thing we never have a shortage of is books. From school sales, garage sales, online, and gifts they find their way here, filling our shelves, and almost every corner of our house. Faith finds physical books so nineteenth century. Every time she sees me enjoying one, she grunts, "You know, Mom, you*

could have thousands of books on the e-reader we bought you years ago." *She doesn't understand that I like the feel of a book. I like to leaf through a book and turn down the corners. I get a rush when a word or phrase jumps off the page and I can take my pen and underline it. As they occur, I can write insights and memories in the margins in my handwriting, not typed in standard fonts. I feel like I'm at work with my e-reader. It's efficient and functional, but does everything have to be efficient and functional? Books are personal. They have personality. Am I being stubborn?* I sigh and tuck my feet under my thighs. *Maybe I am. Right now, though, I don't want to think. Let someone else think for me. Take it away, author!* I adjust my glasses that I conveniently attached to my head earlier. I let the words wash over me.

"Viv?" I feel someone gently tap my shoulder.

"Hmm," I open my eyes with a start. "We have to stop meeting like this. I can't believe I dozed off."

"It's understandable since you didn't get very much sleep last night."

"I'm sorry for my outburst earl—"

He rests a hand on my shoulder. "Seriously Viv, you already apologized, and I already forgot about it," he offers me his hand. "I made us a few sandwiches and desserts. I thought we could walk to the park and eat it there."

"Love the idea!"

"Yeah, well, why not, right?" he blushes. "We aren't centenarians, who can't walk or remember to date once in a while."

"Centenarians? Date? Are you insinuating...?"

"Stop right there," he squeezes my hand. "We don't have to overthink this, label this or analyze. We are just going for a walk. With food. Period."

I nod and release his hand. "I'm going to splash some water on my face. I'll meet you out front." I turn to go, but on impulse, turn back. "Thank you, Qu," I kiss his cheek and run upstairs.

I've always loved this neighbourhood. I knew I was home the first time we viewed the house, and I saw all these huge, magnificent trees surrounding it. These trees line every street within a five-mile radius. This place is so lush and green. Alive. Quiet. No matter what noise is in my head, outside my door is rustling leaves and calmness. I take a deep breath in.

"Beautiful," I exhale.

"Yeah, it is," he agrees, looking at me.

Our strides fall in sync. I just realize Qu's holding my hand.

"Qu, how long have we been on this street?"

"I don't know... years."

"Years," I repeat softly.

"If you could live anywhere, where would you live?"

I eye him quizzically, shrugging my shoulders, "I don't know. Never thought about it."

"Not true! When we were dating, you'd always talk about the different places you wanted to live."

"Well, if you already know, refresh my memory."

"That's not the point. That was then, this is now. I want to know where your mind is now."

I sigh, "Fine, the beach."

"What beach?"

"Qu."

"No, I'm curious. What beach?"

"I don't know what beach."

He inhales sharply and waits.

I spot a bench. Releasing his hand, I head for it. Gently he sits close to me and rests his hand on my knee. He lightly massages it.

"Sometimes I feel like you're pushing me away."

I swallow sharply. "Qu, I am *not* pushing you away." Again, that edge is in my throat. I take another swallow. "Earlier, I was upset because Justin was angry that I was pushing him to talk and, and he lashed out at me. I got all surprised and hurt..." I paused at the irony.

I look at Qu stealthily and realize the irony isn't lost on him either. We both laugh.

"Anyway, If I was pushing you away, would I have agreed to come out with you now?"

"Hmm... fine. What beach?"

"Man, you are like a dog with a bone."

"Well?"

I cross my leg as I turn to face him. "A beach, Qu. That's it! Every great memory I have, every peaceful, calming experience I've had, somehow involves water. Growing up, we always lived near water. I can sit and stare for hours and not get bored. I can fall asleep to waves and feel safe. We shared some amazing kisses on the beach," I playfully nuzzle his neck. "We good now?"

"No."

Okay, now he just wants to fight! What's gotten into him?

"I know you love the beach. I'd have to be an idiot to be with you all these decades and not know you love the water."

"Then I don't understand."

"You're unhappy, Viv."

"What?"

"I know you are unhappy."

Don't cry, Viv. Hear where he's going with this.

"You are angry all the time. You cry for what seems like the smallest reasons."

"Well, that's kind of harsh."

"I'm not trying to be harsh, Viv. I'm trying to be real. I'm trying to be here for you."

I squirm.

"Stop," he holds my knee tighter. "I'm trying to fix whatever is broken."

My hand lands on his arm as I will my tears to stay. "Stop," I breathe.

"No. I need to get this out. If you'd be happier somewhere else, then let's move!"

"It's not about the house or the location. I love our home."

"But if we could move near a beach—"

"I'd still be living in this mind, this body," I pinch my thigh.

Playfully, Qu air-bites at my forehead and thigh.

"I love this mind and this body," his voice is hoarse.

I lift my hands to gently push him away, "I'm sorry, Qu. I'm sorry if I've made you feel—"

"You don't have to apologize."

"Qu," I say as caressingly as possible. "Maybe I need more time away."

"No!"

"I mean just until—"

"No," he stares at me.

"Qu, it may take me some time to—"

"No. Whatever it is, we'll work it out together."

"Qu."

"We'll fix it."

"Qu, I don't even know what *it* is."

With an exhalation, he leans back on the bench. "We'll fix it together."

I link his arm and rest my head on his shoulder. "Sometimes, space and quiet to work things out are good."

"You've had your space. I don't want any more space. Space makes me crazy."

I sigh. *I need to let this drop. Every time I open my mouth, I'm hurting him. And he tries. Then he tries again. I need to let this go.*

I reach around him and pull out a tuna sandwich. Still resting on him, I unwrap it and hold it up to his mouth. Without his eyes leaving mine, he takes a slow bite. *This man makes my heart smile.*

"Fine, Qu. Wherever you live is where I want to be."

NINETEEN

"Viv!"

"Yeah," I rub the nugget out of the corner of my eye. Blearily, I peer to see what time it is. *Is that a three or an eight?*

"Viv, I need you to listen."

"I'm listening, Ma," I reply in groggy defiance.

"Who is it?" Qu nuzzles closer, whispering in my other ear.

Who-is-it repeats, "Viv!"

My eyes shoot open.

"Ma!"

"You need to get dressed and get down here."

I sit bolt upright.

"I'm at St. Christopher's hospital on the third floor."

"St. Christopher's," I repeat, flinging off the covers, feeling for my slippers.

"Hurry, it's—"

"Please, don't tell me yet," I cry. *Where is that shoe!* "There's only so much I can process," I stumble to the door reaching for the knob.

"Hurry, I need you," she sobs.

"Okay," I click off the phone and throw it back on the bed, missing Qu's head by a hair.

"I have to go," I say robotically over my shoulder.

"Go where? It's three," he hesitates, "eighteen in the morning!"

I splash cold water on my face, though I don't need it. The call and chill in the house are sobering enough. "Something's happened and I have to get to St. Chris."

I hear quick shuffling and jangling.

"Okay, I'll let the kids know we're out."

"No, you stay."

"Get dressed," he commands, zipping his pants. He is already down the hall.

Following orders is easier than thinking at this point. Mechanically, I head back to the bedroom and pull on my black yoga pants. *St. Chris'. That's where I had Faith. Where I had Faith.*

"Hello, I'm here to see..." I stop, not sure who to ask for or where.

How can she just tell me the third floor? It seems like there are so many departments on the third floor—Psychiatry, Critical Care—I thought I saw a sign for Radiology.

"Has a patient by the name of Grant been admitted in the last hour or so?" I hear Qu inquire.

I pull out my cell from my pocket. It's slippery in my hand. My eyes haven't adjusted to the fluorescents. Qu's leading me by the elbow, guiding me along a hallway. *Why question him? I'm still trying to make sense of the squiggles on the screen.*

"Viv! Qu!" My mom thrusts herself around me. Feeling strange in my skin, I pat her gently on the back. She grabs my arms hard before embracing Qu.

"Thanks for coming."

"What do you mean, Ma? You call at three in the morning; of course, we are going to come."

"Well, I—?"

"What happened, Ma?" Qu asks calmly, gripping my hand. His other arm still encircles my mom.

"He just stopped."

I wait for her to continue. She's visibly shaking. The words stick in her throat. Qu looks gravely at me. I don't know what to make of anything. Qu steers us towards a set of chairs in the corner. I wait standing. *What does she mean he stopped?*

"We were watching an old movie. Some romantic thing I was pretty much talking through. Then we headed upstairs, and he was slower than usual. He sat on the bed. I was talking about..." she rubs her forehead. "What was I even talking about?"

I want to scream. "Ma," I say firmly.

She looks up, her face is wet. Her tears and words flow and drip off her chin.

"I asked him something," the tears avalanche.

I fish out a tissue and put it in her hand. She barely notices.

"At first I didn't hear him answer, so I was about to scold him, then this mumble," she gestures with the tissue clenched in her hand. "This mumble. I came around his side of the bed. He looked at me, glazed. Viv, he was so scared," she sobs. "And he stopped."

"He—"

"Mrs. Grant?"

"Yes, that's me," Ma feverishly wipes her face and steps forward.

I watch a-ways off as the white coat closes the gap between my mother and Qu. The coat shakes her hand, before running down the situation. All my faculties can grasp are crumbs.

Stroke.

Unconscious.

Stable.

Call.

Intensive.

He walks away and my eyes are mesmerized by his back. I need to sit.

"Viv?"

"Hmm..."

"I asked if you would like something to drink? I'm going to get Ma some tea."

"No," there's haze in my voice. *I don't recognize the sound of my voice.*

He rests his hand on my arm. Instinctively, my hand covers his.

"I'll be back, alright?"

He looks so concerned. I nod, allowing him to sip away.

I look up at my mother, a set of chairs away, consoling herself. *I hope Qu comes back soon. She looks like she can use a hug, and no one knows comfort like Qu, the human teddy bear. 'Hurry back, Qu,' I yell in my mind, hoping to reach him telepathically. She keeps sobbing. Qu. Oh, dear God, did the coat say he was dead? He can't be dead. He can't be sick for long. He's Dad. Old Reliable. The you've-got-a-friend-in-Jesus, dude. It's unnerving how much she's sobbing.*

"Stop crying, Ma," I tell her dryly.

"I, I, I can, can't help—"

"Ma, please."

She blows her nose and rests her forehead in her hands. Her shoulders are shaking. "He's, he's—"

"He's going to be fine, Ma," I say more to reassure myself. *Where's Qu? Seems like an eternity.*

"Oh, Malachi. Thank you, but..."

He holds the cup firmly in her hands. "You haven't eaten. Please, sip this tea in the meantime."

She nods and looks at the paper container in her hands. She tightly grips it attempting to stop shaking. I'm in awe watching them through the glass. *Qu has such a way with him. It's not enough he's gorgeous, he has to be sweet, too? I want to crawl under a rock.*

"Viv!"

"What?!"

"What happened when I was gone? What did they say? What's next?"

"Nothing."

"Nothing?"

"Nothing," I cross my arms resolutely leaning against the back of the chair. *I can't look at him.*

"Fine. Where's his doctor?"

"Dunno."

Qu looks at me in silence before rising and heading towards the nurse's station. I can't stop myself.

"Qu, just go home and make sure the kids—"

"I'm staying," he shoots back, before gesturing for the scrub's attention.

Why? I shake my head, glancing at my mom. *I can't look at her either. Ah! I'm so irritated! I'm so irritating! I tell Qu to leave when I want him to wrap himself around me and never... let me go. Why can't I be stronger? I'm a mental case... A, a freakin'...*

"They said they'd let us know as soon as he's stable," he rubs my arm.

"Filmore."

"What?" he looks at me quizzically.

"The doctor's name is Filmore. Didn't you ask me the doctor's name?"

"No, I didn't," Qu looks me in the eyes, troubled. He holds me tight. He read my mind.

"He stopped."

I stop wringing my hands, glancing up at my mother.

"He just stopped."

"It's alright," I pretend.

"No Viv, you had to be there. I've never seen him look at me that way before," she pauses. "You ever seen those wooden clown toys? The jack-in-the-boxes? The kind with the brightly coloured painted-on eyes?"

"Oh, Ma," I breathe.

"No, Ma, go on," Qu squeezes my hand, nodding at her.

"The clown jumps up with all this energy, shakes and jerks, and the kids laugh because he's got this grin and, in the shock—the pop—it's all so entertaining," she chuckles softly. "But the bobbing slows and the laughter fades as the toy with its painted eyes stops moving." Ma inhales sharply, "Your dad's eyes were like that old toy with its faded paint. At first, I could see his pupils jumping, but then I lost him. He wasn't Si."

Qu crosses over and holds her. "I'm so sorry, Ma."

She grips his sleeves and sobs.

Any other time hearing my mom compare my dad to a jack-in-the-box would leave me in stitches. Now, all I feel is sick. The whole idea is absurd, right? Not just the analogy, but the idea of my dad just stopping. The idea of my dad, the strongest person I know, not being himself. I can't hear that right now. My dad is. Period.

Is...

I jerk up off the seat. "Look, I'm just going to check in on the kids. I'll be right back."

"Viv!"

My purse slips, nearly spilling the entire contents on the floor. I catch it just in time as I get ready to run.

I can't be here. I shake my head. *I can't be here.*

I'm speed walking, but I have no idea where I'm going.

Straight.

Away.

That's all I know.

Maybe if I turn here, I'll find some stairs? Why do they build these hospitals like mazes? Hospitals and airports. Worse than hay mazes! At least those are built for a fun escape. This place is neither fun nor an escape.

Damn! I would pay someone right now to parachute me out of this place! Just eject me out of this blurry red, blue, orange-lined crazy-ass maze! Where the hell am I?!

"Viv!"

Stop yelling after me, damn it. I swipe at my face. *I can't breathe this toxic, heavy, sanitized...*

I trip.

"Viv," he catches my arm, out of breath.

"Damn, Qu."

"Sit."

"I don't want to sit, I have to..."

His grip is tight on me.

Can't breathe. Sobbing steals my air.

"Now!" He drags me to another waiting area.

I sit at the edge of the stiff-backed chair trying to catch my breath.

"Give me the car keys," he instructs.

I toss the bag at him. "Take it." *I have no idea where the keys are. Wouldn't know where to begin.*

"Don't move."

I don't even acknowledge him. Sobs are wracking my body from down deep. *I didn't even know I had anything left to cry. My soul, my flesh, feels dry. I thought all the water was gone. At the very least I thought I had a control switch.*

I wrap my fingers around the hard, cold plastic cup he places in my hands. My grip fails, sending the water flying. Qu wraps his fingers around mine to steady the tremors. Everything is blurry. *Why is he keeping me here?*

"Viv, why do you always choose flight?"

"Not now Qu," I sniff. "I don't even know what you are talking about."

"You, Viv, we are talking about you."

I sit back again. It's weirdly comforting to feel the hard plastic against my back.

"I love you."

"Please."

"I love you, Viv," he draws out every syllable. "I love your family. I love our family. I love us," he pauses, "but I'm done."

I'm cold.

"You have to stop running away from us."

Quakes run through me, pricking bumps down my arms, and leaching sensations from my fingers.

"I wasn't—"

"Look at me."

I can't. Everything is swimming. He takes a nearby tissue and dabs my eyes.

"Look at me," he demands again, drawing out the words slowly. *I'm ashamed.* He tilts my chin up gently.

"We are done running. Flight is no longer an option."

I try to drop my chin. His fingers are fixed.

"No. More. Flight."

"I—"

"We're done," he stands and offers his hand. Sheepishly, I accept. Feet solid on the ground, I attempt an inhale.

"Your mother's alone. Let's go." Without another word, I follow. We retrace our steps one sure foot after the other.

"Ah, you're back," Ma creakily attempts to rise.

"Please, Ma," Qu encourages her to take her seat again with a wave of a hand. I can't lift my eyes.

Qu leads me to a chair. I obey.

The room falls hush. I'm ever aware of my mother's breathing. It's low and despair deep. Just sitting there helplessly. I can't bear to look at her. Qu lets go of my hand and in the same motion, pulls out his cell phone. Tapping away as he leans over, elbows balancing on his thighs. He clicks off, gives me a peck on the cheek and rises to leave.

"I'll be right back," he breathes on my cheek. He squeezes Ma's hand and is gone.

He left me alone! Here!

My head is throbbing with all the internal screaming. *Pull yourself together.* I inhale deeply and intentionally. *She needs me.*

I get up to sit next to her. I take my hand and as gently as I can muster, pull her head onto my shoulder. *Flight is not an option. Flight is not an option. This is where I need to be.*

Every time I close my eyes, I'm back at the hospital looking at my father in his bed. He looks small under the covers. Like his frame has shrunk, leaving only the bone with a thin layer of skin blanket covering it. My mother didn't lie about his eyes, though I wish she had. His eyes are the most unsettling. Coated, darting, and then they'd stop when they rested on me, and he realized he couldn't reach me. At first, he'd moan deep and slow, but his words were lost in translation. Locked away from me. His frustration would drive his head back further into his pillow. Heavy, muted silence. I keep waking up upset.

I have to remember this will pass. Dad will make it. For now, though, I just want to watch these fools kiss in this ridiculous melodrama.

I'd rather be anywhere than in my mind. Closing my eyes is too painful.

"Viv."

"Yes."

"Are you awake?"

"No."

"I made some—"

"Not hungry... thanks," I click the replay button.

"Calls, Viv. I called Etienne and told him what happened. He sends his condolences and says that he will extend your leave. You just need to call him in the next few days and let him know when you think you'll be back."

"Thanks."

I continue gazing at the screen. *Romance and laughter. Isn't that all the world needs? Just two people in love who kiss over and over, passionate, and intense, forever and a day, the more one presses this little circle called rewind. I never want to leave this bed. I love that it's warm. I love that it's safe. Just me and these beautiful kissing fools.*

"Viv."

"Yes."

Qu kneels on the carpet and levels his head with mine. Distracting me. *Now he's crossed the line.*

"Viv."

"Qu," I whine, "get out of the way," I try to move him aside. *Damn, he's built. How irritating.*

"Viv."

"What!"

"You haven't left this room since we got home yesterday."

"I don't want to. Now can I please watch my show?"

"Viv, you keep watching the same scene over and over."

I give Qu my meanest look which turns out to be my most pathetic look. *Aaagh! Damn, he's so handsome even when he's bugging the crap out of me.* I pause the screen and cover my head. *I can't deal with him right now.*

"What's your point?"

"Talk to me."

"No," I retort muffled from deep under the covers.

"Viv."

"Go aaawwwwaaaayyyy!"

"No."

"NOW!"

"I love you."

"Don't be an idiot!"

"I'm not."

"Faith's calling you," I lie.

"Your Ma needs us."

"Stop it!" *He thinks that I don't know that?*

"I miss him too."

"Stop talking—just GO!" I seethe, through clenched teeth.

"No flight option, remember?"

"Now!"

He kiss-pecks me through the blanket. I don't know whether to laugh or cry.

"I love you."

"I-di-o-toe."

"I love you," he plants another kiss.

"You are smothering me," I weakly complain.

"Then come up for air."

"Hell. No. Bye."

He swoops in like the mischievous boy he is and grabs my waist before I can dive out the other end.

"I love you."

"This is not the time."

"OK, you stink."

"That's better."

"Let me bathe you."

"Do I look like a toddler?"

"We need to go and help your mother. She has so many appointments—"

"Not now."

"Viv, I only have so much lieu time."

"Qu! I can't leave this bed! I just... I just..." *I can't speak. Like Dad, I can't find the words.*

"OK, OK," he coos, wiping my tears with the back of his fingers. He takes a deep breath. "What you watching?"

I swallow, "Drivel."

"Hmm..." He rearranges the covers and spoons me as he clicks play. The screen comes alive with lovers' thrusting tongues, heavily grinding, and wildly panting. *Well, this is embarassin'.* He twists his head slowly to the side as he watches the action on the screen. I switch it off and shove the laptop under my pillow.

"Fine. Bathe me."

TWENTY

Interruption of arterial blood to the brain... Arterial, arterial...

My mind grasps.

Blood that carries oxygen... okay, damages brain tissues. Damage to brain cells leads to short or long-term disability... dis-ab-il-it-y...

My eyes linger on the word unseeingly. I grip the pages in my lap.

Dis-a-bil-ity, lacking, loss of ability. Speech, thinking process, mood.

"Can't believe it cost me the same money to celebrate my birthday as it did for that Brujo fundraising we all had to attend last week!" The red-faced man spat into the bleached air. I glare at his arrogance hovering under the 'Quiet Zone' sign. Obliviously, he continues to run his mouth. He is unfazed as he quickly paces while tapping his earpiece. I sigh as I look at the pages in my hand.

Buildup of plaque, strain on heart... Pla-que? I thought that was only on teeth. Jaundice coating. Bacteria. Bursting blood vessels... stress...

"I mean, come on?!"

I shift away from the red-faced man using my back as a cement wall. *Everything seems so pointless. Who cares about frivolous parties, or any function for that matter that gives people occasion to fake good times and goodwill? What is the point of doing anything that isn't tied to the real? The now. No more 'real' and 'now' than sitting here trying to decipher what happened to my dad. No one can tell you. Nobody can warn you. Not even a whisper can alert you to what's to come. I can't believe I am here.* I continue to read the printouts.

"Yeah, yeah, you're right... the booze was top-notch..."

My cement wall isn't high enough.

People of African descent and Asians are considered high-risk groups. We are high risk... risk... exposed to danger... harm... loss... risk...

"Ms. Moji?" A woman appears in front of me. "Ms. Moji?"

"Yes, that's me."

"Hi, I'm Nancy, one of your father's nurses. Your mother is asking for you."

"Thank you," I nod.

Nancy has a pleasant round, almost blank face, which contrasts her chosen uniform. I remember a time when all nurses had to wear the same colour scrubs, usually in some nondescript pastel. Now it seems they can wear whatever scrubs they want. Nancy is dressed in a deep purple ensemble with cartoon characters adorning her ugly, plastic, old lady shoes with the thick white heels. Where did she even find those? Who goes out of their way to buy ugly?

"Ms. Moji?"

She is still standing there. *Why does she look so concerned? Damn! Have I been staring at her shoes this whole time?*

"Yes... Nancy... right. I'll go," I awkwardly rise to follow her down the hall. I catch Mr. Red Face staring at me from the corner of my eye. I shoot him a mind-your-business glare as I pick up my pace. Moving through the hallway, my mind goes back to the pages.

Disability, lack, speech, thinking abilities, mood... What about mood? Will he be angry? Depressed? Mood can imply anything except maybe indifference, right? Maybe indifference? I can't imagine Dad indifferent. What if angry, depressed, sad...? What if I can't get him back? What if his mood becomes who he is from now on? What does that mean? Mood... strain on heart...

"Hi, Ma."

"Viv, come, come, come," she says softly reaching for me with both hands.

Viv, get it together! Don't you dare cry in front of Ma! She needs you. Stay strong. Be tough. I warn myself as I uneasily walk into her embrace.

"How you doin', chile?"

I smile despite myself. I am several decades old and have two young people who I consider my children. Yet here I am. Parenting my parents who still see me as a child. Perception is a bitch.

"I should be asking you that," I reply resting my head on her shoulder with a sigh. *I notice that I sigh a lot, forcing myself to relax instead of relaxing. I've got to cut that out. Remember, Ma needs me.* I jerk my head up abruptly.

"What did the doctor say about Dad?"

"Hmm, nothing."

That's strange. "They didn't tell you anything about his condition or what to expect?" I press.

"Honestly, Dear, I don't remember what the doctor said. I was just glad to see your father. When he was talking... my eyes were only on Dad's face," she smiles at me and pats my arm. "I'm sure he'll be fine."

She starts humming and rocking to a song I don't recognize. The motions give her comfort. Rubbing my arm. Humming. Rocking. Waiting for another sign from Dad that he is with her. I unconsciously find myself rocking with her. *I could use some comfort too.*

"What the doctor say?" I feel Qu's face brush my own before he bends to give Ma a peck on the cheek too.

"Hi. Nothing, I think. If he said anything to Ma before I arrived, I don't know. We've just been here waiting."

"When did you arrive?"

I look at Ma, puzzled. "We never left, did we?" We keep rocking and patting each other's arms. Gazing at each other.

"Viv", Qu clears his throat. "Did you eat?"

"Not hungry. How about you, Ma?"

Qu doesn't wait for an answer. He kisses me on the lips and hurriedly leaves the room. *What's the urgency? We aren't going anywhere.* I look at Ma and smile as we continue to sway back and forth.

Qu returns with sandwiches, salads, and steaming cups of coffee in tow.

"The lineup was out the door. The staff was moving like molasses. It took them forever to fill the orders. Sorry, it took me so long."

"You weren't long Qu," I reply with a smile. *I don't know what time it is or when he left.*

Qu gives me a concerned look. He places a cup in Ma's hand before placing the rest of the food on the side table. Ma lets go of my arm to hold the warmth of the cup in both her hands. Her hands seem smaller and frailer than I expected. Looking around the room, Qu drags a chair beside me. I feel my hand being wrapped around a cup. My gaze leaves Ma's hands for a second. I nod at Qu as he rests beside me.

"You look tired, Ma," Qu comments as he sips.

"Not really, Dear. I want to be awake when Si opens his eyes," she murmurs.

I smile at Ma's pet name for Dad. *I always wished I had a pet name growing up. How mom's name is Althea, but all her friends back home call her Babs. Dad's name is Josiah, but his people call him Roy. Ma always called him Si. Qu, Babs, Roy, and Si will never be found on any of their birth certificates yet are found in the hearts of those that know and love them. I come along and I'm Vivian. Plain and simple. No cutesy, loving alter ego keeping me from evil eyes. Just Vivian. Viv.*

"It couldn't hurt to rest though as you wait. The chair you are sitting on can raise your foot. Look," he picks up a blanket from the cart and places it gently on Ma's lap. Slowly pushing a button on the side of the faux leather lounger, Ma's back slowly reclines, and her legs rise. At first, she seems a bit alarmed, however, she soon relaxes. She balances the coffee away from herself to prevent it from spilling.

"Gracias mi amigo," she chuckles.

I never know what is going to come out of her mouth sometimes. I giggle with her.

"Comfortable?" Qu smiles.

"Yes, it's good," she nods.

"Okay. Well, Ma, I'm going to steal Viv away for a minute. We'll be right back alright?" he says, patting her shoulder.

This is news to me. "Where we going?"

"Short walk," he says firmly, holding my elbow to help me rise.

Ouch. My bones retaliate. When has it ever been difficult for me to rise out of a chair? Why does my whole body ache? I grimace as I creak into a standing position. I let Qu hold the small of my back as we leave the room and turn the corner. My steps are weary. I feel weary. We keep walking slowly, in silence, corridor after corridor.

"Did you want to say something to me?" I finally ask looking up at his face. His eyes are fixed on the far end of the hallway.

"No, I just wanted to walk with you a little. You left early and it's now after 3:00 p.m. I'm assuming you've been sitting in the same spot for hours."

It didn't occur to me. We continue to walk, lost in our thoughts.

Damage to vessel walls... buildup of plaque... strain on heart... bursting of blood vessels... stress... affects blood flow to brain... irregular heartbeat...

"Oh, hi. I'm Nancy. Remember, we met earlier today? Anyway, I was just telling your mother that now that your father is awake, we are going to take him for some further tests," Cartoon Shoes says, matter-of-factly.

My eye traces my mother's drawn face, and my father's frightened face. *I don't remember ever seeing my father frightened before. It's jarring.* I squeeze Qu's hand.

"I'd like to accompany Dad for his tests," I look up at Qu, "do you mind keeping Ma company?"

"No problem."

"Right, so what were these tests for again?" I ask the nurse.

Nancy does her best to explain the purpose of the tests, but I only pick up snippets. I heard he needs a nuclear scan. He fasted for four hours so is ready for the procedure. I nod like I've heard everything else and follow her and the bed out of the room towards the elevator.

We are left to wait in an area with other patients between thin cloth dividers.

I wish he wouldn't look at me that way. All murky-sea-swimming-unfocused eyes. I'd never say it out loud, but it's like he is seeing out of fisheyes and it's unsettling.

Fix your face, Viv. Pull yourself together.

I think I read about this test before. Nuclear scan... nuclear... radioactive tracers. I shiver.

"Dad, it's going to be alright. They are just going to run a few tests," I squeeze his hands, hoping to reassure him. I guess it was enough. Though his voice is lost, he gently squeezes me back.

"Alright Mr. Grant, we are going to put another gown on you," Nancy says, as by rote.

The other male nurse doesn't introduce himself. He struggles to put on the second robe to cover Dad's backside. *I don't know if I should look away or not.* I decide to stand guard only to see the gown expose his behind to the cold as they were flipping him over. *I'm embarrassed for him.* I avert my eyes as they begin transferring him onto the next table.

"I can't wait to have a coffee," the male nurse comments as they continue to adjust him.

"Your shift over after this?"

"Hmm," Nancy answers as if Dad and I aren't in the room. "Oh, shoot, consent form!" she exclaims. "Ms. Moji, we have to inject material as part of the procedure, so we need you to sign this consent form on his behalf."

Material, what material? Upset, I take the form and begin reading it.

1/10,000 have a heart attack from the procedure... Could my dad be that one?

"I'm not sure if I should sign this. Shouldn't my mom sign this instead?"

Both nurses exchange looks. "You're a family member so it's fine," Nancy replies, still looking the male nurse in the eyes.

Do I want to give this to Ma to sign? I don't want her to worry. Looking back at my Dad, I see that he has closed his eyes. He's probably imagining himself far, far away from this cold-ass box of a room.

I hastily sign the form and hand it back to Nancy. Seemingly pleased, she places the form on the counter and continues to position Dad on the slab.

Hands above head.

Plug attached.

Blood pressure cuff and IV completed.

Injection liquid streaming through a clear plastic tube.

"His name?" the male nurse checks his chart.

I answer.

He scans his wristband.

"Done," he responds carelessly, checking the screen of the wand.

*Shouldn't they have done all that before disrobing him and plug-
ging him up to all this shit?*

Feeling almost as powerless as my father must, I continue to
stand guard trying my best not to show my disgust.

"Step out please," Nancy motions me to the door.

Machine begins.

Gradually rolling.

Lower.

Slow.

Stop!

Wait.

Again.

Dad is obviously uncomfortable. His right hand jerks and spasms
over the plug. *I think the plug is tugging at his skin. Is he in pain?*

"Now Mr. Grant, you have to keep still!" the male nurse returns,
admonishing him as he presses the plug.

He's not a child!

Again.

I want to reach out to Dad, but I've been relegated to peering
from outside his space.

"Alright Mr. Grant, we're done," Nancy says to tightly closed
lids. I re-enter. I hope he knows that I didn't abandon him.

More time passes before we wheel back into his hospital room.
Dad's face is moist. I am exhausted. I can't bear to look at either Qu
or Ma.

"Alright, all done. He's tired, so probably give him some time.
When the results are out, the doctor will come by to discuss them
with you," Nancy reports to us before quickly exiting.

Quiet fills the room for a few breaths. Ma rises from her chair
and starts dabbing Dad's face with her handkerchief.

"How you doing, Si?" she coos. I want to break down and cry but choose to swallow instead. I feel Qu against my back, encircling my waist. I lean back, swallowing all the harder.

"Ma, do you want to come home with us for a while? You can have a shower, eat some dinner, maybe rest before coming back," Qu persuades.

"No love, I want to stay with Si. You two go on. You got Faith and Justin. Yes, you go. I'll stay," she replies all the while wiping his brow.

"No, Ma, I'll st—"

"Alright Ma, we'll go," Qu interrupts. "We'll bring you back some food and toiletries. Soon come." Kissing Ma on the cheek, he picks up my purse and takes my hand. I gently release his. I am about to protest but decide not to when I see the intention in his eyes.

"Bye, Ma. Bye, Dad. I love you. I won't be long," I kiss them both before turning back to Qu's hand.

An interruption of arterial blood to the brain... interruption... arterial... I read about this... arteries are those mighty blood tubes... What was it?

Focus.

Muscular walls... imagine it... tubes carrying oxygen from the heart to the mind... interrupted... causing damage... brain damage... interruption...

"What do you think?" Qu shakes my knee.

Startled, I look around me. I run my fingers over the plush couch cushion by my side. I bring myself back into the room. Back into emptiness. The windows are black with night. *I have no idea how we got home, when we got home, what day it is or anything. I don't know what I think about anything besides arteries and muscular walls.* I rub my eyes roughly.

"Sorry Qu, I don't know what you asked me," I shake my head. "Never mind, I'm just going to turn in—"

"Wait, I was asking what you wanted for dinner? The kids got a whole buffet going. Pizza, Chinese..."

I want to vomit.

"No, maybe later," I reply, creaking into a standing position with a yawn and upstretched arms.

"You sure? You haven't eaten anything."

"Yeah, I'm good," I lay a fake smile on him. I immediately see he's not buying it. I brush past him and start to climb the stairs before he can convince me to do otherwise.

I close the door silently and feel a pent-up roar rock my core. I run to the bed and throw the covers over my head hoping to muffle my despair.

TWENTY - ONE

Today, I am happy I started journaling way back when. Having this to do, to organize my thoughts, focuses me while sitting by Dad's bed.

He's still asleep. There's construction so the sole window in here is temporarily boarded up. It's 4:05 p.m., but in here it could be midnight and we wouldn't know the difference.

Being here is so surreal. The floors to floors, beds to beds, ups and downs have been increasingly upsetting. I just came back from Dad's second CAT scan. My dad was again exposed, and vulnerable. Part of me wants to drag him out of here. I know that isn't an option. I also know that if I am not going back and forth with him, who will? Ma? I don't want her to see all this either. She's already feeling depressed and sad enough as it is. As much as I wish I didn't have to be here, I am glad that I am here to speak up on his behalf. I am glad I am here to keep him company.

The nurses (Gayle, especially) are offended by his sometimes-scowling expressions. Not once have they thought about how their actions may have caused it. They talk over him. They roll him over and his bottom is exposed, and his cheeks are stretched. They plug him in.

I stab the page.

The dad I know is private and independent. He is diligent when it comes to his and Ma's affairs. They have no idea how brilliant and loving he is. He is worthy of care and grace. He's just trapped right now. Can't express himself beyond a scowl. For now. But they just see him as this old body!

My anger is rising.

They go about their duties and disregard Dad, who they are supposedly serving. Servicing? Assisting? I don't know what words to use because none of them describes what I have seen. I feel them not genuinely caring for him, or about him, but only going through the motions. Every chance I get I remind them he's real. I'll say, "He's right there! You have a question? Talk to him! Look at him, not me!" It's interesting. The helping profession. Social services. Health services. Are they truly about health, helping and servicing or just putting in time for their next paycheque? It makes me wonder how single patients are treated. I wonder how they treat Dad when no one is around.

I remember Dad once told me that there are angels all around us, holding us up. He honestly believes that. I wonder if he feels angels surrounding him now. Thinking there are angels around him when we aren't by his side, strangely comforts me.

The frenzy has been building, but today I feel more at peace (for what it's worth) than I have felt in weeks. Despite the changes and trauma of it all.

From the panic of not knowing what happened the first day he was rushed here:

~ to admittance forms
~ restlessness

~ *facial contortions*
~ *no talking*
~ *heart attack, and second stroke*
~ *plugs*
~ *tests, CAT scans*
~ *blood transfusion form*
~ *ICU, coronary unit isolation*
~ *monitors*
~ *7 bags of fluid*
~ *infections*
~ *huge IVs, and*
~ *the damn catheter!*

To this morning, seeing him smile slightly and nod in response to my voice. It's a better day! I can't wait until he regains his voice. I long to hear his voice.

I talked to Qu, my rock, earlier. He said to me that we need to take it a step at a time. Just a step. I'm sitting here thinking how I'm going to go through this again and again—all the tests, and forms and vague answers—and then remind myself, again, a step at a time.

On Friday, I had to do a lot of surrendering. I know this sounds crazy, especially since God and I are just getting reacquainted, but I felt speak in my spirit that I did the right thing. Even when the doubt returns, there is this whisper that I have done all I can do. Even Justin said out loud that I am doing right by my dad. I need to hold onto that whisper. Those words. That peace.

I have also been reminding myself not to compare myself to anyone else. I need to get through this the way I need to get through this. Lately, my coping method of choice has been list-making. Lists have always been my go-to, so why stop now?

Number one: I need to go for another walk. I must remind myself not to stay planted in this chair.

Two: Probably do some banking. I could get Qu to do it, but I know that even this small task will help me regain some semblance of normalcy, right?

Three: Make sure Ma and the kids eat.

And the tasks go on and on. For now, I aim to keep it simple. I'm tired all the time. If I can do three concrete things a day, I win!

I also have to figure out how to surrender the shoulds. For instance, why does my family only show up at tragedies? Anne, Peggy, June—I haven't seen them in ages. But for two weeks now, I've been receiving steady phone calls, demanding updates, and offering well wishes. Wishes only, no real offerings of help.

Never mind, it's fine. But why are we all so busy?

I deliberately lay the pen in the spine of my notebook. Hugging it to my chest, I lovingly gaze at my father.

TWENTY - TWO

"Mom?" Justin lightly touches my shoulder.

I'm curled up in the recliner, still hugging my journal. *I must have been super tired.* I dab the drool from the corner of my mouth and slowly unwind.

"Hi love, you just got here? Where's your dad?" I greet him with a sleepy smile.

"I told him I'd find my own way here after school. It's just me," he says, dropping his knapsack beside my chair.

I nod. *So, Faith didn't come.*

Justin turns and strokes Dad's arm. Dad is still. *I don't think he's moved in some time now. The monitors seem steady so I'm not going to worry about it. When he is ready to open his eyes, he will. Let him rest.*

"Grandma told me you had the family meeting with the doctors earlier," he comments, still looking at Dad.

"Yeah, we did," I say dryly.

"How'd that go?" Justin asks, perching on the side of the bed, turning his attention to me.

My first instinct is to shoo him off. *That's Dad's space!* I catch myself as I realize if Dad isn't disturbed, why am I? Looking at Dad, I see that he is still peaceful with Justin stroking his arm. I inhale deeply.

"Truth? It was uncomfortable. It was sterile. I hated every minute of it."

"Why? What happened?" He stops stroking and puts his hands in his lap.

I look in his eyes and see Qu. *How can one boy look so much like his father? People see him and me together and say how much we resemble, but when I look at Justin, I see Qu's imprint all over him. His same concerned, troubled eyes are unnerving.*

"How do I...? It wasn't just one thing..." I push my legs down, forcing the chair upright. I take a sip of cold coffee as I collect my thoughts. Justin intently watches my every move. *I am obviously not going to get away with an evasive response.*

"At this meeting, it was the doctor and the other specialists that have been working with Dad since he was first admitted. They gave an overview of Dad's state when he arrived in the current... state... It was very technical." *In other words, I don't remember.* "It was a lot of this is what we suspect happened, this is the damage to his brain, his heart. This is what we did so far. This is what we are suggesting as a treatment for these organs going forward. These are the risks associated with the options we are suggesting. Blah, blah, blah. I found myself having to keep reminding myself that they are talking about Dad. Not the sum of this faceless person's parts. You know what I mean?"

"I think I do. They were talking about Grandpa like he was an object."

"Exactly!" I exhale. *I needed to say it out loud. I didn't realize how much the meeting upset me until I opened my mouth.*

"They kept referring to the suggested options as part of his care plan, but it didn't feel like caring at all. I hear care and I think compassion, right? They would make suggestions based on how long each action would keep him in the hospital. The entire time they were talking about time and treatment, I was hearing, 'we need the bed.' Move brain and heart along the conveyor belt at a steady clip, please," I snicker darkly.

I ramble on, "They are pushing for shorter hospital admittance, which I get, but don't get at the same time. I mean… I hate that he is here too, but I also don't know if we are ready to have him as an outpatient. Are we equipped to take care of Dad at home? Can we afford extra help for Ma to care for him? We'd need a personal support worker to help bathe him, climb the stairs, maybe with his meds. Ma and I could feed him and get him to his appointments but even that… Ma hates to drive, and I have to eventually go back to work."

"I can help. I get my driver's license soon," Justin chimes in.

I stop. *Listing off all my worries, I forgot that Justin was sitting right in front of me, a part of the conversation.* I reach for his hand.

"Sorry, Justin. I didn't mean to lay all of this on you."

"No, I'm serious, Mom. I can help drive him soon."

"I know you can. I'll probably take you up on that!" *Justin is driving. I love him, and I know he would be a good driver, but my baby on the road with other idiot drivers—idiots like me with lead feet…* I shiver at the thought.

"I was just saying that the family meeting seemed… seemed… like a sham. I can't think of any other way to describe it. A routine meeting with a lot of words. A means to an end to free up a bed," I sigh. "I am more concerned about what happens after he leaves this place. I want to make sure we have all he needs." We exchange smiles.

"I'm sure you will. You always figure stuff out," Justin reassures, letting go of my hand and standing.

"You want another coffee? I was going to get myself one," Justin asks.

Ugh. I hate the fact my kids drink coffee. At first, I tried to discourage them by saying it would stunt their growth, only for them both to tower over me by more than five inches. Foiled. Why fight it?

"Sure. You know how I like it."

"Black, always black. I don't know how you can drink it like that."
Little does he know...

"I don't know how you can drink yours with a ton of milk either," I say smirking at him.

"Whatever," he says as he accepts the bill from my hand.

"What happened?"

"I don't know. I was sitting here and the next thing I know there are alarms, and lights and nurses rushing in and yelling, and I'm pushed out the room. I don't know what happened... He was, he was sleeping," I sob into Qu's chest bewildered. Justin pats my back as I try to control myself.

"Justin, did they say anything to you?"

"No, I was downstairs in the cafeteria. I only got here after Mom was already in the hallway, and they already wheeled him away."

"Did, did, did anyone tell, tell, Ma? F-faith?" I can't catch my breath. *The words hurt.* Looking up at Qu, I see him give Justin a signal. Justin turns and starts tapping his phone.

"Don't worry about that right now," Qu holds me tighter. *I'm falling.*

"But but what is he going to, to, to say? Dad, Dad..." *Words, Viv, words.*

"The doctors are with Dad now. We'll find out what's happening soon," Qu rubs my back as I try to breathe evenly. *Inhale, hold.* The tears are choking. *I'm drowning.*

"I, I, I..." *I don't remember how to breathe.*

"Let's get some water," Qu tries to gently move me.

"No... no... no." *All I know how to do is stammer. This is so frustrating! How can they just wheel him off and no one tells us anything? Just gone with him. What's happening?*

"Faith is getting Grandma and will be here soon," Justin reports as he takes a seat.

Qu and I stay standing, swaying back and forth. I can't control my sobbing. I see Justin lift his coffee to Qu. Qu shakes his head, keeping a firm grip on my back. Justin nods and takes slow sips instead. His knee bounces nervously.

"It will be okay, Viv. It will be okay," Qu calms as he gently smooths the back of my hair.

"Hello, Ms. Grant? I'm Dr. Whitney. I am so sorry, but we tried everything…" the smocked blur continues to inform my mother.

What is he saying? All I hear is wailing. I can't feel my hands. What is he saying?

"Viv? Viv?!"

This wasn't supposed to happen. He was just sleeping.

"*Viv!*"

TWENTY - THREE

It's been a surreal two weeks. I feel like today is the first day I can speak in full sentences. Since Dad...

I don't want to say... left. I've only been able to say a few fragments here and there. I've mostly felt like a stammering moronic mess. I love my family so much, but I just couldn't. I know Ma needs me, but I see her, and I just want to cry, and cry and I lose my voice again. The first week, I went to the funeral home with her, and they were very kind, talking about dates and times and the type of casket we wanted, in these hushed tones like they were speaking in the Vatican. They talked about the location of the plot my parents bought that I had no idea existed. I felt like an idiot. My mom's all nodding and engaged, answering question after question, giving her ideas and wishes. And there I was, supposed to be supporting my mother but instead, my mother was holding court! She is so much stronger than I ever gave her credit for. Only after all this, did I realize how she was prepared for...

I let my pen rest as I collect myself.

I'm a grown-ass woman, blubbering in front of this stranger. A hospitable stranger. A stranger who has probably seen people like me cry uncontrollably, maybe worse even, but I couldn't help chiding myself for being so—

Lost. The only word I can think of is lost. I lost myself when I lost my dad.

The tears keep coming! I'm tired of this. I have to put the journal away.

Frantically wiping my face, I remind myself that I need to get this out once and for all. Well, maybe not for all—for now.

I pick up the journal again.

She asked for the funeral to take place at the end of the month to give some of our relatives back home some time to come and pay their respects. Our family is so large and disjointed. One tree with a million and two branches. Mostly Ma's branches. Dad's and their present community branches sporadically peeking through. It will be an ~~event!~~

That is not the right word. I just don't have the words for anything these days. Events are supposed to be festive. The last thing I want to think of is attending my dad's _________. This is hard.

Ma likes the idea of a celebration of life. Spinning the death into a joyful occasion. I could have vomited all over her when she said that to the funeral director. My mind gets it, but my heart rejects even the notion of shifting the focus to a celebration ~~event.~~

Whatever.

My dad is gone and there is no celebration in that. My dad is gone. My dad is gone, and I didn't get to ask him all my questions yet. I had so many conversations I wanted to have with him. I don't know enough about his childhood. I don't know anything about what he did for a living. All those years of silk ties, business suits and late nights returning from work. I didn't know enough about what made him tick.

He never got to teach me how to garden properly. Or how he made his curry so much better than Ma ever did or could. Where did he get his faith from? Why was he so devout? How could he be so devout and be gone? He was so full of all this faith! He wasn't finished yet! He was just supposed to have slept peacefully and, wake up.

Fuck it! I'm just going to let the tears fall and stain the page.

I can't talk about this anymore. I need to move on. I'm tired of being sad and angry over—everything!

Two days ago, I went into our bathroom, and I didn't recognize my face in the mirror. It's like I wrinkled into a ninety-year-old version of the daughter formerly known as Viv. My hair was all stringy and dull. Dry. Brittle. Even to the touch, never mind the appearance. Just this lifeless, worn out, swab-the-deck-mop.

Without thinking, I fired up Qu's razor and watched the strings fall in one patch clump. It was strange to watch myself do this. It was like I was watching this other pathetic hag with wild, swollen eyes power shave the right side of her head. I turned the razor off and tried to figure out what I had just done. The hair just lay there. I looked up and I don't know how long I stood staring in the mirror at this person's half bald, half scraggly mophead. I remember feeling shocked and strangely relieved that I fired up the razor again and went to town. No more straightening, no more curling, no more hair appointments, no more care! When I finished, I looked like a stray cat and just howled from my gut! Not long after I started screaming, Qu ran in. I think I took ten years off his life. He looked at me, looked at the floor, looked at the sink, looked at the counter, and then back at me. He cried! A big man like that laughed and cried as he palmed my head like a basketball. I sank and laughed and cried with him. It was a sight! He ended up doing his best to shape the massacre I'd created so I looked less like a stray cat and more like an old man.

But yeah, it's gone. It's humbling that Qu doesn't care. I couldn't help but smile to myself when he kissed the top of my head when it was all over. My face, like now, was dry, tear-stained. I was full of fear. I couldn't even speak. But as I sat there on the toilet, I felt myself spark when he kissed me.

Faith had the most severe reaction to what I did. She doesn't even look at me anymore. I feel like she's been even more hostile towards me than before if that's possible. I've barely seen her this past month, to be honest. I don't remember seeing her the entire time I was in the hospital. When I do see her, she seems to avoid me. I suspect I've lost her trust ever since the beach.

Now that I think about it though, I've been missing-in-action way before the beach. That was just the crux.

I have to figure that out. I've been so inside my head. Neglectful. I don't even know how the kids feel about this whole thing with Dad. I should know.

My tear-stained face is beginning to hurt. I lay the pen down and head to the washroom to wash my face. *I need to stop for now. I'll try again tomorrow.*

TWENTY - FOUR

I take a slow look around the room and breathe it in.

The service is tasteful. It is amazing how many people showed up to pay respects to Dad, especially on a rainy day like today. People who I haven't seen in years. People I knew of but could never place a face to if I were tested. Back home people. Past work colleagues. Past neighbours. Present neighbours. Domino cronies. Church friends and family. Their seniors' groups. His mechanic. The mailman! Is that Dour? Can't be.

I am happy that Ma has this community around her that stretches way beyond me, Qu, and the kids. I think about that sometimes and forget. Being an only child, I wonder, not often mind you, what life would be like if Qu left me. Would I have a community to rally around me? Or were they always there for Qu but less for me? I forget that Ma has always been social. She always found people. Chatted with people in the street. Cracked jokes and offered treats to whoever she came across. Hard not to have that in your DNA when you have as big a family as she does. Coming from where she does, perhaps. I forget that about my mother.

The small chapel is packed. The hallway outside the space is teeming with even more people. Why didn't Ma opt for the church? It's a bigger venue and I'm sure the pastor would have agreed. I must have asked her this already. Holding her hand, sitting in the front row, I forget what her reason was. *It doesn't matter anyway, right? We are here, they came, and I just need to be present. Focus.*

I would not have chosen that casket for Dad. This casket screams Ma's taste.

Dad isn't materialistic. Ma and Dad's house is full of stuff that migrated in with Ma after her many ventures over the years. It is not full of Dad's stuff. He could care less about stuff! He had a few suits, lots of shorts and t-shirts, a couple of ties, maybe three shoes in good repair. A few more favourites in bad repair. He liked a good watch. A couple of Swiss timepieces. Don't ask me brands, but they had to be good, solid watches. Lots of food. Yes, my dad loved a well-stocked kitchen. But fancy knick-knacks and antique furniture and ornate framed pictures? Dad wouldn't tolerate any such frivolity if it weren't for my mother. She loves a sparkle! Gold here. Gold there. A thrift shop find that may remind her of something else or be just odd enough that she couldn't bear to leave it on the shelf.

Is that why she chose that thing? My eyes, again, roam over the casket in disgust.

This whole casket thing reeks of Ma! If I was in my right mind when we were making the funeral arrangements, I would have stopped her from choosing this monstrosity. Where do you find a white engraved casket with white satin inlay in a fan pattern, with twelve (why twelve?) bright, oversized, brassy gold handles on all the sides <u>and</u> corners, accented with yet <u>more</u> cryptic engraving, on a foundation of, oh yes, more brassy, tacky gold! If Dad didn't love her as much as he did, he would come down right now and rebuke her in front of all her tribe!

I try not to laugh under my breath.

That's not Dad though. He loves her. Loved her. I'm just going to try and stop making direct eye contact with... I can't even call it a casket.

Ugly box.

I clear my throat.

Hard though. The person impersonating my dad is laid inside. I fidget in my seat.

<u>That</u> *is not my dad. Even when my dad was sleeping, he never looked like that. That guy is grey wearing brown foundation. That guy has his hands on his abdomen. Like he's covering up a growling stomach. That guy is way too thin and lifeless to even have the audacity to call himself Josiah Grant.* <u>Mr.</u> *Grant to that stranger. Tell the audience my dad has left the building.*

Jerking my eyes from the ugly box, I focus on my aunt who is speaking. I try to catch up, but I can't follow what she is saying. Whatever she said ripples a chuckle throughout the room so it must have resonated. *I need to be more present.*

I squeeze my mother's hand and gaze at her profile. *She's so beautiful, my mother. She looks almost hopeful. Sad, but hopeful. Whatever Aunt Sissy said must have given her some peace... maybe. I hope.*

"...and there was never a mango Roy didn't like!" Sissy exclaims as she slaps the pulpit.

Another ripple of laughter erupts around the room. *So? Who cares? Please tell me she has not spent the last few minutes talking about Dad's favourite foods. He was so much more than taste buds! I can't look at her or ugly box right now.*

Looking at my lap, I try to reason with myself.

Funerals are meant to clean up everything anyway, right? I mean we want to say goodbye and only remember the good stuff about... I glance up. *Ugly box. I can't expect anyone to go up there and tell the whole truth like... Dad loved to walk around his house in his underwear no matter who was visiting or was fond of sucking his teeth when he disagreed with you. Or... or... Damn! I can't think of anything bad about him either.*

Sighing, I take another slow look around the room and note all the bright colours.

Everyone's wearing their best. Fireball oranges, yellows, and reds. Royal blues and ocean turquoise. *I forgot that Ma asked people to wear cheery colours. You can tell the ones, particularly from church, who didn't get the memo.* Sombre dark dresses and black suits pepper the congregation. *Got to love church hats though! They must be very old hats or hats that they made themselves because where can you buy those amazingly outrageous hats now? The artificial flowers and lace and height; so beautiful, and creative in their unique way. I'm surprised Ma didn't wear any of hers. She loves a good Sunday hat. I wonder if they are wearing them to honour Ma, too.* I sigh deeply.

Too bad I couldn't convince Faith to do the same and honour me. So rude! She tells me she'll wear what she feels comfortable in because Grandpa wouldn't care! Damn her, I CARE! First, please me, <u>then</u> *Grandpa, damn it! Rolls up here with some simple black mini dress and sparkly hooker heels. She makes me want to scream! We ain't in no club! She ain't grown yet! Ugh, I have to let this go... Be grateful she came at all, and we didn't argue the entire way here—only part of the way. Count my blessings.*

My eyes float back to the stage as my cousin reads a passage from the Bible.

I'm glad Todd is open to doing this for Dad.

I didn't know if I would have my voice back, so purposely didn't put myself in the program.

"This is one of Uncle Si's," he looks at my mom lovingly, "Favourite verses," he begins.

"First Timothy 6:12 AMPC reads, 'fight the good fight of the faith; lay hold of the eternal life to which you were summoned and, for which, you confessed the good confession of faith before many witnesses.' One thing I know about Uncle is that he lived his life faithfully and had no regrets. He worked hard, he loved hard, and he gave hard. He fought the good fight." Todd wipes a tear from his eyes before rushing, "Rest in peace, Uncle Roy," and bolts from the stage. *Why he have to tear up like that?* I gently let go of Ma's hand to rummage around my purse for a tissue. A melody of amens reign.

More and more people go to the platform, sharing anecdotes of Dad on the island.

I have hazy memories of the island. I haven't been back in years. Even if I had, the pictures they drew of back home were raw, vibrant, rich, and utterly foreign to me. The world they painted was so unlike the well-manicured mixed congregation, neutrally coloured walls, tastefully chandeliered salon, and comfortably cushioned chairs we all sit on now. Intermittent calls and responses of 'praise Gods' and 'I know I'm blessed' now fill the air, affirming Dad's world. Video slides of a young, cherry-cheeked handsome bachelor in baggy, pleated pants, cut to more recent video slides of a grey-whiskered, balding, and slightly round-bellied older man. My dad. It was all so stark. His smile was the same. The way he posed for the photos was the same. The passing of time, though, is funny. Sitting in this room, listening to his people recall Roy, Si, and Mr. Grant, and seeing him projected in front of me, I forgot how he used to look. How he physically held himself and took up space. How he looked at me growing up. Even the way he looked at me before the hosp—how did he age overnight like that? I—

My thoughts are interrupted by two strangers standing by the wall.

"What's this? Church?" One of the rental pallbearers smirks at his colleague. They are both standing at the front to the side. Unbeknownst to them, their comments are audible to everyone in the front row. His partner in crime inches closer to his ear.

"What's he doing? We gotta get moving before the Chan party arrives!" he whispers loudly. "Umm," he curtly grunts.

I'm about to stand up and deliver a beatdown when I feel a hand on my shoulder. Scowling, I see the funeral director looking decidedly concerned at me. I try to quell my anger. "Excuse me, I don't mean to disrupt your family and friends' tributes for your father, may he rest in peace, but unfortunately, we now need to bring your father to his final resting place."

I look into his blue eyes, knowing what he is saying, but not wanting to accept it. My mother's head is hung as she cries into Dad's kerchief. I nod and begin to slowly rise. I catch the eye of Pastor Jay, who immediately stops mid-sentence on the stage. I turn to face our family and friends. A hush falls over the room.

"Sorry, everyone. I, I want to thank you all for coming on this grey day to honour my dad. Though I know most of you, for those who don't know me, I am Josiah's daughter, Vivian. I wasn't going to talk today, but…" *Hold it together.* "But as my dad would have said, make your plans and prepare for God to laugh." Some more chuckles and a few amens embrace me. "As much as I would love to stay here and continue listening to all the stories you have about my father and well wishes for my mother," I give her hand another squeeze without looking at her, "unfortunately the time has come for us to take Dad to… to take Dad…" *Hold it together.* I shake my head.

"It's time. Please join Pastor Jay in a closing prayer before we head outside. We will also be having a gathering at the house afterwards. The details are in the program. Umm, Pastor?" I look at him expectantly before dropping back on my chair. I lift my thigh to pull out the purse I unceremoniously crushed in the attempt to get all eyes off me. The Pastor begins.

"Let us stand," he gracefully levitates his arms. Chairs shift as people jostle themselves to rise in obedience. He tightly shuts his eyes and his voice booms.

"Heavenly Father, we thank You for eternally keeping our brother, Josiah. We thank You for the time You allowed our brother to share his life with us."

"Yass, Jesus, yaaass," some women murmur in unison.

"We thank You for all the benefits you have bestowed to us Father, for all the suffering and insults You bear on our behalf."

"Amen!" The temperature heats up in the space.

"Most merciful redeemer, friend, may we continue to know You more fully, love You more deeply, and follow You more intimately…"

"Gloorryy!" another woman jumps in agreement.

"….every day we draw breath. Thank you once again for your Spirit that empowers and prepares us to pursue the life You have created for every one of us, that we are not captive to fear or worry, knowing that whatever happens this year and years to come—"

"Yaaasss!"

"You protect us and keep us. You deserve all the praise! And we all say this in the mighty name of Jesus—"

And the room erupts with resounding amen, amen, and amens, as Pastor Jay wipes his brow.

Music is cued as people prepare to watch the closed ugly box travel down the aisle.

I feel empty.

It's raining buckets out here. It's cold. There are pools of water on the narrow road leading to the cemetery. So many hands on my arm and hugs around my shoulder as people pass Ma and me on their way into the downpour.

I'm over it. No one touch me!

Outwardly, I smile and nod with every passing.

Hands cover heads as people try to figure out how to follow the hearse and miraculously not get their hats, perms, or weaves, wet in the process. Huddling under a few umbrellas, couples start to hold each other and run in step, every which way to the parking lot. Faith stands beside me looking out the sliding doors.

"I guess we should follow?" she half asks half states.

"Yeah, we'll take our car," I reply dryly. I have another thought.

"Ma, why don't you and the kids go with Qu first," I say, squeezing her hand. "I'll make sure everyone leaves before riding to his tree with Todd." I look beyond Qu and make eye contact with Todd.

"Yeah, that's fine, Aunty. We'll see you in a bit," he confirms, returning my gaze.

We all fall silent. No one makes a move to leave the hall. No one reaches for an umbrella. I place Ma's hand in Faith's.

"Alright, I'll see you soon," I say, dragging Todd by the arm out of the circle.

A few feet away, Todd stops me. He strokes my arms and smiles at me, "You alright?"

"As alright as I can be at a funeral."

"I mean are *you* alright? Why don't you want to drive up with Qu?"

"Why you making such a big deal of this?"

"Viv," he continues to stroke my arms.

It's so irritating that he knows me so well. I don't have the energy to bullshit him.

"I'm not ready to go to the tree just yet."

"The plot?"

"Yes."

"But you'll allow me to take you there, right?"

He's so irritating.

"Of course! What kind of daughter would I be if I didn't say goodbye to my dad at the tree?"

"I'm not judging you; I'm just asking."

"Well..." I sigh. "You don't have to judge me. I judge myself just fine."

"Aaahh," Todd gives me a hug. *Why is everyone in my family— alright, almost everyone in my family—so tall? It's like being a house cat in a family of lions.* I encircle his waist and lean my forehead against his chest.

"I hate this day so much," I muffle into his shirt.

"I know," he breathes.

"I was this close to faking a brain tumour so I wouldn't have to come," I confess.

"Whooo, see how much you've grown!" he teases, causing me to giggle. I may be a few months older than him, but it has always seemed like our birth order was reversed.

"Right? Give me props, damn it!"

"No one says props," he corrects.

Exasperated, I lift my head, "Just give me this."

He holds me tighter. "Alright, I'll give you props, only because it's you," he kisses the top of my smooth head. "Ready to go?"

"No," I release him and inhale deeply. "But let's go anyway."

We can't reach the tree. Every road leading to my dad's plot is congested. The soggy grass lining each side of the paths are choked with SUVs, minivans, and cars. *Rainwater is a curse for my people. Good thing the hearse led the way, or they would have blocked Dad out of his resting place just to not have to walk too far in the rain.* We hear a commotion, but I can't figure out why. *It's a cemetery. Do we have to have any reason for drama here of all places?*

Todd covers my shoulders with his suit jacket and opens the blue umbrella to shelter us. We weave between bumpers, car mirrors, and doors to the shivering cluster of people.

As we draw closer, the source of the commotion is revealed. There is a tractor and four men in dirty army green overalls trying to force the crowd back. The rain is hitting the top of the ugly box, now in what seems to be encased in an open-top vault casing. The tractor operator is manoeuvring it into place. The mud tracks keep tearing up the ground every time the tractor moves. I didn't realize until now that Dad's plot was in the newer part of the cemetery, therefore not all the grass and shrubbery has finished being planted. Just hills of mud and this lone tree.

The claw lowers into the hole and repeatedly grabs more mud and water. With each excavation, there's awkward dumping on the other side of the hole. The ugly vaulted box lies on the other side of the hole, in the pour, directly opposite this growing mound of brown-black sludge.

He's getting wet.

Swinging on chains, this hydraulic crane finally lifts Imposter Dad above the hole attempting to get the box into position. I watch the vault dangle. Back and forth. Just dangling there. This thing. This ugly box.

But isn't there a human inside? I don't understand. Why is there a tractor involved? Why is this box up there so high? I crane my neck watching as the ugly box is eventually lowered into the ground. I still don't understand what is going on.

"Why don't we all sing Amazing Grace?" I hear Pastor Jay suggest in the distance.

Miserably, the mass starts to sing off-key as the tractor shovels dirt over the ugly box. They are upset, but, like me, I suspect they don't know how to react. The rain lightens to mist as the chorus also peters out. Flowers are intermittently tossed into the hole. People fling embarrassed farewells in our direction. My voice abandons me, again. I nudge Todd to leave. I start walking without him towards the car. Kids dance hide and seek amongst the vehicles as I pass. My heels keep sinking. I'm trembling. Despite myself, I hold onto the words of Amazing Grace.

How sweet the sound... that saved...

I'd do anything to crowd out the spectacle that is my father's final goodbye, even if it means replaying that blasted song in my head.

"Please take me home," I say to Todd, gripping his jacket tighter around me.

I can still hear the tractor humming.

TWENTY - FIVE

"Viv."

"Hi, Qu. Sorry, but I just need to go home."

"Where are you now?"

I look at Todd, who is concentrating on the road. Jaw tight, he is lost in his thoughts. It took us a while to get out of the cemetery. Dodging other mourners, we had to back out of the lane for what seemed like half a block before being able to safely three-point turn out of there. The entire time Todd was gripping the steering wheel and cursing under his breath. I look away.

"I'm almost home. Todd took care of me," I squeeze his forearm in thanks. He doesn't respond. Frustration is still written all over him. I return my attention to the phone.

"Qu, I will be at Ma's house in an hour or so. Two, tops. I just want to pull myself together before facing all those people. Cool?"

Silence. *I never know what silence means when I'm talking to Qu. Particularly these days. Silence could mean anything. Maybe I was pushing it when I mentioned two.*

"Alright. An hour," Qu retorts.

I knew it! "Alright, see you then. Love you," I say praying to hear it back.

"I love you too. Soon." Click.

A rushed love you, but I'll take it. It's not fair for me to leave him with my mother. I need to pull myself together quick! I gingerly return my phone to my purse.

"Here we are," Todd announces as he throws the car into park. His voice is tense.

"Thanks, Todd," I say hugging his neck. "Will you head over to Ma's?"

"I got some things to do, but I might check in with her later."

"And me?" I fake a pout. My attempt to joke falls flat. *Try again.*

"If I don't see you later, I'll just call you next week for coffee or something," I offer.

"Yeah, call me. Take care, Viv," he says as he gives me another hug.

Standing on the porch, I wave as he honks twice and speeds off.

Clothed in a towel, I examine my closet. *I don't know what to wear. If I could just roll up there in yoga pants, I'd be so happy. Wait, didn't I just chide Faith about the evils of being comfortable over appropriately fashioned?* I grimace.

I take out a contemporary rust-coloured wrap dress and hold it up against me. Looking in the mirror, I note that I look less devastated than I did a week ago. Every week, a little less sad though my heart is still mending. *Try not to feel... anything. Impossible, but a feat I still pursue. Feel nothing. Show up. Be present. Move on.* I drop the dress on the bed and search for a statement jewellery piece that will distract from my bald head. *Maybe a clunky brass necklace? Hoop earrings? Feathers? African beads?* I sort through all the jewellery I've collected over the years. I drop piece after piece. Vexed, I slam the boxes shut.

If they can't figure out I'm a girl from my dress, then to hell with them all! I rub my head and fall back on the bed.

I got to get moving.

Lying down feels good. The house is so still. No one is asking for anything. Or offering me condolences.

My bed. I love my bed.

Focus.

Qu. Ma. The kids. Right. I can rest later. It will be fine.

"Oh, you're here," Qu places his hand in the small of my back.

"Yeah, sorry it took me so long. I just needed to change," I reply, giving him a quick kiss on the cheek.

"Okay."

I look up at him, expecting him to say something else. Nothing. Awkward silence. *Why is he looking at me like that?* "Alright, I'm just going to go over here," I say, jerking forward with nowhere in particular in mind.

"Oh dear, you're here!" Ma calls from the living room. As she walks towards me, I fight the urge to bolt.

"Yes, we've established that I am here now," I retort for God knows what reason. *That sounded catty. I didn't mean it to come out that way.*

"No, I'm glad. I was wondering if you were alright," she said, hugging me. "Todd dropped by for a second and just left. I thought you would be together."

That traitor. I thought he was going to blow this off.

"No, with the funeral and rain and mud and all," I start to over-explain, "I just needed to—"

"That's fine dear, I'm glad you are here now. Go get yourself something to eat in the kitchen. So many people brought casseroles, rice and peas, vegetables, chicken, desserts—there is so much!" she says with a weak smile. I look into her eyes. I hope she reads in mine that she does not have to pretend either.

I pat her hand, "I'll be right back."

The house is still packed with family, friends, and neighbours. Heading to the kitchen, I pass people I recognize, but couldn't name if you paid me. I nod politely as I breeze past them, hoping none of them will dare stop me with any well wishes. Under the radar is my only goal.

"I see you like the tomato salad," a fellow dodger comments as I fork more onto my paper plate.

"Yeah, tomatoes," is my snappy comeback.

"Did you know Mr. Grant very well?" he asks smugly.

"Something like that," I reply giving as much attention to the spread of food in front of me. *Maybe if I don't make eye contact, he will move along.*

The muncher nods and continues to smile knowingly as he spoons boiled carrots into his mouth. *Ma wasn't kidding! She won't have to cook for a month from these leftovers alone!*

"Well, I'm Jerry. I live about two doors down. It's nice to meet you," he offers his hand.

"Nice to meet you, Jerry," I limply shake his hand and return to the table of delicious.

"It was a wonderful service," he shares, unfazed by my rudeness. "I noticed you were sitting beside Mrs. Grant in the front row."

I sigh and rest my plate. *So busted.*

"You got me. I'm Viv. My dad is Mr. Grant," I confess. "If you must know, I just wanted to get some food, find a corner and talk about anything but the service." *There. I said it.* Picking up my plate again, I resume shovelling food onto it, hoping Jerry will get the hint. He doesn't.

"I had a feeling. I sometimes see you come to the house with your kids. I must have not seen you for a while, though. I didn't know you changed your hairstyle."

I stop, mid-scoop. *One Mississippi. Two Mississippi.*

"It looks good by the way," he adds quickly. "I just didn't recognize you at first."

How should I take that? Whatever.

"Thank you, well, I—"

"I was at my aunt's funeral earlier this month and it was just me and the funeral staff. Aunt Mildred was in her nineties and mean as dirt! Even the PSWs would just rush to look after her, then get out of there. But let me tell you, being in that room with just the funeral director and the urn was depressing. Can you imagine?" he asks.

I just stare at him. *How do I get out of here?*

"*Nothing* like today's service, though. I don't go to church let alone a *Black* church."

Why he have to say it like that? This man is getting on my nerves. Who let his lily-white ass in here?

"But today's service for your father! That was church! That place was so full of warmth. Full of love. Your father was so loved, Viv. He was a good man," he looks at me with glossy eyes.

I can't speak past the lump in my throat. *All I wanted was some food to stuff back any emotions and then Mr. Jerry has to go and say that! I hate you, Jerry.*

"Hmm, yes. Thanks," is all I can utter before running into the hallway.

"Viv!"

Damn it.

"Hey, Viv! Over here!"

A corner, Lord. All I want is a corner and these damn rice and peas!

"Hey...you," is all I manage to say. I know who he is but can't remember anyone's name today. The old man gives me a long, tight hug before releasing me to peer into my face. I feel a shiver go down my spine as I look back into the face of my father.

"It's been so long, Viv. I think the last time I saw you, you were still carrying a baby on your hip," my father's cousin, Dante, reminisces fondly.

I nod my head, trying not to cry. "Wow, I can't believe it has been that long, Uncle. That baby is now a facety teenager," I joke-not-joke. I sharply jut out my chin in the direction of Faith, standing in a group on the other side of the living room.

"I can't believe Roy's gone. That just leaves me the elder of the family," he concludes wryly.

It sounds strange to hear him say that. Uncle lives back home so he was never around when I was growing up. A few visits here and there, spaced out over years at most. I would never consider him the surrogate elder of our family. Dad still holds that mantle.

I swallow my feelings. "Yeah, I guess so," I lie, trying to be polite. I play with my food with my fork. "So, where is Aunty Joni?" I ask, scanning the room.

"Oh, I left her and the other women chatting somewhere in the family room," he replies disinterestedly. "I was just heading to the kitchen for a drink. You want anything?" he offers.

I was going to refuse but think better of it. "Yes, if there is any ginger ale, I'd love one. Thanks, Uncle," I accept, squeezing his hand.

"Right back," Uncle smiles.

Briefly watching the back of his jacket, I return to scoping out a spot to sit and eat my food in the shadows. *Two down.*

I can't remember the last time there were so many people in this house. Though I am happy my mother has so many people around her, I find this all so overwhelming. There aren't any spaces. Without thinking, I turn to the staircase and start climbing to my parents' room. The voices dim with each stair. Closing the door, I can breathe again.

There is too much stuff in this room, I think as I slowly walk to the bed. This was the last place Dad was before going to the hospital. *I don't know why that comforts me. Like I'm closer to Dad here than I was earlier at the funeral home. That's crazy, right?*

The grains are catching in my throat. *Why am I crying again? All I do is cry. Where is the water coming from? I should be a desert by now. This is crazy! I just washed and reapplied my makeup, damn it! I'm going to eventually have to go back down there, show my face, looking like a freak. I can't stand this.*

Why did he have to go and die?

With that thought, I lay the plate on the floor and cover my face. *Why did you have to die, Dad?*

You were supposed to rest, get a good sleep, **recover**, *then go home. You had no right to die!*

Ma needs you. I need you. You were supposed to come back home. Come back into this room and live for another forty years! That was the plan.

I am violently convulsing now.

Why did you have to go and ruin our plan? My plan.

It's not fair!

You had no right to die!

You had no right!

I turn and reach for the tissue box before laying on the bed. On his side of the mattress, I curl my knees up to my chest.

This is ridiculous. I was supposed to come here, greet, and entertain the guests, comfort my mom, that's it. Instead, I'm a blubbering idiot child in a... in a...fetal position. Apanasana. Wow, the things you remember in the most bizarre times.

Why can't I do something as simple as supporting my mother? That's all I had to do.

Support Ma.

Dad, you would be so disappointed to see me like this.

Another flood of tears washes my face.

Dad would want me to be strong. He'd be like, Viv, stop wasting time.

Or would he?

I blow my nose and wonder.

The last time I was here he was pretty laid back, right? More "be and let be."

I stare up at the ceiling.

Are you mad that I am crying now, Dad? Wherever you are, do you see me crying and are you sad to see me this way?

I turn back onto my side and dab my ear.

I miss talking to you, Dad.

I miss not being able to tease and joke around with you.

I want to hear you call my name just one more time. Okay, maybe not just one more time.

I wish you were here.

You need to get through this the way you need to get through this. Allow yourself the space to grieve.

The salt is caked around my eyelashes and tracked on my cheeks when I crack open my eyes. The sun is beginning to peek through the curtains. The house is still, and I can feel someone else beside me. At my back, my mother snores softly. Her hand is resting on my hip. *I didn't mean to fall asleep.* I try not to move so that my mom will stay peaceful. It's no use. She stirs and gradually opens her eyes.

"You awake, chile?" she half yawns.

"Yeah, I didn't realize I had drifted off," I say sheepishly.

"Hmm, no worries. I was happy for the company," Ma replies warmly.

I try to smile, but the dryness hurts my face. I slowly unravel myself. My muscles seem to have degenerated.

"I'm just going to wash up. I'll be right back," I murmur.

"Kay, Dear," she says, turning from me for her second round of sleep.

I notice my purse on the side table. I pick it up before shuffling to the door.

"Qu?" I half-whisper into the receiver.

"Viv, you're awake?" Qu mumbles back. *He obviously isn't yet.*

"When did you go? Why didn't you wake me up?"

"What do you mean? You were exhausted and Ma said that you could stay. I think she wanted you to be there with her."

Of course. It just dawned on me that Ma would be in the house by herself, pretty much for the first time. Sort of. She has mostly been staying with us for the past few weeks. There are also a few extended family still staying here now, but she will be totally alone soon. I don't remember my mom ever not sleeping beside my dad. Sleeping in that room without Dad must feel lonely. I guess.

"Alright, well, I'll head home shortly, okay?"

"No rush. The kids and I will just be knocking around here today. We'll see you soon," his voice trails off. *I think he's asleep.* His snore confirms it before I click off.

I gently open Ma's door and step inside. Lifting the blanket, I slip underneath hoping not to disturb her. It is soothing listening to my mother's breathing. I close my eyes and try to still my thoughts. I let the quiet envelop me, when—

"Qu and the kids, okay?" I jump at the sound of her voice. *So creepy! I thought she was asleep.*

"Yes, they're fine. Still sleeping. I mean Qu answered, but he was still half asleep."

"Oh, that's good, Dear."

Ma falls silent again, so I close my eyes and snuggle deeper into my pillow.

"It was a lovely service."

My eyes pop open again. "Yes, lovely service," I concur. *I should just let it rest, right? Or should I?*

"But Ma, what was the deal with the casket?"

"What about the casket?"

"It wasn't enough that it was ugly—"

"It was *beautiful*," Ma corrects, jerking her head around to glare at me.

"But the crane? The tractor? It was all so... so—"

"I know. I was horrified too."

"You were?" *Really?*

"I didn't stick around long at the cemetery or much downstairs," I continue, "but I didn't overhear anyone even mention it."

"I think it was so bizarre people didn't know what to say," she says matter-of-factly.

"I mean, Dad was in there..."

"Hmm hmm..."

"Dangling," I hedge.

"Like a giant rapper's pendant on a gold chain," Ma chuckles. I burst into laughter with her. *The image is so stupid!*

"A macho giant's chain!" I exclaim, wiping my eyes with the back of my hand. "Is it sacrilegious to say that?" I ask trying to control myself.

"Was it sacrilegious for the funeral home to dangle my husband in the air, in the rain for everyone to gawk at? Probably." Her face slowly softens as she reflects.

"Probably sacrilegious. Good thing Dad wasn't in there," I say before I catch myself.

"Yeah," Ma replies, surprisingly.

I gape at her. *Well, that was unexpected. She agreed with me.*

She continues to look at me lovingly as she covers my hand with her own. "We are all spirit. The minute your dad passed, the only thing that was left was his shell. Si is gone. Si was not in that box. Only his shell," she says more wearily. "My Si is gone. No one can hurt him now."

I swallow, "No one can hurt him."

Spirit's eternal.

TWENTY - SIX

"You're back," Qu smiles at me.

Way to state the obvious. "Yes, I am back," I say instead, making nice by giving him a peck on the lips.

He continues to rinse the dishes as I rest my purse on the counter. "How's Ma?" he asks.

I love that he calls my mom, his mom. He never called her Mrs. Grant, even when we were dating. Strange. I should have known then that we would be together. Ma, not Mrs. Grant, was a hint of things to come.

"She's alright. We had a good talk this morning. First in bed, then over a light breakfast. Even as I was leaving. She walked me to the car, and we just kept talking." A thought occurs to me, "So, how is your mom?"

Qu pauses, resting his wrists on the side of the sink. "Funny you should ask. I gave her a call this morning. They are alright. I'll probably take a drive up there later this week."

"Sounds good. We should all go."

Qu was silent. *My instincts about what his next move will be are totally off these days.* I reach around him to grab some cold water.

"How are the kids?"

"Hmm," Qu grunts. "I don't know. They have been holed up in their rooms for most of the day. I only see them occasionally grab a bite to eat before disappearing back into their rooms."

I lean against the counter facing the kitchen as I sip. "I know I should go check on them," I say haltingly. I'm convincing no one including myself.

"I guess you should," Qu smirks while flicking water at me. I feign irritation.

"I know," I pout as I wipe my arm.

Qu shuts off the faucet and wipes his hands on a nearby tea towel. He leans on the counter beside me, following my gaze. "You want to run, don't you?" he finally says.

"Who said anything about running?"

"That look in your eyes, for one."

"Shut up, Qu!"

"Then go upstairs and check on the kids."

"I said shut up! I'll go when I'm ready." *Irritating.*

"Sure, you will," he says, dropping the towel on the counter and walking away.

He is testing me. What? He thinks I'm just going to leave. Again. Not see my kids. God, I hate when he's right. I'd love to escape to the beach right now if I thought I could get away with it.

I drop my head and sigh. *Face the music, Viv. I can't prove him right.* I trudge up the stairs to Faith's room.

"Knock, knock," I say as cheery as I can.

"Why do you say knock, knock instead of just knocking?" Faith rolls her eyes.

Off to a great start! Inhale, exhale, try again. "You know me. Just trying to be cute," I joke as I bounce on the bed beside her.

Faith shrugs, "Whatever."

"Wh-a-t-ev-er," I drawl as I tap my hands on my lap.

"Is there something you want?"

"No, I just haven't seen you much these past few days. I was at Grandma's—"

"I know. We left you there."

"Right, as I said—"

"Everything's fine, Ma. I miss Grandpa, but I'm fine. The service was fine. The reception was fine. I slept fine. I ate," she says haughtily. "So, now can I please just go back to talking to my friend?"

"What friend?" I try to peer at her phone before she clasps it to her chest.

"It's just Chris."

Chris who? Boy Chris? Girl Chris? "Chris who? Boy Chris? Girl Chris?" *Damn! I said that out loud.*

"Mom!" Faith shrieks! "They can hear you!" she mouths exaggeratedly.

She looks so mortified; I laugh before I can catch myself. "Great! Let me introduce myself and tell them about the time you thought the Easter Bunny—"

"Mom!" She jumps up onto her knees.

"Alright, alright. Wow, touchy," I continue to snicker as I make my exit.

"Aaahh, she is so annoying," I hear her tell the screen as I shut the door behind me.

And my work here is done, ladies and gentlemen.

I crack the door open and see Justin lying in bed with his book open on his face. I stand there for a few minutes. *If he's faking, he is an incredible actor.* He didn't stir once. I gently close his door.

"Well, I am here to report that I have officially checked on the troops, Captain," I salute Qu before flopping onto the bed beside him. He hugs my waist and rests his head on my chest.

"Nice," he replies. He closes his eyes and smiles. "You gonna wash up?"

"I did, at Ma's. She had some of my clothes still there. You didn't notice this wasn't the dress I was wearing last night?"

Qu lifts his head and gives me a once over. "Nope," he concludes, dropping his head back into his sweet spot.

"Nice," I rub his hair playfully with my knuckles before resting my head against the top of his.

"So, I was talking to Ma."

"Hmm."

"And she told me so much I didn't know."

"Like what?"

"Like they both left the house to us when they pass away."

Qu remains silent. *Nothing?*

"Does that surprise you?" I ask.

"No, you are their only daughter."

"Did you know that my dad had some stocks and land back home?"

Qu gives a long sigh. "I'm not surprised. Your dad didn't talk much about what he had but they also never did without. I assumed Dad had assets."

"Well, I was surprised. Apparently, Ma and Dad had discussed their wills, insurances, assets, as you put it, way before his... his... attack." *I hate that my voice still catches when I think of Dad.*

Qu hugs me tighter and exhales. "That's a good thing, right? I mean that Ma and Dad had a plan."

"Yeah, I know. But still, it was a bit strange for me to hear Ma talking about their assets with me. Talking about what would go to me, you, and the kids. Talking about what she envisioned about her future. Just talking about..."

"Life without Dad," he finishes my thought.

"Yeah," I breathe.

Qu rises and rests on the headboard. He lifts me onto his lap causing me to laugh.

"What are you doing?"

"I'm getting closer to my sexy—"

"Qu, I'm trying to be serious."

"Yes, I can tell," he says as he continues to snuggle my breasts.

"I'm telling you about Ma and Dad's will."

"Go on," he kisses my arm.

"Dad left you all his expensive watches."

"Hmm, hmm."

"But the land back home, he left that to Ma."

"Hmm," Qu moans, seemingly enjoying himself.

"I think Dad left us enough to cover most of our debts."

"Hmm," Qu nibbles.

I doubt he is hearing anything I'm saying.

"And Ma said that though the house is for us when they both die, she was thinking of giving it to us sooner."

Qu stops mid-kiss. "What?"

I put my hands on Qu's cheeks. He looks freaked out. "Ma is thinking of giving us the house sooner than later."

"I still don't get it. Why would she do that? Does she want to live with us?" Qu sits bolt upright, and his arm loosens around me.

"Ma is thinking of retiring back home. When she does, she wants us to take the house."

Qu's head hits the board. *The stunned look on his face is a little frightening. How do I make this better?*

"What do you think?" Qu finally asks.

"Well," I start, "hear me out," I swallow before launching in. "As I was talking to Ma more and more, her idea of moving back home didn't seem that outrageous to me. Her talking about her future kind of got me thinking about where and what I want to do in the future, also."

I pause. Qu is still looking at me frightened. "What about our future?" he says deliberately.

Don't chicken out now.

"What would you say if I decided to quit my job?"

"What?"

"Quit my—"

"I heard what you said but don't know why you said it."

"Do you know since I went on leave, I haven't thought about work once?"

"You were burnt out. Dad was ill."

"Yeah, maybe. I mean, of course, you are right, but also I still haven't been missing work."

"You love teaching."

"I loved teaching."

"You aren't making any sense. You have *always* loved teaching."

"Not lately, no. I've been mailing it in for at least the past year now."

"What?"

"I burnt out."

"Yes, you were overworked, I get that, but teaching—"

"I haven't found joy in teaching for some time now. I don't know what it is, but for the first time in a long time, I think I could step away from teaching and still be alright."

"But why now? Teaching is—"

"Qu, please just hear me out," I shift off his lap to better face him. "I showed up every day to the same job that I started to care less and less about, every day, to pay the bills. I didn't complain about it."

"You complained about it."

"Fine, I complained about it, but I was willing to do it and keep paying the bills. But we may not have a mortgage soon. We will be able to pay off most, if not all, of our bills with the inheritance. What if we sold this house? Or rented out this or Ma's house?"

"So, bottom line, you are saying you don't want to work?"

"What I am saying," I hesitate. I can't look at him. "What I am saying is, I don't know what I want to do. I want us to think about options. One of those options could be that I don't teach anymore," I try to explain. "All I do know is, I don't want to keep living as we have been living. I want us to think about—"

"How we've been living."

"Sorry. What I mean is..." *I can't find the right words.* "Don't you want to be happy?"

"What makes you think I'm not happy?"

Happiness was not written all over his face.

"Qu, I've been a mess. Admit it."

"Don't start."

"Qu, you too, work a job that you are barely appreciated for."

"My work isn't that bad."

"Alright," I resign, holding him close. *It doesn't make sense to continue. Now is not the time. Right now, I just need to hold him and let him know I'm here. Be still.*

It has been two weeks since Qu and I talked about the future. I can't figure out how to bring it up with him again without melting down or backing down. How can you tell the one person who knows you the best that they don't know you because you are just discovering things about yourself? I'm trying to know who the real Viv is and the whole thing is confusing and ridiculous, and I don't know where to go from here.

Well, that's not completely true. So far, I decided to tell Dour I wasn't coming back for the rest of the semester, which is ending soon anyway. Temporary fix, but a fix worth celebrating anyway.

I also decided to go back to volunteering. I've been missing my women at the shelter.

Yesterday, Carol from the haven invited a few of us over to her house for an evening hang. It was just what I needed. After taking the kids to swimming, I swung by her place. Unfortunately, or fortunately, depending on how you look at it, I ended up being the first person there. We spent that time together just admiring the changes she made to her home. Carol loves to decorate and frequently changes her environment. Bold art and colours everywhere. The lighting, pictures, instruments, and spaces she creates is inspiring. I love how she mixes antiques and contemporary furniture with this flair only she possesses. She even created a meditation room upstairs that is sparsely furnished and lined with walls of books and instruments. A plush carpet anchors the room. I found myself dreaming of how I could spruce up our own home.

As wonderful as Carol's house is, the main reason I want to write about yesterday's outing, is Chloe. Chloe was the second person to arrive. I knew of her, but we never had a shift together. She has a heart-shaped face, a large afro which she braided at the front, and she draped her curves in shades of orange. I was struck by how many blessings and love coated every word she spoke. She didn't have a sour word to say about anything or anybody.

Much later in the evening, Chloe shared with the group that she was recently diagnosed with terminal cancer. She is not on any treatment and doesn't claim the diagnosis. Instead, she decided to take some time off and simply live her life. I am awed by her determination to praise God and be thankful for all things, including the diagnosis. Who does that? That is still hard for me to understand and accept.

According to her, she has good friends. She has a good relationship with her ex-husband who has since remarried. She has a twelve-year-old daughter who she adores. Chloe even talked about how last month she lent her van to a friend, and it broke down. Instead of being angry, she talked about how she enjoyed reading on the bus and the freedom of not multitasking with the absence of ready transportation. Friends call her and offer her rides to the grocery shop. She described her church as very supportive. She talked about how her piano gave her joy and how she was strongly considering getting certified so she could share her gift more widely.

To look at Chloe, you would think she was the healthiest woman on the planet. I had no choice but to write about her. I don't want to forget what she shared. I don't want to forget her, period. Funny enough, listening to her speak reminded me a little of Dad. Dad is was thankful for everything. Unlike Chloe, he didn't talk about all his business, but still, for me, there were whispers of him when she spoke. Particularly, the belief in living without regrets no matter what life deals you.

If Dad's passing has taught me anything, it is that we all need to live purposefully. For instance, how do I use my words? To hear Chloe talk about her daughter made me feel a little ashamed. I talk about Faith and Justin like they are nuisances. When I go into their rooms, they would rather talk to their screens than me. They must sense that my words don't glow when I call their names.

I'm excited for Chloe because her life and energy are a testament to us all. Forty-six and strong! Forty-six and thriving! Diagnosis be damned!

Faith passes me in the living room, glued to her phone. When I clear my throat, I notice she quickens her pace.

"Come here Faith, I want to talk to you." Friendly, I pat the cushion beside me.

"I didn't do anything!"

"I didn't say you did anything."

"So, what now?"

"Sit down and you'll find out."

"Ugh," she stomps over to the couch. Dropping her phone onto the coffee table, she looks at me with fire in her eyes. She is ready to face off.

I clear my throat again. *Why is this so hard? All I want to know is what she is up to and how her day has been. Instead, we are already starting a fight.*

"So, what do you think of my hair?" I ask, singsongy, as I relax my arm along the back of the loveseat.

"Really, Mom? You called me over here to ask me about your stupid hair?"

"Why you have to call my hair stupid?" I wince.

"Can I just go please. I've got things to do," she huffs.

Inhale, exhale, try again. "What do you have to do?"

"Forget it. It's nothing."

"So now you have nothing to do? Which is it?"

"Mom! Seriously, what do you want?" she yells.

"I want to have a conversation with you without it being a brawl!" I scream back at her.

We both stare at each other, breathing heavily. *That went from 0 to 100 in four seconds. What is wrong with me? With us.*

Try again.

"Can we start over?" I finally say, composing myself.

"Mom, I have nothing to say to you," Faith responds, picking up her phone.

"I don't understand. Why don't you have anything—"

"Why all of a sudden do you care?"

"I've always cared. I just..." I'm shocked. *Why is she trying to hurt me?*

"Cut the act, Mom," she snorts.

"What are you talking about Faith? I'm not—"

"Mom let's just drop it. You don't want a conversation. You want to tell me what to do. So, what do you want?"

I slump in the chair. *I feel deflated.*

"You say all these things and don't expect me to have any feelings about them? How can you sit there and tell me, your mother, that you don't want to have a conversation? That I don't care?" *Hold it together Viv.*

Faith falls quiet. *She is still glaring at me, but I don't know what she is seeing. I don't know if she sees me.*

"What do you want from me, Mom?"

I want to choose my words carefully. It's difficult since I have no idea what will set her off. How can I speak truth to my child and also not sound or appear wounded by that fact?

"Can you please sit here for five minutes and have a real conversation with me? That's what I want."

I wish I could read her mind. She is still glaring at me. Maybe it would be easier to just let her go.

"Fine. Five minutes," she scrolls to the clock app and clicks start. *Rude gal.* "Seriously. A timer?"

"Ticktock."

"Is this the kind of relationship you want to have with me, Faith?"

"Does it really matter what I want?"

"You are speaking to me in riddles, Faith. What do you mean does it really matter? Of course, it matters what kind of relationship you want us to have!"

Faith crosses her arms and looks away. "Say what you need to say."

"We *are* wasting time, Faith. Why don't *you* just tell me why you're so angry with me so we can stop the bullshit."

I see her body cringe. *I rarely swear in the house but that seemed to get her attention.*

"Fine, Mom," she faces me, but her fire is replaced with pain. *How have I hurt her?*

"You are not here."

"Again, with the riddles. I'm right here."

"No, you are not. You are not here," she launches in. "I give you my papers to read. You forget. I have practice. You forget and don't pick me up. You take off to the beach. You don't tell anyone. You don't cook. I give you this important note, a form for a scholarship, and it is still sitting on your dresser. I had to get Dad to fill it out last week. You spend most of your time in your bed. Grandpa's ill. You don't even tell me. I found out from Dad. Grandpa isn't even Dad's dad! Grandpa dies. You flake out and don't even drive with us! Friggin' reception? You're MIA! You spend more time at the women's shelter than you do with us. Do you know I am a woman too? Do you know that I am even flunking math *and* English? You are a *teacher,* and you don't have a clue about what I am doing in school! The only time you seem to know that I exist is to tell me to clean my room and wash dishes or to tell me I'm wrong and…"

I see Faith's mouth moving, but I went partially deaf. She hates me so much.

How did I not notice for so long that I haven't been here, even when I am here? I don't know what to do. Her words stick to me like this heavy gooey alloy that I can't seem to scrape off.

"Faith, that's enough!" I hear Qu's voice boom. Her eyes remain pointed at mine.

"Well, that wasn't quite five minutes, but may I now be excused?" she says sarcastically.

"Faith, hand me your phone and go to your room," Qu demands.

Trembling with anger, she crosses the room and slaps the phone into his palm.

"And Faith, this is not over. Stay in your room until *I* tell you you can leave."

"Of course, you would take *her* side," she huffs under her breath.

"You want to add a week of grounding?"

"No, sir," she mumbles heading for the stairs.

Once she's out of earshot, Qu looks at me with confusion. "What was that about?"

I gulp and try to make light of the assassination. "Oh, your daughter despises me, is all," I say shortly. I can still feel the word goo on my skin.

He starts to walk toward me, but I raise my hand to stop him. "I'm alright Qu," I lie. I don't want the gunk to ooze onto him too.

"You want to talk about it?" he asks, an arms distance away.

"No, I think we just need to go to our corners," I smile weakly. "Regroup for round 567."

"Viv," he says sadly.

"I got this," I say, creaking into a standing position. "I just need some fresh air."

I pat his chest as I walk away.

TWENTY - SEVEN

Thank God the sun is out. It's a relief that I don't have to find socks and shoes, or worse yet, boots, to go outside. I'm glad I bought these hiking sandals last year. They are ugly as sin, but man are they easy on the arches.

I quicken my steps up the small hill.

You know it's a new season when you see heaps of yard waste and old broken possessions lining the streets. Funny though, I don't see many people out doing the thrash and dump. Only the afterthoughts. The results of the purging work.

I take a deep inhale as I continue to climb the slight incline.

I've always loved the mature trees in this neighbourhood. Come to think of it, I always like old more than new stuff in general. Look at those big expansive branches. The thick roots may be warping some of the sidewalks, but it's a small price to pay to preserve the trees. Providing beauty. Providing shade. Providing cool. Small price for so much.

I don't want to think about Faith, yet I can't stop thinking about Faith. No shrubbery in the world could erase the look on her face. She was so angry, and I still forced her to talk. She asked me about that note in the car weeks ago and I still didn't read it! I forced her to spew that filth all over me. I deserved it. I've been an absent mom! She has a right to be angry.

So now what?

I know I have to pick up the last conversation with Qu too. It's kind of tied to what Faith was accusing me of anyway. I've finally admitted I am not completely alright.

I laugh softly.

I hate to admit it but thank God for Dour. He didn't fire me outright, but he certainly could have! Thank God, he gave me this time.

I am usually so... prepared.

I turn the corner and keep marching.

Existing on coffee.

Four hours rest and up.

Responsible and always on the ready.

Prepared.

Constantly doing.

And then this year dropped.

And all I want to do is sleep.

And I can't sleep!

I keep climbing.

Just thinking about sleep makes me want to park my ass on a bench and watch the world pass me by. Good, I chose hills with no benches in sight. I can't hide behind sleep.

Why am I so rest-less?

Why am I so off my game?

If Dad were here, he'd tell me simply, "Snap out of it!" Like that Moon movie.

SNAP OUT OF IT!

Snap out of WHAT?

What is IT?

What is this...unease?

I start listing all the ways I should be fine as I continue climbing.

I am married to this incredibly sexy, smart, loving man! (Damn, Qu.) There are women in the world who are literally sacrificing themselves to have one child and I have two with no more than a wink from him (Damn Qu, again. Well, one child hates me but anyway.)

I have a great home. Soon I will have two homes through very little effort on my part.

I have a great teaching job! There is a nation full of teachers scrambling for substitute gigs and I have a full-time, union and pensioned teaching job that I am tenured in.

I am healthy. No cancer. No heart issues. Nothing broken, not even a chipped nail!

AND, for the first time in what seems like forever, I don't have any money issues.

My steps slow as I start to pant.

But...

I lost my Dad.

I'd give back the money and the house if it meant getting back my dad.

But...

He's gone.

SNAP! I'm a grown woman. It's not like I'll immediately be shipped into emergency foster care. I'm freakin' blessed!

So why do I feel so messed up? Why am I still grieving?

Besides Dad, I have it all.

God, how can I have it all and still feel...

Still feel...

Like this? I still feel the alloy on my skin.

I stop mid-stride and place my hands on my knees to catch my breath. I wasn't running, but again the air is trapped inside me. I scan the street for asylum and eye a corner coffee shop not too far in the distance.

"Sold," I decide as I make my way towards the entrance.

"Good morning, what would you like today?" Bright teeth shine at me through the plexiglass.

Not you too? I have no idea what I want.

"Sorry, I need a second."

"No problem, take your time. It isn't that busy," she beams.

I concentrate on the shifting screens above her head trying to figure out if I want hot, cold, salt, sweet, petite, large...

"I'll have the large, iced vanilla latte, with non-fat almond milk. Could I also have a spoon of whipped cream in a plastic cup on the side?"

Her smile fades a millisecond as my order settles in. Teeth reappear. "Whipped cream on the side," she taps.

"Yes," I confirm.

"Alright, that will be $6.49. How would you like to pay?"

I lift my phone for her to scan.

"And your name is?" she asks, with her marker poised.

"Viv."

"Well, all right *Viv*. Your order will be right over there shortly," she motions to the side counter.

"Good morning, what would you like today?" Bright teeth greet the next customer over my shoulder before I have a chance to thank her despite getting my name wrong.

It's nice here. I should get one of these bistro sets for the house. I could then just lounge on my patio with a much less expensive sugar fix. Speaking of home, I can't go back there without having made a decision.

How am I going to face Qu and Faith?

I tip the tiny pink spoon into the whipped cream before savouring it in my mouth for way too long.

Or maybe I could just sit here, continue being MIA and soak in the sun?

Another self-indulgent taste.

Sugar is love.

I let the froth float around my mouth for a spell.

Right. Flight isn't an option.

Do I want to stop teaching, or do I just need a break? Is it about the women and the shelter or the teenagers and the high school? Is it about formal or informal teaching? Is it the subject matter?

Man, I could use a beach right about now. The world's perfect when you're just sitting by the water.

"Snap out of it," I chide myself.

What would it mean if I decided not to go back to the high school? Remember the look on Qu's face when I told him I may not want to go back? Mind you, he was concerned that I meant not working period.

I like to work. Sort of. I mean, I like to feel like I have a purpose. Like I'm doing <u>good</u> work. You know... Why does that sound bitter to my ears? Maybe if I flip the question. What do I <u>like</u> about teaching?

The whipped cream is gone no matter how much I keep scraping the sides of the tiny plastic cup. *How shameless would it be for me to ask for another spoon of cream?*

"Forget it," I rebuke myself as I tap the container on the other side of the ceramic crushed tabletop, dropping the offending spoon beside it.

Teaching... I couldn't make up my mind in high school because I was interested in everything. Teaching was the only thing that came up consistently when I took all those career aptitude tests. Was I confused? Afraid? No. I complied with a machine so I wouldn't have to think about making a real choice. Teaching was tangible. A solid profession. I thought I could pull it off successfully.

I can't complain. I don't mind teaching and the pay is enough for us. I should be grateful. But now this... This is the first time in my life that I want to make a <u>real</u> choice.

Let's take some things out of the equation. Forget the aptitude tests. Going back to school. The bills. The kids, who are pretty much grown. Forget Qu. Forget all the things that I have been using to justify <u>not</u> choosing.

But... They have been such big parts of my life. The main parts of my life. How can I separate them from me?

How can I start thinking about what I?

Me.

Alone.

Wants.

It feels selfish.

I sip the mostly water latte and set it down.

At least I enjoyed the whipped cream as an appetizer. Six dollars worth of coloured water with lots of ice. Yay.

Stop changing the subject. Focus!

I look around and watch the stray people pass by. There are very few people on the streets these days. *It's weird. Such a beautiful day, yet people are indoors indulging in air conditioning. I hear more humming than chatter.* I let my mind drift as I sip my latte laced water. The occasional car drives by. My eyes follow their movement along the road until they disappear.

The longer I watch the world, the calmer I feel. My breath begins to even. I drop my eyes and absentmindedly watch the straw twirling my ice... As it shrinks...

A whisper.

Be honest about how you feel.

You are hurt and this is hard.

A pause.

Take a step anyway.

Take a step and know the road will expand.

I continue to stir my ice, sitting in the whisper.

TWENTY - EIGHT

Is that Qu? The wave from down the street tells me that my intuition is correct. Even though I can't see his face, I know the way Qu moves. I know his gait. I keep walking towards him without hastening my pace.

"I was looking for you," he says, gently taking my hand.

"I had a lot on my mind," I smile at his profile.

In silence, we swing our arms like metronomes. Both of us are lost in our thoughts.

As we near our driveway, something in me pulls back. Qu senses this.

"We goin' in?" he asks. He stops and faces me. His hand doesn't release mine.

"Yeah," I reply without making a move.

We wait.

"You want to sit outside for a while?" I stall.

"It's getting chilly," he hesitates, "you want to sit in the car?"

"Sure," I say before realizing I don't have the keys.

"Kay," he grins, jangling the car keys off his index finger.

Opening the door, he holds my elbow as I slide inside. Firmly shutting the door, he circles the car and nestles into the driving seat.

After putting the key into the ignition, he pushes the button on his seat causing it to slowly recline. He still has the jazz playlist cued. I stop his hand from pushing the power off. He lightly rests his hands on the steering wheel and relaxes.

Waiting.

"We should talk," I begin.

"I'm listening," he responds with his eyes closed.

"I don't have all the answers."

"I don't expect you to. Just tell me what's on your mind," he says. He sounds exhausted.

I exhaust him.

"Faith is angry with me because I haven't been around lately. You told me in the hospital that I can't keep running away. You're both right. I'm sorry."

"Look, I'm more interested," he turns his head to look in my eyes, "in why you want to run. Why you still aren't around."

I feel like we have been around this mountain a million times.

"Me too. I'm getting better though, right?"

Why is he just staring at me?

"Fine. I am starting to figure out why I am *still* running away too. It's just going to take me some time to do that. Definitely more than an afternoon's stroll."

He's unconvinced. "I think you know, and you don't want to say."

"I have nothing to hide from you, Qu. I'm telling the truth," I sigh. "I'm sorry to disappoint you," I lay my head against the seat. Pushing the button, I recline to Qu's level looking up through the sunroof. Warmth and silence envelop the car as we both look up at the sky.

"Take a step and the road will expand," I find myself whispering.

"What?"

"Take a step and the road will expand. It was something that came to me earlier today."

"Hmm."

More silence embraces us.

"I think I've been feeling like I've lived this expected life, but now I want to try something different."

"Different how?"

"Different in the way I work, mainly. I haven't been feeling like I'm growing or contributing as much as I could. I've been feeling like I am in a rut."

More silence. More unspoken questions.

Speak.

"I also think it would be good to go back home for a while."

Where did that come from?

"Back home? To the island, you mean?"

"Yeah. When Ma was talking about developing the land and giving us their house, I found myself wondering if Faith and I should go and help her. Just for some time…" I let my words hang above us like branches. I continue. "I haven't been back home in a long time. I miss the sea wall. I miss the air there. I want to be there more, lately." *Enjoying the stillness.* "It would be good for the kids to know home too."

I smile at the sky. Feeling brave. Qu says nothing.

Maybe if I try another angle.

"You know, it's like how we have papers that say we are citizens. We have property papers that say we own this house and land. We got university papers to say that we are educated. We have staff cards to say we have a stake in the companies we work for. But ultimately, we don't. The way people view us, we are not citizens. We are not Indigenous or even the bank, so we don't own this land. We will never know enough. And companies can quit our ass anytime it suits them!" I laugh at the irony.

Qu's voice is gruff. "Viv, we know who we are. Wherever we step foot, we belong. We are educated. We *do* own this property. I don't care what people think! Who the fuck cares what they think as long as *we* know who we are!"

Whoa....!

"Yes, Malcolm X. I get that," I pat his hand. *Well, that failed. What if...*

"I'm thinking a bit differently," my hand continues to caress him. "You saw my dad hanging high above the ground the way he did, and then sunk into the depth of it a moment later? I will never forget that." My eyes never leave the stars. I'm trying not to tear. "I've been thinking about that a lot lately too. My dad was so amazing, but at the end of the day, he's gone. The funeral staff treated him like an object, not as a man of character or great wisdom. He was so much!" I swallow. "He quietly built this legacy that we now get to enjoy. But in the end, he's gone."

Keep going.

"A big part of who he is, sorry, was, is the island. I want more of that. No one can take the island away from him and my people because it's more than just land. My heritage is there. A good piece of my dad... is there," I look at him hopefully.

He nods, "How long are you thinking of going for?"

"I am nowhere near planning the details of it all. Like before, I am just talking about possibilities."

"And your work? Your job?"

I turn on my side. "I am thinking of taking the rest of the semester off." *I'll break it to him later that I already talked to Dour.* "But what would you think if I switched from teaching formal education to popular education?"

"I don't understand what you mean," he draws out cautiously.

"Instead of teaching in the public school system, what if I taught in nonprofits or on the island or something like that," I explain excitedly.

"Teach what?"

"Well, I don't know yet. Again, these are only incubating ideas right now. All I know is I know a little about a lot of different subjects. I have over a decade of teaching experience, love working in the community and if I taught back home, I'd learn more about myself and where I come from in the process." I lean closer to Qu with my head resting in my palm. Qu's eyes are staring skyward. I can see the wheels turning.

More silence holds us.

The gruffness doesn't leave his voice. "You are talking like a single woman. How can we raise kids, and you are overseas?"

My heart drops. "Qu, wouldn't you want to do this with me?"

"Viv, I have a job!"

"So? Qu, you are brilliant! You've worked for this company for years and they still don't recognize how brilliant you are."

"Viv, both of us can't just fly up and start new careers! We can't afford—"

"Who says we can't afford it? For the first time in forever, we don't have to just get by."

"I'm fine working where I'm working."

"But is that all you want to do?"

His breathing is heavy so I can't tell if he's frustrated or mad or upset or what.

Wait on him, Viv.
You don't have to push.

I rest my head and obey.

After a long while, he speaks, "This is all happening too fast. I don't want to make any decisions based on feelings or what-ifs."

I wait. *I don't want to be defensive.* "I'm not pushing," I breathe.

"Well, no offence, but it feels like you are."

"Offence!" I exclaim playfully Judge Judy style.

He grabs my hand and shakes it. "But why now? If you were so unhappy all this time, why now are you blowing it up?"

"Wow!"

"Well, do you want honesty or sugarcoating?"

"Honesty," I say slowly assembling my thoughts. "Well, I could chalk it up to Dad being gone, but I think the wake-up call came for me on the beach. but then again, the freak-out was before the beach," we both laugh.

We fall back into the silence.

"Sad that it took that to make me realize I, we, need a change."

"Hmm."

"We need to dream again," I continue looking at Qu's profile, lovingly.

"Hmm, dreams don't pay the bills."

"And couldn't we dream *and* pay the bills?" I chuckle looking back at the sky.

"I don't know," he says kissing my barely-there afro. *He must know that turns me on.*

"Alright. Let's figure it out together," I squeeze his hand. "I'm ready to go inside now."

"Hey, Justin," *I'm surprised to see him sitting in the living room by himself. Waiting.* He rises at my voice.

"Hi," he answers, wiping his palms on his jeans.

"Everything alright?" I stroke his arm. *He doesn't look right.*

"I was going to ask you that. You were out on the driveway for a long time."

Qu and I exchange now what looks.

"Yeah, we just had a lot to talk about. Nothing to worry about," Qu reassures.

"Well, it's a little too late for that," Justin replies looking straight at me.

"Look, I'm thirsty. You want to go into the kitchen and talk?" I suggest, gently steering Justin in that direction.

"All of us?" Qu asks, inching towards the stairs.

Now, who's the coward?

"No, it's fine," I pull a face at Qu over my shoulder as Justin and I walk down the hall.

"I wonder if there is any more pop in the fridge," I ask myself. No Ting. *Figures. Groceries evaporate as soon as they hit the front door. I should be drinking water instead anyway.*

"You want water too?" I lift a glass at Justin.

"No, I'm good," he says firmly with his hands folded on the table. *I feel like he's about to give a deposition.*

"Alright," I say, sipping as I take a seat across from him. "What's on your mind?"

"You and Dad getting a divorce?"

I spit out the water, spraying his arm. With barely any reaction, he reaches for a napkin and methodically dries himself off.

"Sorry, what?"

"Are you leaving Dad? Us? Getting a divorce?" he says faking aloofness.

You must be scared. "No, absolutely not. Your dad and I are in this for the long haul," I try to reach for his hands. "Why would you think I was leaving?"

He shrugs and draws his hands off the table. I feel a sharp pang. "I dunno."

I fall back against my chair and start twirling with my glass. *How many times has it been that I can't find my words or collect my thoughts?* I turn my glass with my fingers a moment longer. *What do I say to him?*

You don't have to push.

I inhale deeply and look at my beautiful son sitting in front of me. Anxious.

"I'm sorry that I have not been around for you, Faith, and Dad for the last few months. I've been trying to figure out what to do differently in my work, and in myself," I exhale. "I'm sorry if it seemed that I was pulling away in all this figuring out stuff."

His face seems to soften at my apology. His hands reappear on the table, and he begins to tap. "Is that all? That's my entire life! Figuring out stuff," he scoffs. "You should have just said so." He gives me a small grin. *I'll take it.*

"Easy for you to say! I'm the mom! I'm already supposed to have it all figured out!" I playfully poke his finger.

"Sure," he laughs sarcastically. Though I'm laughing with him, part of my heart sinks.

"So, what have you figured out so far?"

"So far, I'm thinking of carving out time for myself. Maybe take some more time off work, spend more time with all of you and Ma. Maybe volunteer some more at the shelter and other nonprofits around here."

He shrugs again. "Except for taking time off work, it doesn't seem like much of a change. It sounds like you figured out nothing."

I could get defensive, but with the day I'm having it seems futile. I tap his temple. "You would be correct, Sherlock."

He nods. "Okay. Is that it?"

"Yeah, that's it. But remember Justin, if your dad and I make any major decisions we would totally tell you and Faith before moving forward."

"Nobody says 'totally' anymore, Mom," he teases me, imitating his sister's deadpan tone.

"When did Faith get in here?" I jokingly lift his hand and look underneath.

TWENTY - NINE

It's been a great few weeks. After talking to Qu and Justin it seems to be getting easier talking about making changes. Mind you, small changes to start. I think they, especially Qu, started to get antsy when I was brainstorming big changes like leaving the school board and going to the island. Once I talked about taking off just one semester, Qu seemed to calm down. I then decided to talk to Dour about possibly changing schools and grade levels. There may be some Grade 12 philosophy, and world politics course positions opening in two secondary schools closer to home.

The more I think about it, I realize I still love teaching but need to change what I am teaching and who I am teaching. These subjects are interesting and new for me. I already have some ideas about what I can add to the curriculum to make it more relevant for the students.

I also sent my resume to some post-secondary schools to test the waters. The teaching schedule for post-secondary is more flexible than high school, so I think it may be worth a shot.

In the meantime, as I am off work, I accepted more shifts at the shelter. I like facilitating the youth reading circles and even arts and crafts programs. I discovered I have a knack for painting! I like dabbling in acrylics. Most of my pieces are abstract, but it doesn't matter. It's a lot of fun! It's easier for the women to open up to me as we are sitting side by side, experimenting with colours. Anyway, as I'm supporting the women and their children, I am also learning more which is... Unexpected.

When I first started volunteering my attitude was, I was there to help displaced women, but these past few months I am realizing that volunteering is more reciprocal. I am growing so much as I give.

At the end of the month, Ma, Faith, and I will be leaving for home. I have barely packed. I don't have any intention of packing much anyway. We'll be staying with Ma's older sister, Aunt May, and her daughter, so I figure what I forget they'll have, or I'll do without. I will be away for four weeks and then Qu and Justin will come and join us for two weeks before we all come home together. I've already talked to Qu about going home for at least a month, annually, from now on for both of us! He needs to be refreshed and reconnected with his family just as much as I do. It will also be good for the kids to know more about where we come from.

As for the house, we are undecided. We haven't been able to agree on what to do: sell, not to sell, rent, not to rent, move, not to move. I've decided to rest my defences for the time being. Until Ma's house is built, she will be going back and forth. We have time. The world won't fall apart if I wait until I am sure in my spirit of what to do next. There isn't any reas—

"Mom?" Surprised, my ink streaks the page. Putting the pen and book aside, I give Faith my full attention.

"Come in," I invite her, patting the space beside me.

I realized after apologizing and explaining to Justin what was on my mind, I needed to do the same with Faith. Granted, she wasn't as quick to accept what I had to say. It is what it is. But at least now she is looking for me. I don't always have to chase her.

She closes the door behind her and crawls over the bed to sit beside me. She rests her head on the headboard. Gingerly, I tilt her head onto my shoulder, feeling her resist at first before relaxing.

"What's up?"

"Nothing much. I finished my homework and checked all my messages," she says with a moan.

Teenage angst is so weird.

"Hmm," I reply fighting the urge to tell her what to do next.

"Do you know what's for dinner?"

"No, it's Justin's night to decide."

" 'Kay."

"Did you want to do something together? Go for a walk? Play cards?" *I am not going shopping, so not suggesting that.*

She groans like I've asked her to climb Mount Everest.

"Nooo," she says lazily.

"Alright, what then?"

She shifts closer to me, linking my arm. "Can I just sit here?"

I nuzzle the top of her head with my cheek. "Of course, Faith. As long as you want."

Five fifty-eight a.m. burns red hot.

I rub my eyes allowing the light to enter. I gently nudge the soft snorer. Chickens peck at the wire outside the window. The sound of straw sweeping the yard greets my ears. The smell of green banana and callaloo wafts.

"Ma," I whisper, "it's a new day."

The snore continues without missing a rise or fall.

READING GROUP DISCUSSION QUESTIONS AND WRITING PROMPTS

I hope you have enjoyed the novel *Yielding: Life Unraveled.*

Below are some questions to help you further reflect on the themes explored.

1. Viv was living her life on autopilot but received several signs that eventually pointed her back to self-awareness. Think of a time in your life where you were operating on autopilot or experienced an event that caused you to rethink the way you were living. What were the nudges that brought you back to self-awareness? How were you changed?

2. When Etienne Dour met with Viv, he meant to be supportive of her. She believed however that she was being punished. Have you ever had an intention, but the person you were talking to believed you had an ulterior motive?

How did they respond? How did you try to address the miscommunication?

3. Viv felt overwhelmed. She decided to start writing her thoughts to better understand how she felt and why. How do you cope when you feel overwhelmed? How do you sort out your thoughts and feelings?

4. Have you ever run away from someone or something? Who? What? Why? How did this impact you and those you love? If you could change the past, would you run away again?

5. Qu went to the police station and experienced several microaggressions. What message do these microaggressions reinforce? How do you think these behaviours may have affected him?

6. Culture is fluid and we often take it for granted. How did the culture of Viv's parents impact Viv as an adult? What are some instances in which we see Viv resisting being like her parents? Why do you think she does this?

7. Viv kept putting off talking to Faith and Justin about why she left. Why do you think she did this? How do you think this may have impacted Faith and Justin without Viv knowing?

8. *Yielding* was purposely written in the present tense and doesn't mention specific locations, dates, or events. The book, however, was written in 2020, the year of Covid. During a conversation between Viv and Gabe, they talked about planes crashing which some may think is a reference to 9/11. Think of one global event that has had a huge impact on our collective perspective, psyche, and way of life. Can you remember the day, time, and circumstance you first heard of this event? How has it personally changed you since?

9. Viv started to think of her spirituality and what it meant to her. Has there been a time in your life where you either questioned your faith or wondered if you even had any faith?

What made you start questioning? What did this lead you to discover about yourself?

10. Is having it all—healthy family life, careers, marriage, great wealth, and happiness—attainable or unattainable for women, particularly racialized women? Why? Why not?

11. Yielding means to give way under pressure and soften resistance. In which areas of your life have you yielded to develop something within yourself or give yourself space to reflect on your next direction?

12. Which character in the book do you identify with the most and why?

www.ingramcontent.com/pod-product-compliance
Lightning Source LLC
Chambersburg PA
CBHW071417200726
48294CB00002B/425